BLOOD AND ROSES

BLOOD AND ROSES

Best wishes to Gretchen & Mark — transcontinental friends!

A JAYNE TAYLOR NOVEL

ANN TONSOR ZEDDIES

Ann Tonsor Zeddies
sigalivis @ aol.com
anntonsor @ gmail.con

A PHOBOS IMPACT BOOK
AN IMPRINT OF PHOBOS BOOKS
NEW YORK

PHOBOS
IMPACT

A Phobos Impact Book
Published by Phobos Books
200 Park Avenue South
New York, NY 10003
www.phobosweb.com

Distributed in the United States by National Book Network, Lanham, Maryland.

Cover by Zuccadesign

The characters and events in this book are fictitious. Any Similarity to actual persons, living or dead, is coincidental and not intended by the authors.

Library of Congress Cataloging-in-Publication Data

Zeddies, Ann Tonsor.
  Blood and roses : a Jayne Taylor novel / Ann Tonsor Zeddies.
    p. cm.

ISBN 0-9720026-7-7 (pbk. : alk. paper)
    1. Government investigators—Fiction. 2. Human-alien encounters—Fiction. 3. Espionage, Japanese—Fiction. 4. Nuclear weapons—Fiction. 5. Conspiracies—Fiction. 6. Single women—Fiction. 7. Orphans—Fiction. I. Title
    PS3576.E36B58 2005
813'54—dc22
                                        2005007012

∞™ The paper used in this publication meets the minimum requirements of American National Standard for Information Sciences—Permanence of Paper for Printed Library Materials, ANSI/NISO Z39.48-1992

For Diane Silver, in memory of a funny, inspiring, and encouraging lunch at which she told me my next book should be about a heroine.

And for Toshio Ishida, my childhood playmate, who taught me about the *tanuki* when we were four years old—in memory of singing "Shojoji no Tanuki Bayashi" and dancing—pon poko pon pon pon!

Does Mum . . . still believe
That there's no Devil and that youth is bliss?
As certain as the sun behind the Downs
And quite as plain to see, the Devil walks.

—Sir John Betjeman,
"Original Sin on the Sussex Coast"

BLOOD AND ROSES

CHAPTER ONE

THE DEVIL BEHIND THE LINES; OR, SHOOT FIRST, PRAY LATER

Picardy, France, 1917

Jayne Taylor surveyed the devastated landscape warily as she slammed her dented, cranky camion to a lurching halt. The dust cloud raised by the truck's passage over the rutted road settled slowly. Jayne reached under the seat for the nonregulation pistol she kept hidden there. Relief workers were supposed to be noncombatants, but more than once a show of force had saved her from serious inconvenience.

"Hello," she called.

She'd heard something—or thought she had. Now she wondered. Even the birds had abandoned the ruined countryside, after its latest pounding by retreating German artillery. Fresh corpses from both sides lay buried in the rubble. Stragglers and looters might be lurking, too—though Jayne worried more about blowing up her precious truck on an unexploded mine. The truck was a lifeline for the

1

refugees who depended on the relief supplies it carried. Jayne risked their welfare as well as her own by detouring from the main road after some phantom sound.

But Jayne dreamed at night of wounded, broken bodies trapped beneath the rubble—and woke up screaming. She had to be sure. She couldn't leave without searching. She was no Red Cross nurse, but she could at least offer transport to an aid station for a human survivor. And if it was merely a wounded farm animal, well, heaven knew they could use the meat.

But now that she'd stopped, she no longer heard the sound. She shrugged, and was about to put the gun down and reach for the gearshift. And then something moved in the ruins—a clatter of stone on stone, a muffled curse, a faint high-pitched cry, cut off suddenly.

"Who's there?" she called sharply, raising her weapon to the ready.

A shuffling shape dragged itself over the remnants of a wall. It was human, but so ill-formed that it seemed monstrous at first. Then Jayne realized it was two figures, one clutching the other tightly and dragging it along. Both were covered from head to foot in the powdery white dust that coated everything since the bombing.

She thought this must be an overlooked survivor, carrying a companion who needed help. Both of them stumbled and tripped over long robes as they climbed the piled stones. The big shape wore fabric bunched around its head as well, and Jayne finally recognized the draperies as the habit and black veil of a nun. The smaller figure wore a lighter robe of white—a novice, perhaps.

Jayne struggled to make sense of it. Where had they come from? But she started to relax, all the same. Of all the dangers she could have encountered, displaced nuns were the least of her worries.

"Mes soeurs," she called. "How can I help you?" She
lowered the gun, about to reach for the door handle and
let them in.

Then the smaller of the two shrieked—the same high-
pitched cry that had originally brought Jayne to a halt.

"Look out!" the voice said in French.

Jayne froze in shock as the voice choked off, and the
big nun pulled a Mauser automatic pistol from beneath her robes and pointed it at the younger woman's
head.

"Get out of the truck," the nun said, voice rasping and
harsh with dust. "Leave the keys."

"Madame, je vous en prie," Jayne protested. The woman
must be mad—crazed with shock, perhaps. "Please! Put
down the gun. I can help you."

"Give me the truck," the nun said. "Now—or I kill
her." A murderous nun? Jayne wasn't as surprised as she
would have been, once upon a time. The stench and roar
of endless battle had a way of twisting even the gentlest
of people.

One of the nun's arms tightened cruelly around the
younger woman's neck, shaking her for emphasis. The
captive's eyes fixed desperately on Jayne's face, and her
mouth opened in a tiny squeak of protest, like the beak
of some fragile bird caught in a cat's claws.

The nun spotted Jayne's gun. Perhaps she had raised it
in an unconscious gesture of defense. The big nun actually smiled, looking from Jayne to the girl, and suddenly
Jayne was looking down the barrel of the Mauser. She
couldn't give away the truck. But she'd have to, unless
she could think of something fast. The nun's eyes were
insanely blue in a mask of dust.

"Hands up," the nun said. "Drop it. Or I kill you both."

Jayne knew she was dealing with a madwoman. Surrender was the only sensible response. She saw the nun's

grasp on the girl relax just a bit as Jayne's hands rose to obey the order.

And the girl screamed again, inarticulate words tumbling over each other.

Faster than Jayne could think, long before the meaning of the words had cleared in her mind, she'd let the barrel fall to point at the big nun's head, and pulled the trigger. The sound of the shot slammed into her ear, and a round dot appeared on the draped figure's forehead, first black, then red against the dust. The big form collapsed backward, pulling the captive down as well. The gun arm jerked convulsively skyward, pulling the trigger, but without aim, then fell wide, casting the weapon aside.

A nun. She had killed a nun. If there was a hell, Jayne had just reserved a prime spot in it. She scrambled out of the truck and dropped to her knees beside the two strangers. She pulled the nun's habit open. Beneath it were the gray wool jacket and the insignia of a German NCO. The nun was a German soldier. She felt for a pulse, but there was nothing. The flesh felt cold and rigid, as if he had been dead for hours. His head lolled sideways. A thick trickle of liquid spilled from the wound and meandered sluggishly through the dust. Jayne looked away.

Maybe she wouldn't go to hell after all. Why didn't that make her feel better?

Her mind played back what the girl had been saying, just before the shooting. Now she understood it.

"Tirez! Tirez! Ça n'est pas la mère supérieure, la mère est morte!"

Shoot! Shoot! That is not the mother superior. The mother is dead.

As gently as possible, she pulled the girl away from the dead man's grasp.

"You're safe now," she said. "Are you all right? Are you hurt?"

The girl's arms were stick-thin under the heavy robe she wore. Her face was thickly masked in dust. The white powder caked her cropped hair, even her eyelashes. She tried to speak, but coughed instead, one frail hand going to her bruised throat.

"Come, I'll give you a drink," Jayne urged. Holding on to Jayne's arm, the girl shifted a few feet from the corpse, but when Jayne tried to raise her, she curled up against the broken stones, shaking her head.

Jayne let her go and hurried back to the truck to get her canteen. She pulled off the scarf she wore around her hair and wet it to wipe the dust from the girl's face. She tried to make the girl drink, but after only a sip the girl again shook her head.

"*Non, non,*" she whispered. "*Mes soeurs*—the sisters will be thirsty." She tugged at Jayne's hand and pointed. "There—they are waiting. I went out to get them water and—I have been very much delayed."

This time, when Jayne tried to help her stand, she rose to her feet and led Jayne haltingly through the rubble.

"You have sisters?" Jayne said. "Where? Are they hurt?"

The girl stopped and pointed dumbly.

As far as Jayne could see, the world had been shaken and pulled down to one level, from the blasted and burned tree trunks to the towers spilled on the ground like a handful of toy blocks. She tried, without clues, to make sense of the scene before her.

A tumbled slope that might have been a staircase. Bits of smashed glass, bearing traces of dulled color. Fragments of scrolled stonework. A church, perhaps? Yes—she could still make out a sketchy rectangle that had formed the walled convent garden. Dust shrouded a few broken rosebushes, their petals spotted with a deeper red. And in the shadow of a broken buttress—

Jayne rested her hand on the girl's shoulder and gently turned her away.

Mes soeurs. The other nuns. Those whose black-clad bodies now lay beneath the unforgiving weight of stone saints and fallen angels, giving off a still faint but pervasive scent of mortality.

The girl struggled weakly to turn back.

"I stayed with them," she said. "Then I came out to get water, and he caught me. I have been away too long. I must take them water. I must wash their faces—cover them—I cannot leave them so."

"Come with me," Jayne said. "What is your name?"

"I am Soeur Madeleine," the girl said. "I cannot go without them. I must—"

Jayne took her hand, and the girl flinched. The delicate fingers were scraped raw, blackened with earth and grit. Had the novice tried to dig the others out, or to bury them? Perhaps she had tried to free them first, but yielded at last to the knowledge that they were dead.

"Come, Madeleine," Jayne coaxed. "We must go and—and find a priest. The priest will care for them. Wouldn't that be best?"

She could feel Madeleine relax, clinging weakly to her arm.

"Oh, yes, a priest," the girl said gratefully. "Bring the good father. He will know what to do."

Jayne very much doubted it. She doubted that any man on earth, or any god in heaven, knew what to do with this vile mess.

The body of the dead German, half-wrapped in its stolen robes, still barred their way. Jayne had to step over it, and kicked it in passing.

"Bastard," she said furiously.

She felt Madeleine flinch.

"Oh, no," the girl said pitifully. "We must pray that he will be forgiven. Pray to forgive."

They could never know if he and his kind were responsible for all of this, Jayne admitted to herself. The Germans, the French, the Americans, and then the Germans again—all had bombed and shelled, raped and beaten this once-lovely fragment of earth. Who could say when the church had fallen? Who could say what color the uniforms had been, under all the dust?

But you're the one who made me kill you, she said to the dead man. *I'll never forgive you for that.*

She'd seen it in his eyes, even before she'd seen the sleeve of the uniform beneath the Mother Superior's habit. At the last minute, she'd seen that look that said he'd kill her anyway, once she lowered the gun. Perhaps because he enjoyed it, perhaps because killing was the order of the day. At the last minute, she'd found that she had whatever it took to kill him first.

Never. Never forgive.

The girl had no obvious injuries, but she huddled against the door, as far away from Jayne as she could get. Jayne wanted to take her back to the clinic, get her out of the truck, but she had to finish her rounds for the day. She had no choice. The villages—or what was left of them—depended on the cans of milk, the bread, the blankets and vitamins for the children she still carried in the back of the truck. She drove as if pursued by the devil or the Boche, as she'd heard the French soldiers call the Germans, bouncing and grinding over the rock-hard, rutted clay.

By the time she returned to the supply depot, it was clear that something was very wrong with the young nun. Drops of sweat stood out on her pale face. She tossed and muttered, and no longer responded to touch or voice. Jayne bypassed the depot and pulled up in front of "headquarters"—the official-sounding name they

7

gave to Madame de Grace's dilapidated town house. A couple of aides were just going off shift. Jayne called them to help carry Madeleine into the clinic that occupied the rooms downstairs.

But as they lifted the girl, she struggled and called piteously for help. She kept screaming something about "*le diable.*"

The devil. The devil has stolen Mother Superior. Don't touch me! Devils!

Jayne changed her mind.

"Not the clinic—take her up to my room, please," she said.

The aides exchanged glances, shrugged.

"What is it?" Jayne said.

"She's delirious," one of the young men said. "Looks like typhus to me. We've seen a lot of it lately."

"Well, in that case, she certainly shouldn't be taken into the main ward," Jayne panted as she helped drag the litter up the narrow stairs. "If she's contagious, she'll be better in isolation."

They set the girl down carefully on Jayne's bed.

"Your funeral," the aide said, but she knew that the words masked concern. "Make sure you burn that bedding afterward—even if she survives."

"I do know how to wash my hands, thank you very much," Jayne said, waving them out of the room.

But when they were gone, she stood helpless before the girl's distress, wondering what to do next. She knew she needed to examine Madeleine and bathe her, but the girl only screamed and clutched her robes around her when Jayne came near. Jayne left her alone for a moment and went in search of Madame de Grace.

As Jayne entered the hallway, Madame was just coming down the stairs from her room on the top floor, dressed in her threadbare best.

"Oh, Madame, I'm so glad to see you," Jayne said. "I need your advice, if you have a moment."

Madame had obviously been bound for some other errand. But she put aside her hat and the gloves she had been about to pull on.

"Always a moment for you, *chérie*," she said.

The older woman owned the house, as well as most of the property outside of town. Before the war, her family had presided over a chateau and half a dozen villages, with their holdings of land and timber. The chateau and the farms had been devastated, first by the Germans who had dispossessed her, then by her own countrymen as they battled to drive the Germans out. The only family property left standing was this town house, which she had opened to the relief agencies and the medical clinic. Here she still presided, wearing her ancient hats to the meetings of the Secours aux Blessés Militaires with as much dignity and presence as she might once have worn a tiara to a ball.

"In my room, please, Madame," Jayne said.

Madeleine was lying down when they entered, but jerked upright and huddled back against the wall, hugging her knees, at the sound of their voices.

"Ah, the poor little soul!" Madame exclaimed. "*Mon dieu*, she's wearing the robe of a Carmelite!"

"Yes, I found her near a destroyed church on the road to Grécourt."

Jayne glanced at the frightened girl, unwilling to describe the scene in detail. She didn't know how much Madeleine could understand in her current state.

"It seems she was the only survivor of the convent."

Madame sank down into the single wooden chair by the bedside. Her face revealed lines of grief, though her posture remained upright and correct as always.

"*Bon dieu*. That lovely little church. It has always stood on that spot, even through the Revolution. Gone now."

She shook her head and seemed to put her personal feelings aside.

"*Tiens*, we do what we can for the living. This poor girl needs to be made comfortable."

"And that is why I need your help," Jayne said. "Her name is Sister Madeleine. She was so afraid of the aides that I brought her here, where there's some privacy. I need to examine her. She has no obvious wounds, but there is something wrong. Her mind is disturbed. The boys downstairs think she has typhus."

Madame handed Jayne a key from the bunch she kept fastened to her belt, and rolled up her sleeves.

"Go to the linen closet and bring me a clean sheet and towels. In my room you will find a clean nightgown folded in the dresser. Bring that also, then fill the tub with water. I shall help you bathe her."

By the time Jayne had filled the tub with buckets of warm water brought one by one up the stairs from the clinic, Madame had actually coaxed the girl out of her heavy outer robe. Madeleine sat on the edge of the bed, shivering in her white inner garments, her eyes still big as saucers.

"The nuns bathe under a sheet, for modesty's sake," Madame explained. "We drape it, so—and now, if you will assist me—"

At last Jayne was able to lower the girl into the tub. Madeleine still would not allow Jayne to wash her, but she seemed to have confidence in the older woman.

"Perhaps if you would step out for just a moment," Madame suggested.

When Jayne returned, Madeleine rested quietly in bed, enveloped in one of Madame's voluminous, old-fashioned nightgowns. Madame sat by the bed, smoothing out her dampened sleeves and tidying her hair.

"The Secours aux Blessés will have to get along without me today, I fear," she said. "But that poor girl has been wounded just as surely as the soldiers downstairs. I fear she has endured a great outrage—you understand me?"

"Do you mean, she was raped?" Jayne said bluntly.

"I cannot be sure. We may never know for sure. She is feverish, and her mind is wandering now. When she is herself again, she may not remember. She may choose not to remember."

"I understand," Jayne said.

But Madame still gazed at the girl with a puzzled expression.

"What is it?" Jayne said. "Do you think she has typhus?"

"That is just the puzzle," Madame said. "She is unwell. You are right about that. But if this is typhus, it is not typical. *Et voilà*—this hand—"

She turned back the covers to display the girl's right hand. Now that the caked dirt had been cleaned away, the skin appeared painfully red and swollen, as if it had been burned.

"Merciful heavens," Jayne said. "No wonder she pulled away when I took her hand. Perhaps she was burned on hot debris. But I didn't see any signs of a fire."

"There are burns on her chest, like these," Madame said. "On the right side. As if she had been carrying something hot that burned both the chest and the hand."

She crooked her arm to demonstrate someone holding a dangerous object.

"But why would she carry something that burned her?" Jayne said.

"An astute question." Madame nodded thoughtfully. "I wish that I knew the answer. But come—we'll have the

11

boys carry this tub away, and we must go downstairs to the clinic and scrub with the doctor's nasty soap."

Jayne wasn't satisfied, but she sensed that Madame didn't wish to pursue the subject in Madeleine's presence. She scrubbed with disinfectant soap until her skin was red, then left instructions for the aides to look in on Madeleine at intervals, and returned to the depot to supervise the loading of the next day's relief shipments.

By the time she finished, it was late. Darkness had fallen. The chirping of crickets had been replaced by the occasional rumble of distant artillery. Jayne recalled that she now had no bed to sleep in. She went to her room to check on Madeleine, and found that someone had already set up a cot for her at the foot of the bed where the sick girl slept. Pinned to the top blanket was a note inviting her to step upstairs to see Madame.

She climbed the steps wearily. She would rather have fallen into bed—but she knew that as soon as she stopped working, she'd have to face what had happened that day.

"Sit," Madame invited her, as soon as she entered. "If you wish tea, I will have Marie brew a pot. I thought perhaps this would be more suitable."

She gestured to the bottle of red wine that sat opened and breathing on the dressing table.

"Thank God," Jayne said fervently. "Madame, you are a genius."

The older woman smiled. "No," she said. "But I have walked with genius."

She poured the wine.

"*Salut,*" she said. She tasted the wine and nodded.

"That comes from our own vineyards," she said with satisfaction. "As you know, Picardy is not, for the most part, wine country. Nevertheless, my late husband created some vintages that were considered quite drinkable, even in Paris."

Jayne savored the heady perfume of the wine. Perhaps a glass or two would let her sleep. In the meantime, she was more than happy to be carried out of this place and time by an old woman's reminiscences.

"Had he been the younger son, rather than the older," Madame continued, "I believe he would have pursued a medical or scientific career, like his great hero, Dr. Pasteur. Even as an amateur, he continued to take the greatest interest in scientific matters. He installed in our chateau a telescope and a little laboratory where he could perform analysis of our wines and sometimes diagnose crop sicknesses. He kept up with the latest advances in chemistry. Before the war, we entertained many of the leading scientists of Paris."

She paused for a healthy swallow of wine.

"Happy memories of those times returned to me today—and yet, perhaps not completely happy. It was the wounded hand of that poor girl that reminded me."

Jayne realized that she had misjudged this conversation. It was more than idle chat about times long past.

"I recalled a summer evening in 1903," Madame continued. "Marie Curie had just received her doctorate in science. My husband and I were invited to the celebration. In the evening, we sat in the garden, and Monsieur Curie proudly demonstrated the luminosity of radium for us. He carried the rare element in a tube coated with zinc sulphide, which fluoresced brilliantly under the bombardment of the rays. It was a glorious sight— brighter than the moonlight. Our hearts thrilled to be present at the beginning of a new age of science."

The yellow candlelight in the room was soft and forgiving, but Jayne thought that Madame showed her age more than usual tonight.

"I have shaken hands with Fritz Haber," Madame said. "Now he manufactures gas for the Germans. And Harry

Moseley—dead in Turkey. Even that enchantingly beautiful light, apparently so harmless—well. I saw Monsieur
Curie's hand, with which he held the tube aloft for our
admiration. It looked just as Madeleine's does now.
Swollen and inflamed, as if it had been burned. When I
asked, Marie admitted that constant exposure to the radium rays caused some discomfort, but she insisted it
was a trifling matter. Now I wonder."

Jayne felt that the wine had slowed her mind. She
could not grasp what Madame was saying.

"You think that Madeleine was exposed to radium?"
she said. "How is that possible?"

Madame shrugged. "I merely observe, like a scientist,
that the two phenomena—Monsieur Curie's hand and
hers—appear identical. I have no explanation. Indeed, I
hope I am wrong, for if I am right, it could mean that one
more terrible weapon has been unleashed upon the
world. It is possible that what ails the little nun is not typhus at all, but the result of some kind of radium
weapon."

"Good heavens," Jayne said. "We must return to the
bombed church tomorrow, and search the rubble. If the
Germans have a new weapon, the authorities must be
told!" She remembered just in time that she did not give
the orders here. "I mean, if you think it wise, of course."

"I do think it advisable," Madame said. "Though I
hope this is all just the fumes of a fine vintage gone to an
old woman's head. In any case, we must finish the job, as
you promised Soeur Madeleine, and see that the nuns
have a decent burial."

She refilled the glasses, and then tapped Jayne's arm.

"And you, my friend," she said. "I see in your eyes that
you, too, have suffered today. You have not told me all. The
boys downstairs are full of admiration. They say you have
fired on the enemy. Drink up, and tell me your story."

Jayne choked, and took refuge in a fit of coughing.

If she told Madame the truth, would Madame turn away from her in horror? Would she revoke her rarely granted friendship? Best to find out right away, she thought wearily. She wished she had a pocket handkerchief. She had no intention of weeping, but she felt that her nose might start running any minute.

"I killed a man today," she said defiantly. "And I'm not sorry."

Madame said nothing, but after a moment, Jayne felt the older woman patting her hand as she had Madeleine's.

"A German soldier had disguised himself as a nun," Jayne said. "He took Madeleine hostage. He was choking her. He tried to take the truck. I shot him."

"And if you had not," Madame said, "you would be lying in the dust now, along with the girl. The children would have no bread, the relief service would have no truck. And I would be mourning the loss of another good friend."

"I'll have to resign from the relief service," Jayne said. "I promised to remain neutral."

Madame gave her a shrewd look.

"But you have not endangered our noncombatant status, because no one saw you shoot," she said.

"Perhaps not, but the story is already spreading," Jayne said. "When we go there tomorrow, everyone will see the body. They'll assume it's true. Anyway, the point is that I broke my word, whether anyone can prove it or not."

"And so you feel a need to make reparations?" Madame said. "Perhaps you should confess to the good father when he comes to see Sister Madeleine."

"You know I'm not Catholic."

"So, I will assign you a penance," Madame said. "You will continue to do this work you do so well, and say nothing of what happened today. You will make sure that for the life that was taken, two lives will be lived. Yours and Madeleine's."

She raised the glass that held the last of the wine.

"To you, *chérie*, and to me, and to this bitter century that dawned in so much hope. We have all survived another day."

In the morning, Jayne accompanied the soldiers who drove down the Grécourt road. Their official mission was to bury the good sisters. Only Jayne would be searching for more than a decent grave. She wore her pistol tucked into the back of her trousers now. Under the seat of the truck seemed too far out of reach. Her stomach was jumping with nerves—and perhaps with a touch of a hangover as well, she thought ruefully. Her upbringing by good Presbyterian parents in Delaware County, Pennsylvania, had not equipped her for French social life, even in these times of scarcity.

The soldiers invited Jayne to stay in the truck while they excavated the remains of the convent, but she forced herself to stand by and watch. She was alert for anything that might have the appearance of a weapon, or a scientific artifact, but she saw nothing. A couple of twisted candlesticks were the only objects that emerged from the ruins. The bodies of the nuns were lifted out as gently as possible, and quickly wrapped in blankets and tarpaulins and laid on litters for transportation to the graveyard.

One of the bodies drew shocked murmurs even from the hardened poilus—a woman older than the others, her bare head exposing cropped gray hair, her body clad only in voluminous monastic undergarments. It was the mother superior. Someone had stripped her of her outer robes before she died. The soldiers began to curse the

Boche before they remembered that a priest was present, and subsided into shamefaced muttering.

Under pretense of turning aside to recover her composure, Jayne searched for the body of the soldier she'd killed. The dead man had apparently vanished into thin air. She could not even be sure of where the body had been lying. Dust covered the place where his blood had flowed. For a moment, relief flooded Jayne's heart. She must have imagined it. She hadn't shot anyone, after all. Or perhaps she had shot him, but he hadn't died. He'd only been unconscious. When he'd come to, he'd walked away.

Then her foot struck a hard object that clattered. It was the Mauser, right where she'd seen the soldier drop it. Jayne picked it up and wiped it on the hem of her coat. She remembered the cold, lifeless feel of the soldier's body under her hands, and shuddered. He'd been dead all right. And therefore it followed that she had killed him. What happened to his body was a mystery, but it couldn't change that fact.

As soon as Madeleine seemed able to understand, Jayne told her that the sisters had been properly buried. Madeleine nodded, silent tears trickling down her pale cheeks.

"I'm sorry for your loss," Jayne said awkwardly. She was afraid to hug Madeleine, afraid she'd cower away and babble about devils again. But the girl stretched out her good hand, pleading for Jayne to approach. When Jayne came close enough, Madeleine clung to her.

"Your hands are warm," the girl said. Jayne realized that she was weeping silently. "I'm sorry I called you a devil. Please forgive me. You have been very kind. Tell me your name. I will pray for you."

"It's Jayne. But I know it doesn't sound right in French."

Madeleine stumbled over the sound, repeating it to herself.

"But it is like Jeanne," she said finally. "Jeanne d'Arc, the saint of Lorraine."

"The names may be similar, but I'm no saint, either," Jayne said.

"Please tell me one thing," Madeleine said. "The reverend mother—she too is laid to rest?"

"Yes," Jayne said. "I promise you, I saw with my own eyes. She was—she was dead, of course, but in all other respects, I assure you that all was in order."

She ransacked her memory for some reassuring detail.

"I'm not Catholic, so I'm afraid I don't know the right words, but the priest said the prayers. There was a blessed candle, holy water . . . a cross for each grave. You must get better soon, and then you can see for yourself."

"*Dieu merci,*" the girl sighed.

"There is one thing you could tell me, in return," Jayne said cautiously. "Why is it that you have been so concerned about the mother superior, in particular? Why have you spoken of devils?"

Madeleine shivered. For a moment, Jayne was afraid that she'd reawakened the girl's nightmares, but then Madeleine sat up straighter and looked her in the eye.

"You will think I am superstitious," she said. "A silly little girl. And you are so brave, like a soldier. But I assure you, it was not my fantasy. A soldier came. He was wounded. He threatened us and said we must help him. He did not understand. We would have helped him anyway. He was still one of God's creatures.

"The reverend mother placed him in the chapel and watched with him all night, trying to heal his wounds. But when she came out—she was not the same. She spoke so strangely. I touched her hand, and it was cold and hard, like a skeleton beneath the skin. It is said that the devil is cold to the touch, always very cold. And so it was. So then I knew. She was not herself. The devil had taken her."

"But Madeleine . . ." Jayne fell silent, baffled. She had no frame of reference to cope with this. "How can that be?" she said finally.

"It was no soldier," Madeleine said with conviction. "It was a devil. After I found the reverend mother's body, I knew that. And the soldier walked again, as a devil. You saw him walk. But you saved me from him."

She squeezed Jayne's hand weakly. "And you saved the reverend mother, too. She lies in consecrated ground, beneath a cross. So I can be sure the devil has left her now. It is well."

Her eyes closed, and she slept again.

Jayne sat by the bed for a long time, looking for an explanation that would fit the phenomena. Radium burns and devils walking—the old nightmares and the new. She refused obstinately to be content with mystery. Surely there must be some rational way to understand all this, an explanation that Madame Curie and the great ones like her could accept. But Jayne Taylor could not find it.

At any rate, the devil had left her with two souvenirs. The sixteen-year-old ex-nun and the German pistol went with her everywhere. By the time the Kaiserschlacht rolled back the Western front again, Madeleine and the Mauser had become her best friends.

Le Havre, France, 1920

"What will you do next, *chérie*?" Madame said.

Jayne wished people would stop asking her that.

She peered through the curtain of rain that fell between her and the docks, but couldn't see the smokestacks of the liner that waited to take her back to the United States. Rain and fog blurred even the other side of the street. Under the awning of the small café where she and Madame enjoyed a last, fortifying glass of Calvados together, raindrops still splattered in and dampened her skirts.

"What a nuisance it is to be properly dressed again," she said, trying to pull her feet farther under the table.

"Will you return to your college for young women?" Madame said, refusing to be deflected.

"Not now," Jayne said. "Not until we have the children settled down."

Her gaze strayed to the corner of the street, where Madeleine, partially sheltered by Madame's big old-fashioned *parapluie*, was playing with the children. Jean-Luc and Henri were jumping back and forth across the puddles, splashing each other and shrieking with laughter.

They'll ruin their shoes, she thought, but then shrugged. *They'll have plenty of time to dry out on the boat.*

Hildegarde clutched baby Lucille to her chest like a big doll.

"Stop it, you're getting the baby wet," the girl scolded. But Jayne noticed that she didn't miss a chance to stamp her foot in the water and splash the boys in return.

"We have to find schools for them, I suppose," Jayne said. "Now that Maddie has been officially released from the order, her dream is to start a school of our own. Did she tell you about that?"

"But of course," Madame said. "A school for peace. No military drills, no spanking with rulers; instead she will teach them to tend gardens and treat all the world with kindness. A school where these children and others like them, made homeless by war, can learn to build a better world. A beautiful dream. But a big responsibility for you."

Jayne thought about how she'd feel if she were about to say goodbye to all of them. Yes, it would make life easier. But she simply couldn't imagine it. Madeleine needed a fresh start. Jayne and Madame agreed about that. She needed a new home, unscarred by war, where she wouldn't see reminders of suffering and death wherever she turned.

And the others . . . well, they'd turned up, one by one, each a reminder that in a world of a million deaths, every loss was still a unique tragedy for one unique human being. During the year Jayne had spent helping to resettle refugees after the war, she'd searched for the families of these children, too. But they'd vanished without a trace. They had no one left but Jayne.

"It will be hard for you to care for them, without a family," Madame said.

"But they are my family," Jayne said. "They brought Maddie back to life. Look how happy she is with them. And they have nowhere to go. I couldn't possibly leave them behind."

Madame smiled. "No, you could not," she said. "Others could, perhaps. But not you. You take it upon yourself to do what needs to be done. For this I admire you, my friend."

"You should not say this of me, Madame," Jayne said, blushing. "You are the one who has helped us all to survive this war."

"I ask you to promise me one thing," Madame said. "When all is settled, you must take the time to complete your studies. You have a fine mind. A new day is coming, in spite of all foolish attempts to hold back the dawn. All our best efforts will be needed in this new world, women as well as men. Perhaps you will come back to France one day and meet Madame Curie as an equal!"

"You overestimate me," Jayne said.

"I think not," Madame said, rapping her heavy gold rings against the table for emphasis. "But in any case, promise me that one day you *will* return to France. For you have become like family to me, as well."

The deep, melancholy sound of the boat whistle boomed through the fog.

"Time for us to go," Jayne said. Madeleine and the children came running.

Kisses on both cheeks, a babble of *"au 'voir, Madame," "au revoir, mes enfants"*—such a swift parting after years working side by side. There was no good way to say goodbye, Jayne thought.

Madame settled her hat at a becoming angle again.

"You will forgive me if I do not come to the gangplank and become wet like a baby duck," she said. "Write to me when you arrive. I shall stand here and wave. *Bon voyage!*"

Jayne glanced back again and again at the majestic figure waving an unfurled handkerchief, until the rain veiled Madame from sight.

New York Harbor, 1920

A week later, Jayne stood on deck, watching for the first glimpse of the Statue of Liberty—again through mist and rain. As the familiar form came into view, holding her torch aloft, Jayne startled herself by laughing out loud.

"What is it?" Madeleine asked. "What is so amusing?"

"The statue," Jayne choked. "Doesn't it look just like Madame in fancy dress?"

Suddenly she felt tears spilling from her eyes.

"What's wrong?" Madeleine said.

But Jayne could only shake her head. She should be thinking *I'm home*, and instead she was longing for the exile she'd just left.

I made myself a home inside the war, she thought. *And now that I've come back to my own country, I feel as if I'll never be at home again.*

How could she explain that to Madeleine, who had truly lost her home? Jayne could feel Maddie press closer to her side, already dreading the unknown city, with its crowds of strangers.

"Don't worry, *chérie*," she said. "Delaware County, Pennsylvania, isn't like New York. You'll like it there."

But it took forever to get there. The health inspector had to examine all of them. Jayne showed her French adoption certificates for the children, properly attested with all the official seals and signatures, and an impressive-looking contract guaranteeing that she would be responsible for Madeleine Guerin, hired as governess for the children. The official pored over these documents for so long that Jayne clutched the roll of bills in her pocket, desperately trying to calculate whether the inspector would be amenable to bribery, and if so, how much it would take. But in the end it seemed his hesitation was due mainly to nearsighted-ness, and he finally let them go.

Jayne had her hands full on the bustling dockside, with a pile of luggage too heavy to move, four children too excited to hold still, and Madeleine, trembling so badly in the rush of the crowds that Jayne was afraid she'd faint. Jayne stood on tiptoe, trying to spot a cab. In-stead her eye was caught by the back view of a man in the crowd. He seemed somehow familiar. Eager for a friendly face, Jayne leaned out to see better, to identify him.

She felt as cold as the icy water off the dock. She'd have known the cropped hair, the flat stare, the jerky movements anywhere. He wasn't in uniform anymore—of course not—but even with him wrapped in a long dark overcoat Jayne recognized the man she had killed. It was the German.

Jayne's first thought was to scream for someone to stop him—but for what? He'd committed no crime, at least not here, on American soil. Her second thought was that Madeleine must not see him. Already she was too upset, too frightened by the hubbub of strangers.

She placed a comforting arm around Maddie's shoulders and turned them both to face in the opposite direction.

"Is that a cab?" she said. "Taxi! Taxi, please! Over here!"

With Madeleine's attention occupied by the arrival of the cab, Jayne stole a chance to scan the crowd again. The man had vanished. Perhaps he'd never been there at all.

Badly shaken, Jayne welcomed the distraction of climbing onto the train with all their bags and boxes, the older children overexcited and the baby screaming. Jayne felt better once she'd tucked Madeleine into the window seat and distracted the children with Hershey bars and peppermints from the candy butcher.

Delaware County, Pennsylvania, 1920

By the time they reached the Radnor station, it was getting dark. As they climbed down, Jayne peered into the twilight, wondering if her old neighbor had ever received the message she'd sent—and if not, how they'd get home. The children huddled together behind her, all quiet for once.

"Jayne Taylor."

She recognized the deep, quiet voice at once, and whirled to find that he'd come quietly up behind them.

"Salem Cope!" she said. She vigorously shook the callused hand the big man extended to her. She could have hugged him in sheer relief. "You did get my message! Thank you so much for coming. We sorely need a ride home."

"It will be my pleasure, Friend Jayne," he said. "We've missed a good neighbor since your mother passed on and you went away. It will be good to have you home again."

"I hope you brought the wagon," she said. "There are rather a lot of us."

With some difficulty, she maneuvered Madeleine from behind her so she could make proper introductions.

"Madeleine, may I present an old family friend, Salem Cope. Friend Salem, this is my dear friend Madeleine Guerin. And behind her, you can see Hildegarde, Jean-Luc, and Henri. The baby is named Lucille, after my mother. I've adopted them," she added. Salem did a good job of hiding a look of relief. His expression barely hinted that for one shocked moment he'd thought they might all by hers by natural means. To his credit, a broad smile soon spread over his face.

Madeleine curtsied deeply in her most polite manner. Jayne could see that she was terrified of the big man looming over her in his dark suit and broad-brimmed hat.

"M'sieur Cope," she said, in a voice that was barely audible.

But he did not tip his hat or nod in return.

"Madeleine Guerin, I am most pleased to make your acquaintance," he said. "But as I am of the Society of Friends, I need no vain titles of worldly honor. I know you mean it kindly, but I'd be best pleased if you would call me Friend Salem, as Jayne does. Brother Salem would serve equally well.

"Please wait here. I'll bring the wagon."

He loaded the baggage as if none of it weighed more than a five-pound sack of sugar. He let Hildegarde and the boys sit on the bench with him, and won their hearts by letting them handle the reins for his team of black draft horses. Jayne was glad to sit in the wagon bed with Madeleine. It was too dark to pick out any landmarks, but Jayne happily breathed in the smell of the hedgerows and fields.

"The Society of Friends are also called Quakers," she explained. "They don't believe in what they call worldly titles, so they don't say Mr., or Mrs., or Sir. They don't bow or kneel, and they don't take their hats off to anyone."

"*Une autre espèce de Protestant?*"

"Yes, I suppose so. But don't say '*espèce de Protestant*' as if we were some kind of weird beasts! Just about everyone in America is a Protestant."

"*Tiens,*" Madeleine said faintly.

"Anyway, Salem Cope and his wife Clementine were friends of my parents for many years. Their farm is next down the road from ours. My father delivered all of their babies. They are good people."

The wagon turned down an overgrown lane, and Jayne felt a pang of anticipation. But Salem pulled up his team.

"I meant to ask you, back a ways, if you wanted to go on to our place first and stop for supper. Your little ones must be hungry."

"Oh, thank you, Friend Salem, but I'm eager to get home. We have some bits and pieces with us to make up a supper. I just want to see the old place, and get them under a roof and into bed."

The farmer laughed. "Clemmie said that's what you'd say. She said, 'Mercy, the child will be longing for her own home. She won't want to come by here and put on her company manners.' But she told me to make sure you knew she'd be expecting you at your earliest convenience."

He clucked to the horses, and they plodded on. Soon light shone out from behind leafy branches.

"Goodness, there's a light on."

"Yes, Clemmie took the liberty to ride over and air out the place for you. She banked up a fire on the hearth and in the stove to take the chill off. Put a little something in the pantry for you, too, seeing that she didn't think you'd be coming back to the house with me."

"Thank you, Friend Salem. And please thank your wife as well. It's good to be back."

As the sound of hoofs disappeared down the lane, the children apprehensively edged away from the vast darkness until their backs were against the door.

"It's very dark here in America," Hildegarde remarked in a quavery voice.

"It's too quiet," Jean-Luc added loudly.

"Where are all the people?" Henri said. "Have they been blown up?"

Jayne flinched at the question, but decided not to respond. Soon, she hoped, quiet and peace would become unremarkable to these children.

"Come on, move," Jayne said, pushing between them to open the door. "Get your bags inside, and then let's eat! Let's see what Sister Clemmie left in the pantry for us! It's sure to be good."

Jayne stirred up the fire in the stove and added wood till it blazed up. It was spring, but the warmth was welcome. Madeleine exclaimed in pleasure over the contents of the pantry. Gently slapping Jean-Luc's greedy fingers out of the way, she put bread and butter, slices of sausage and cheese, and an apple pie on the table. The children pounced on the food, but after only a few bites they were already falling asleep, their heads nodding toward the table.

"I suppose we should get them up to bed," Jayne said. She hadn't even looked at the upstairs yet.

"Nooo," Henri protested sleepily. "I don't want to go in the dark. Want to stay here."

Jean-Luc just wriggled out of her grasp and slid to the floor every time she tried to pick him up.

Jayne shrugged helplessly.

"Wait here," she said to Madeleine. "I'll reconnoiter conditions upstairs."

Beds were made upstairs, but the rooms seemed cavernous and gloomy by night.

"Well, maybe just this once . . ." Jayne muttered. By the time she felt her way downstairs with an armload of blankets and comforters, Madeleine had fallen asleep, slumped on the corner bench by the hearth.

"Just this once," Jayne announced loudly, but no one stirred.

"Just this once, understand?" she repeated, as she rolled small bodies onto soft pallets and propped Madeleine with pillows.

"And without washing hands," she sighed, as she extricated a crust of jam-smeared bread from Hildegarde's sticky fingers. "Oh, good lord, what kind of parent am I going to be? This is a fine mess I've gotten myself into."

She was glad of the firelight and companionship as she made up a sleeping roll for herself on the hearth rug. The image of the German haunted her, though she told herself there was no way he could ever have found his way to Delaware County, even if he'd had any reason to try. Probably he'd never found his way to the docks of New

York, either. She'd only imagined it, under the stress of the moment. She'd heard of stranger things happening to returning veterans. Shell shock, they called it.

Anyway, she had the Mauser tucked under her pillow, just in case.

CHAPTER TWO

BENEFITS OF COLLEGE EDUCATION FOR YOUNG LADIES

What will we do next, Jayne?" Madeleine said. Her big blue eyes stared guilelessly at Jayne over the rim of her breakfast mug of café au lait.

Merciful God, how I wish people would stop asking me that, Jayne thought. Then she experienced a swift pang of guilt. She had acquired the habit of using strong language overseas—French oaths picked up from the soldiers, and their English equivalents, which she got away with because nobody really understood what she was saying.

If I'm going to raise a batch of children in polite society, I simply must *learn to ameliorate my speech,* she thought. *And you're living with a former nun, too! How can you be taking the name of the Lord in vain!*

"But *vraiment,* Jayne, what must we do?" Madeleine said. "They are so kind, your—" She stumbled over the word "neighbors." "—but look how fast Henri eats this sausage. And the milk—nearly gone already! They cannot feed us forever."

Dammit! Jayne thought. And then, *Only one way to stop them from asking that question: Answer it.*

"Well, the first thing we'll do is give everyone a bath. And burn these clothes."

Madeleine and Hildegarde gasped audibly, in unison.

"Burn our *clothes?*"

"Yes. We have to look like Americans now. Not like refugees."

Privately, she thought that would prove difficult. The treatment these children gave their garments would reduce them to ragamuffin status in minutes, even if they'd come fresh from Wanamaker's.

"*Et puis?*" Madeleine ventured. "Then—what?"

"And then," Jayne said firmly, "I will get a job."

She said it, and now she had to make it happen. She finished her breakfast and foraged for resources. She'd made a cursory search of the house already. The dusty barn held a faint, nostalgic scent of horses, and the gig they used to pull when her father was alive. Propped in a corner, she found her bicycle and repair kit. She pumped up the slack tires. They still held air.

"Hallelujah!" she said, hoping it wiped out her earlier exclamations. This little machine was their only tie to civilization, as represented by the railroad station and the city it led to.

"We should keep a team again," she said. She looked around the barn. Yes, they still owned all the paraphernalia of the stable—pitchfork, muckrake, harness. "No! Maddie, I have a better idea. We need a truck of our very own."

Now the job appeared to her not just as an irksome necessity but a glorious vision. It had to happen.

"Horses are the past. But the future is ours, Maddie! We just need a truck to drive us there. And I'm going out to get one."

The house boasted one modern convenience, at least—the telephone. Dr. Taylor had installed that, over his wife's protests. Jayne remembered her mother complaining that now patients could pester them at any hour, and her father's reply that they'd do it anyway—but if they called him on the phone, at least he wouldn't have to be seen in his nightshirt.

Jayne picked up the receiver and rang the one person she could think of who might have usable connections. She only hoped that Kensie was still in town, and had not yet left for some elegant watering spot.

The voice at the other end of the line was familiar—but then, all butlers sounded alike, she thought.

And thank goodness, Kensie was at home and would be pleased to receive Miss Taylor's morning call.

Jayne thought briefly of asking her to send the car, but decided not to push her luck, in view of the favors she hoped to ask for later. The bicycle wasn't the most graceful means of transportation, but it preserved one's independence.

"Oh, this hideous thing," Jayne muttered, settling a hat on her head and pinning it down viciously, in anticipation of the long ride to the station. The children watched in awe, as if she were a knight putting on her armor. She even tucked a pair of gloves into her otherwise empty handbag. Madame had impressed upon her the prudence of dressing for the destination—whether that was the opera or the field hospital. At the last minute, she tucked her gun into the handbag, as well. She knew that was ridiculous, but simply felt naked without it. She'd spoken with enough veterans to know that many of them felt the same. Probably there were enough concealed weapons walking the streets of Philadelphia to start another war. The thought made her laugh, and then frown.

"I'll try to be back by dark, Maddie. Work on getting these ragamuffins clean. And inventory the house, if you have any spare time. Look for dry goods, canned goods, garden seed, anything we might be able to use. Get the boys started on spading up the kitchen garden, if they need an object for their energies. If anything goes wrong, or you get worried, you can use the telephone. Ask the operator to let you speak to Clementine Cope. She'll help you."

"Darling Jayne!"

Millicent Griscom Kensington swept down the stairs with outstretched arms, as if Jayne were her long-lost sister. Jayne was more than happy to be escorted rapidly out of the clutches of the butler, who held her unfortunate hat at arm's length as if it might turn and bite him.

Soon she found herself seated in a snug yet wildly expensive drawing room, leaning against Oriental cushions, resting her feet gingerly against a Persian rug, and sipping fragrant tea from a Limoges cup.

"My dear, you've simply shocked poor Thompson," Kensie said. "I believe he thought I'd given up my dreadful suffragist friends once I left college."

"How would he know that I'm a dreadful suffragist?" Jayne said. "Do I have a mystic mark on my forehead?"

"You have that *hat*, which is surely just as effective," Kensie said, rolling her eyes. "And your dress! Oh, I was so looking forward to your call. Just back from France! It sounded lovely. I thought I'd get a private viewing of the latest fashions. But I can see you haven't changed a bit. And your dress . . . well, that clearly hasn't changed since 1917."

"What's wrong with my dress?" Jayne said. "It's practically new. I only wore it a couple of times before I went to France."

"And since then, a war that consumed half of Europe has drawn to a close, an epidemic has decimated our fair city, women have won the vote, and the Prohibition amendment has passed. And waists have been lowered, skirts raised, and necklines greatly simplified. You look like a refugee from the attic."

"That is unfortunate," Jayne said. "I'm all dressed in what I hoped was my best, because I'm about to go and look for a job. In fact, that's why I came to you. I hoped you might recommend something."

"Oh!" Kensie looked startled. "I thought you might want a vacation after all your adventures overseas. I hoped you might go with me to Bermuda. Really, it's deadly dull there without a friend to amuse one."

Jayne smiled and thanked her for the kind, if impractical, thought. "That's why I need the job, you see," Jayne continued. "My father's legacy might do for me to live on, but it's not enough to support a family.

"Anyway," she teased, "I haven't a thing to wear at a fashionable resort. Refugee from the attic, remember?"

"Dress is no obstacle," Kensie said. "I could have fixed you up. In fact . . ."

She looked Jayne over again and shuddered delicately.

"Come upstairs with me now and let's see what we can do. We can't have you going out like a poor relation."

"Kensie! No!" Jayne protested in vain as she was dragged from the sofa by a soft, well-manicured hand with surprising grip strength. "I can't possibly parade past Thompson dressed in your castoffs. I didn't come here to beg!"

"Oh, didn't you?" Kensie said. "I know you too well, Jayne Taylor. You were going to beg me for the inside story on some form of employment. Which I will be happy to give you, but only if you let me dress you to my own satisfaction first. Beauty by any means necessary! I shall not hesitate to use blackmail."

"This is just like that scene from *An Old-Fashioned Girl* where Polly's immoral cousin dresses her up in inappropriate finery," Jayne complained.

"Piffle," Kensie said. "That's what you get for reading uplifting works for young ladies. You get quite a wrong view of life. You should have done as I did: straight from the nursery to Mama's French novels. Then you wouldn't have these scruples."

She pulled items from her closet and laid them out for consideration.

"Can't you just sign up as a nurse, or whatever it was you did Over There?" Kensie said.

How many times will I have to explain this? Jayne thought. "I wasn't a nurse. I have no interest in becoming a nurse."

"Good for you," Kensie said. "It sounds a horrid profession. I'm sure one does not meet nice people. Or if one does, they will be missing a limb, or an eye, or something. So inconvenient." She held up a navy blue middy blouse. "Why not be a teacher, then?" she said. "You'd make an excellent teacher for indolent young ladies or naughty little boys. This blouse would be perfect for the job—I can't think why *I* ever bought it. Though I'm sure dress wouldn't matter much, as long as your cuffs were nice and starchy and your ruler ever ready. I'm sure I could recommend you to any number of select academies."

"Kensie! Stop teasing!" Jayne said. "It's not funny. Poor Madeleine is going to have to sew them overalls out of old curtains if I don't find some way to make money."

"Sorry, sorry," Kensie said airily. "Hmm. Would Your Ladyship care to be a secretary? I might inquire among cousin Clement's shipping enterprises. I'm sure he could find something for you. Something proper and not too taxing, for an independent-minded young lady."

"That's just the problem," Jayne said. "And do be serious for once in your life. I cannot take a proper lady's job, because a proper lady's wages simply won't do. I need a man's job with a man's pay."

"You don't ask much, do you?" Kensie said. "With all the veterans coming back to the city, it's hard enough for a man to get a man's job." She flounced onto the edge of the bed and sat there, bouncing gently to aid reflection. "Just what abilities have you brought back from France?" she said.

"Keeping track of stores and inventory," Jayne said. "Map reading. French. I can field-butcher a sheep or cow. I drive and maintain trucks."

She took a deep breath.

"And I shoot people," she said bitterly.

"Well! That is quite a list of qualifications," Kensie said. "Let's give this some thought. And let's finish our tea while we're about it. I'll have some brought up fresh. Fresh, and a little stronger." She winked at Jayne and rang the bell.

"Adelaide, please bring us another tray. Strong tea this time," she said to the maid.

"Oh, and leave that dress on," she said to Jayne. "No need to change. The color is charming, especially when your eyes flash indignantly, as they did just now."

When the tray came up, the teapot exuded the unmistakable scent of alcohol.

"Let me pour," Kensie said. "Cheers!"

She raised her teacup.

"This may help us to think constructively."

Jayne sipped gingerly. The cup was filled with a well-aged, respectably dry sherry. "Where did you get this? Isn't it against the law?"

Kensie shrugged one shoulder.

"Scruples, scruples. The law was never meant to apply to people like us. They're trying to keep the working classes out of the saloons, not curtail the legitimate pleasures of their betters. Or so my brother Rodney says. He has a little man who delivers a regular order. Strictly under the table, of course, but I'm sure not illegal."

I'm quite sure it is illegal, Jayne thought. But she didn't say it, for an idea had begun to form in her mind.

"How did your brother make contact with this little man?" she said.

"The details are a bit murky, but I believe he met someone at a prizefight, which would be quite out of the question even for you, Jayne, so don't even think about it!"

"Please try to remember," Jayne said.

"Why? Are you planning to order some sherry?" Jayne saw the light dawn slowly on Kensie's face. "Jayne! You can't!"

"If you would be so very good as to make a note of a name and address," Jayne said sweetly, "I would be so very much obliged."

"Oh, anything for an old school friend," Kensie said, screwing up her eyes. "I'm thinking, I'm thinking . . . Oh! Yes."

She found a silver pencil and a sheet of engraved notepaper on her dresser and scribbled rapidly.

"Here's the name. He works at I. Goldberg on Market Street. The army-navy surplus place. Rodney said he was told to go to the guns and ammunition department and ask for this fellow, then tell him he wanted to speak to a Mr. Hoff."

"Kensie, you are a brick," Jayne said. "I have to go. Give Thompson permission to dispose of my hat in whatever way he finds fitting."

"I shall," Kensie said. "And I'll have the rest of these things boxed up and sent to you. Don't buy too much for your kiddies while you're in town. Wait until I see what I can pilfer from Rodney's little monkeys. And do let me know if you change your mind and want a nice job as a secretary for some overfed industrialist."

"I will," Jayne said. "And thank you for everything! I must run for the train."

"Oh, no, darling, thank *you*," Kensie said. "I must say, knowing you is as good as a novel. And not the improving kind."

CHAPTER 3

RUM, HOOLIGANS, AND SHENANIGANS

Jayne dashed through Wanamaker's like a commando on a foraging run. She bought overalls and sturdy shoes for everyone. Frilly castoffs from Kensie's pampered nieces and nephews might be all right for Sundays, but Jayne knew they'd never stand up to everyday wear from her little squadron. She paid the extra charge to have them shipped to the station. She couldn't pose as a Main Line socialite with her arms full of bags and boxes from the children's department.

Then she sought out I. Goldberg on Market Street. Decidedly down-market, she thought. Half the ground floor was in turmoil as stock clerks maneuvered heavy dollies through aisles already piled high with stacks of uniforms, boots, boxes of belts. The familiar smell of wool and canvas permeated the area. Jayne even thought she could smell the dust of France again, imported on boot soles and muddy crates.

She found her way to the manager's office. He wasn't a "little man" by any stretch of the imagination. He looked about three feet wide. His nose had been flattened by a punch at some point in the past, and his massive hands looked as if they'd be more comfortable holding a meat cleaver or a sledgehammer than the stub of pencil he was using on a stack of invoices. He looked up suspiciously as she approached.

"Whaddaya want?" he said.

Jayne stood her ground and gave him a glacial stare, not speaking until he got the message and stood up.

"Miss," he growled grudgingly.

She rewarded him with a smile. "Do I have the pleasure of addressing Mr. Ignatz Karpinski?"

He looked as if it took him a minute to recognize his own name. Kensie had said her brother was initially introduced to him as "Iggy the Polack."

"Yeah, that's me. What can I do for yez?"

"I believe we have a mutual friend—Rodney Kensington. He suggested you might be so kind as to put me in touch with Mr. Hoff. I have a business matter I'd like to discuss with him."

"Yeah . . . Max." Jayne watched the wheels revolve in Iggy's skull. A conclusion was reached. "He ain't here right now."

"Do you know where he might be reached?"

The spark of suspicion flared again in Iggy's close-set eyes.

"Nah. I don't know nothin'."

He turned his back on her.

Jayne stepped up to the counter and rapped briskly on it.

"Why, Mr. Karpinski," she said sweetly. "I hope you weren't about to give me—what is it they call it? The 'brush-off'? I'm sure Mr. Hoff would be sorry to lose Mr. Kensington's business."

She watched Iggy choose the path of least resistance.

"He eats at Corona di Ferro some days," he said. "Down at the Italian Market."

"Thank you," Jayne said. He'd already turned away again.

Jayne coolly stared past the shirt-sleeved men who gave her the once-over as she entered the restaurant. Some of them weren't bad-looking at all, she noticed. Their light summer clothing highlighted well-muscled arms and shoulders. The place smelled of rich tomato sauce and sharp cheese. She'd never known there was so much to savor in the heart of Philadelphia. A waiter in a sauce-stained white apron approached, then turned tail at the sight of her expensively tailored dress. She overheard the words "swell dame" as he buttonholed the maitre d', who then hurried toward her with deference.

"Mr. Hoff, please," Jayne said, handing him her card.

"Please, lady, yes, this way," he said, bowing her toward a table at the back of the room. The table showed signs of a larger party, but currently held just one man.

Jayne thought of Kensie and her friends, and readied her most lockjawed Main Line manner.

To her surprise, the man at the table rose to greet her. Short and sallow, he looked like a clerk in a corner store. But he wore his dapper dark suit with assurance.

"Oh, Mr. Hoff, I do hope you won't think it forward of me to introduce myself," she said, extending a hand about six inches in his direction so that he might grasp her gloved fingertips. "Yes, thank you—if I may." She allowed the maitre d' to seat her. Then she scooted her chair a few inches sideways, blocking the corner of the table to make it impossible for Hoff to leave again as long as she remained seated. She didn't want to allow him an easy escape from the conversation.

"Iggy said you were here about Kensington's business," Hoff said.

"So you were expecting me."

"Yeah—Iggy phoned me. You can't be too careful in matters of . . . business," he said. He had a shrewd, good-humored smile. For a criminal, she thought, he wasn't entirely unattractive.

"Well, Mr. Hoff, I'll be frank with you," she said. She felt that beating around the bush with this man wasn't going to get her anywhere. He wasn't some chinless family scion—he lived by his wits and would not be easily bamboozled. "I am not in fact a representative of Mr. Kensington. Though I am a family friend, and I was referred to you through him."

Hoff's expression hardened immediately. "What do you want?"

"Mr. Hoff, I want a job."

"Oh? What do you propose to do that would be worth my while?"

Oh no. She could see where this train of thought was going, and it had to be nipped in the bud. She dropped the Main Line act.

"Stock and inventory. Drive and maintain trucks. And I can handle a gun. I want to drive for you."

He threw back his head and laughed, a harsh barking sound.

"Oh, you're good, you're good," he said. "You really had me going there for a minute. Who put you up to this? Was it Waxy? You tell him he nearly got me there."

"Mr. Hoff! I'm serious."

Hoff shook his head appreciatively. "A broad like you, comes in here dressed all la-di-da for a garden party, and then you tell me you want to drive my truck. That's rich." He eyed her again, making her feel that Kensie's dress was much too thin. "I'll tell ya what, if you mean it about the job, I can fix you up with something at the club. You've got class."

Jayne raged in inner fury against the flirtatious skirt and the pretty, fragile shoes. She wished she had her boots on—she'd give Max Hoff a kick in the shins he'd remember for a long time. "I do mean it, but I have no desire to work in a club. I drove trucks for three years in France. That's what I'm good at, and that's what I want to do."

The humor died out of his face. "Okay, that's it. Joke's over. It was fun while it lasted, sugar, but now Boo Boo's got work to do."

He started to rise. The table's edge caught him across the thighs, forcing him to sit down again.

"Get out of my way," he said. His expression had gone from smile to snarl in seconds, like that of a dangerous dog.

His order was punctuated with a ping and a crack, as a hole appeared suddenly in the wall just over his head. Jayne had heard that sound before, in the fields of France, and she knew what it meant.

"Down!" she shouted, flinging herself to the floor. She propelled herself under the table and grabbed Hoff's arm, yanking him out of the chair. He had the presence of mind to push the table over, providing at least a thin layer of cover between them and the shooter. Jayne was still looking around to see where the shot had come from when Hoff bolted toward the nearby kitchen door. He hadn't invited her along, but Jayne followed him anyway.

They burst through the kitchen, past a row of comically astonished faces, and out the back door into the alley. Hoff headed for a truck parked against the opposite wall of the alley, but another shot ricocheted off the bricks, forcing him to hit the deck again.

Jayne took cover in the doorway. She thought she'd spotted the shooter this time—holed up behind a broken window, farther down the alley. A sniper's position. That meant he was a second man, placed here to prevent their escape. So, logically . . .

Just as the thought completed itself in her mind, the original assailant burst through the kitchen door, in hot pursuit. Jayne grabbed the lid off a garbage can just in time to hit him in the face with it, dropping him in his tracks.

Her mathematics professor at Bryn Mawr had been right. Realizing the correct solution to a problem brought its own modest satisfaction, she reflected, as she pulled the gun from her handbag. She fired a couple of shots in the direction of the broken window, to get the sniper's head down, and crawled rapidly behind the garbage cans to a point where she was no longer in the line of fire.

Damn, she thought. *There goes another pair of stockings.*

She belly-crawled across the cobbles, grimacing at the thought of what this was doing to her new dress.

Kensie will kill me if these goons don't do it first, she thought.

She reached the truck and took cover behind it. Glancing back, she saw that Hoff had managed to backtrack to the cover of the garbage cans, but the window shooter still had him pinned down. Taking a chance that the shooter would be too busy to switch to her as a target, she stretched up and through the window, and grabbed the handle of the driver's-side door. As the door swung open, she tumbled in—and collided with the large, dense body of the man who had just jumped in from the other side.

"What the hell!" he said, as they bumped heads. Another volley of shots sounded, as Hoff exchanged fire with the sniper.

"Boss! I'm coming!" the man in the car shouted.

"Rocco!" she heard Hoff yelp in return. "Where the hell have you been?" The barrage of expletives that followed was drowned in more gunfire.

Rocco—if that was his name—then tried unchivalrously to shove her back out the door. "Get the hell out of my—"

She elbowed him in the face, knocking him back enough that she could reach the electric ignition and press the switch.

As the motor rumbled to life, she kicked him in the shins and got her foot on the accelerator. Keeping her head down, she put the truck in reverse and veered backward toward Hoff's position, scattering garbage cans in her wake.

"Get in!" she shouted. Wisely, he didn't try to climb into the cab, exposing himself to further fire. He threw himself over the tailgate onto the truck bed. She roared out the end of the alley at the top speed the truck could attain in reverse. She narrowly missed a horse-drawn delivery wagon, but that was all to the good, as the driver pulled up in confusion, blocking the road and effectively preventing immediate pursuit.

She pulled around a couple of corners at random and cut across the trolley tracks just in front of an oncoming car.

"Are we being followed?" she said.

Rocco turned and looked back.

"You're clear," he said. He glowered at her, but a muscle twitched as if he wanted to laugh. "But the boss is hopping mad," he added.

She pulled up and waited while Rocco helped Hoff out of the back of the truck. She smoothed down her hair and brushed a stray shred of rotten cabbage off her dress. Nothing could really make her presentable again. She chose to remain seated, and thus less visible when the two men came around to her side of the truck.

"So, do I get the job?" she said.

Hoff chose to ignore her until he had finished dressing down Rocco. She could see the big man's ears turning slowly red as the invective continued.

"Where the hell were you?" Hoff said, once he'd returned to coherent speech. "I told you to wait outside with the vehicle."

"Yeah, boss, but I'd been out there for three hours," Rocco said. "I went down the alley to, you know . . . to go. I was only gone for a minute."

"Yeah, well, while you're pissing up a wall, I coulda been killed. I don't pay you to shake it in the alley. I pay you to drive."

"It was some of Luciano's boys, boss, I'd swear," Rocco said. "I wasn't expecting that. I thought you told me the New York bunch weren't going to be a problem."

"I'll be talking to them later," Hoff said. "After I finish with you, you dumb palooka."

The gangster turned his maddened gaze on Jayne. All traces of a sense of humor had vanished.

"And you, dolly, what the hell are you playing at? I get shaken up like a gin fizz because some piece of skirt hijacks my truck?"

Jayne smacked the Mauser down onto the dashboard. She refused to let this man intimidate her.

"I saved your life, *boss*. You think I did that for kicks? I can shoot, I can drive, now do I get the damn job or not? Looks to me as if I can handle it better than some of your boys."

"Could be," Hoff said. "Could be—but what's your angle? A high-class broad like you—why would you want to put your pretty little face out there to be shot at?

You want a job, I got plenty of jobs in the back end. Working the counter, working a desk if you're too highfalutin to show your gams."

"Sure," Jayne said. "Plenty of jobs in the back, for half the pay! I can do a man's job, I want a man's pay. It's that simple, Mr. Hoff. No angles."

Hoff pursed his lips thoughtfully. After a moment, he shook his head.

"Nah. Nah, I can't see it."

Jayne knew she was losing his attention. She had to speak up. Desperately, she said the first thing she thought of.

"You know what? You're right, Mr. Hoff! Who could see it? Who'd ever believe someone like me could be running booze? It's ridiculous, laughable. And that's just what the coppers are going to think, too.

"I'll be dressed just as I am—er, just as I was—and even if the bulls stop us, they'll never believe I'm up to anything."

She fluttered her eyelashes at him—hating it, but ready to try anything.

"Butter simply wouldn't melt in my mouth," she said sweetly. "If you want an angle, Mr. Hoff, *there* is your angle."

The grin returned to Hoff's face. He gave Rocco a shrewd look.

"The little lady might have an idea, at that," he said. "Rocco, you're off driving for me and back on deliveries. And since she's so job-happy, I'm gonna give her one— as your partner. Maybe she can keep you out of trouble."

He chuckled at the dumbfounded expression on the bigger man's face.

"And if either of yez screws up like this again, I'll tie you together and throw you in the Schuylkill, and you can arm-wrestle to see who goes down first."

Jayne wondered why she'd ever thought this man had a pleasant side.

"You—what's your name?" Hoff said.

"Jayne Taylor."

"You wait out here. You—fathead—you come in the joint with me and phone Iggy to come get me. I ain't driving with you again today."

He started to walk away. It took every ounce of determination she could summon for Jayne to stick her head boldly out the window and call after him.

"Hey! Boss!"

Hoff turned slowly, as if he could not believe his ears.

"What now?" he said.

"I'm not hired till we talk money," Jayne said.

"You are some piece of work," Hoff said, almost admiringly. "You'll get the same as Rocco, here."

"Hey!" Rocco protested.

"Cash in an envelope, Friday afternoon at the pool hall in Society Hill. Thirty a week, as long as you're driving. You don't drive, you don't get paid, so stay healthy, get me?"

"I get you," Jayne said. She slumped in relief, thinking, *Thirty times fifty-two . . .*

But Hoff wasn't through. She jumped as he stuck his head back in the window.

"And one more thing," he said. "If ya got one of them occupational health problems, don't even think about the hospital. A dame ends up over there, they're gonna ask way too many questions. We got a house doc—specialist in lead poisoning, if you get my drift."

"Yes, boss," Jayne said. "I, ah, I get it."

Finally, he was gone.

Jayne stared stonily ahead, ignoring glances from passersby who wondered why a nice young lady was sitting in a truck outside a greasy spoon on Second Street.

Finally a well-polished new sedan pulled up. Iggy the Polack went into the café—she recognized him—and shortly after that Rocco emerged and rapped on the driver's-side door.

"Move over. I'm driving."

Jayne almost obeyed. They'd be a lot less noticeable if she let the man drive. But if they started out that way, he'd expect to be the driver every time. She wasn't going to let that happen.

"You're too kind," she said sweetly, leaning against the door so he couldn't reach the handle. "But I can do it."

He climbed into the passenger side with ill grace and slumped into the seat. She studied him covertly as he stared silently out the window. She caught him glancing at her surreptitiously, once or twice, but took care not to meet his eyes. They were brown, she noticed, and his skin was tanned, but fair underneath, at the nape of his neck and under the jaw. The coloring didn't really match his jet black hair. She looked again at the back of his neck. The wispy locks there were sandy, not dark. He'd dyed his hair. She felt certain that his name was not Rocco and that he wasn't Italian.

When they had reached open countryside, he gestured to a shade tree at the side of the road.

"Pull over, willya?" he said. "I need a smoke." He climbed out and sat down on the running board. Jayne wondered if she should get out or not. This might be some kind of ploy to ditch her and take off. But it could also be the moment for a truce negotiation. She walked around the truck and took up a position leaning against the bumper, where she could keep an eye on him. He took out a slightly crumpled cigarette, tapped it straight, and lit up.

"Holy Mother of God," he said to no one in particular. "She can drive."

He pulled in a lungful of smoke and sighed as he exhaled. Then he seemed to notice that Jayne was there.

"Oh, pardon me. You smoke?"

"No, thank you," Jayne said primly.

"Yeah, I know—it's a dirty habit," he said. "I picked it up in the war. Can't seem to break it."

"It's one of the habits I avoided picking up in France," Jayne said.

"Speaking of things you've picked up," he said, "where did you get the gun?"

Jayne pressed her handbag against her side, feeling its weight, just to make sure she'd re-stowed the Mauser safely.

"I brought it home with me," she said. "Let's just say that the man from whom I received it will not be needing it again."

"Fighting the Hun, eh?" Rocco said.

Jayne shrugged. "I'm sure you're aware that relief services workers are official noncombatants. We were not authorized to participate in hostilities."

"Then why the piece?"

"Let's be realistic, Mr.—" Jayne paused.

"Smith," he interjected.

"Mr. Smith—if you say so. I imagine that in your line of business, realism is one of the necessary qualifications. I drove truckloads of valuable supplies through devastated countryside. I would have run like a bunny from armed German troops, but one cannot always avoid the odd smuggler, straggler, or sniper. Or just the ordinary man who feels that a woman alone is a target of opportunity."

"Ever killed a man? I notice you kept missing that guy in the alley."

Jayne gave him points for being observant.

"I meant to miss. Why should I kill for someone who had not yet committed himself to paying me?"

"You didn't answer my question."

Damn. She had hoped to distract him.

"I don't think we know each other well enough—yet—to sit around telling war stories."

"I don't give a damn about your war stories," he said. "What I want to know is if you know how to plug a target in a real-life tight situation, or if you only know how to take the gun out and wave it around."

"If there's any gun-waving going on here, it's not on my part," she said. "We were just *in* a situation, and I think I handled myself all right."

"For Pete's sake, why do you want to get mixed up in this kind of show?" he said. "You want to be one of those independent types, working girl, whatever, fine—why can't you be a teacher or a nurse? Sing in a club or something, if you have to walk on the wild side!"

He gazed at her speculatively.

"You wouldn't be too bad-looking if you'd make a little more of yourself." His hands indicated cleavage in a manner she found irksome. "Dress up. You know."

"I am motivated by the same thing you are, Mr. Smith," she said coldly. "Money. The long green. Cold cash. Do you have any idea how many hours I'd have to toil as a nurse to earn the fee I can get from your boss? Furthermore, I don't like nursing. Or dressing up. I do like driving trucks. And I'm good at it."

"College girls!" he growled, as if it were a curse word. "I suppose you think it's all a big adventure, huh? This is a tough, dirty job. It's no fit place for the likes of you."

"Funny," she said coolly. "That's what they all said when I dropped out of college to work behind the lines in France. I didn't get that so much when I was the only one for miles to bring in clean water and food and bandages.

"Now it seems the jobs that pay are the ones that are too dirty for a woman. They're all right for the likes of *you*—you can take your money and run—but the only place for the likes of me is back home on the farm starving, because no woman can get a job that'll support my— that will support me."

She'd almost slipped there. Best not to let these people know she had family.

He flicked the stub of his cigarette to the ground and ground it beneath his heel.

"Fine. You sweet-talked Boo Boo into this. I can't talk you out of it. But there's one thing I'll never believe—that a girl can guard my back. I'll be watching you."

Not exactly the truce she'd been hoping for, Jayne thought as she drove on toward the train station. But at least he'd accepted that he was going to have to work with her. The defeated set of his shoulders told her that.

"I'll be getting off at the Radnor station," she said.

"Going somewhere on the train?" he asked. "The mood Boo Boo's in, he could send us off on some wild-goose chase any time. And you better be ready—if you really want this job."

"Don't worry. I'm just going home. I left my bicycle at the station."

"Bicycle?" He put his head in his hands in mock despair. "I'm teaming up with a suffragette on a bicycle. It's bad enough you're a skirt—if the boys hear you're a skirt in bloomers I'm dead on the street."

"No bloomers. Scout's honor." She smiled sweetly at him, and was pleased to see him blush.

"Look, why don't we just put the bicycle in the back and I drive you home," he said.

"No, thank you," Jayne said. "Another time, perhaps."

"It's getting dark. Will your ma be waiting up for you?" he said, as she pulled up at the station and let him climb into the driver's seat.

"Sadly, no. Nor will my father be on the porch with a shotgun to discourage not-so-gentlemanly callers. My parents have passed away."

"No one to keep the home fires burning?"

He was obviously trying to find out if she had some kind of guardian or male partner in the wings, she thought. She was almost flattered by his curiosity, until she realized that it was professional, not personal.

"I tend my own home fires," she said coolly. "Where shall I meet you tomorrow?"

"Be here at seven. I'll pick you up. Try not to be caught speeding on your bicycle."

He had the audacity to wink at her before rattling off in a cloud of dust.

Jayne strode to the end of the platform, doing her best to ignore with dignity the occasional disapproving look aimed at her short hair and muddy garments. She retrieved her bicycle from the lamppost where she had padlocked it.

It was a long, tiring ride home. Her legs ached from pedaling, and her back ached from jouncing over pebbles and ruts. But sore feet and shabby clothes were a small price to pay for independence. She leaned forward over the handlebars and dreamed about driving home someday in a truck of her own.

No one was on the porch to meet her as she dismounted and leaned her machine against the gently sagging porch. She limped up the steps and let the screen door slam behind her.

"Maddie! *Je reviens!*" she called.

She was greeted by a torrent of French at high speed and volume. In the distance, the sound of a shotgun echoed through the woods.

"Is everything all right?"

She stepped into the kitchen, and met a cloud of steam that smelled good.

Madeleine turned from her post at the stove, pushing damp tendrils of curly copper hair back from her flushed face.

"*Morte de ma vie!*" the younger girl exclaimed. "*Les enfants* will be the death of me. Look, they 'ave bring me fish, but not clean them. Now they take the gun for rabbits. *Le bon Dieu* grant they don't blow up themselves. *Tiens!* The job! You *réussi?*"

"Yes! I have succeeded!" Jayne said, raising her hands in a victory gesture. "Max Hoff has hired me to drive trucks! With Mr. Rocco Smith, my new partner. I am to meet him at the station at seven o'clock tomorrow. Just think of it, Maddie—this time next week, I'll be picking up my pay! Thirty dollars a week! I'm making as much as a police officer."

Madeleine hugged her and began to waltz clumsily around the kitchen with her.

"Stop, stop," Jayne laughed. "I'm all muddy. And garbagy. You'll get day-old cabbage in your soup."

Madeleine stepped back in dismay. "*Et je suis* stickee!" she said. "I am spill everythings when *ce méchant* Jonny say, 'Boo!'"

She scrubbed at Jayne's lapel with a corner of her apron, but only succeeded in blending a smear of frosting into the mud.

"Just leave it," Jayne said. "I'll scale those fish for you while I'm still grubby, and then I'll change into something decent while they're cooking. I hope we're eating soon. I'm starved."

"This Max 'Off, he doesn't buy you the lunch?" Madeleine said. "He is not *gentil.*"

"No, not very," Jayne said, slipping a layer of newspaper under the pile of bluegill. "Anyway, he really didn't have time." She'd been about to say, "He didn't have time before the shooting started," but stopped herself. What Maddie didn't know would not alarm her.

Jayne hunted through jumbled kitchen drawers for the fish knife. Maddie had heard enough gunshots for a lifetime, she thought. Even the sound of the children hunting in the fields unnerved her. Jayne hoped to earn enough money soon that they could stop hunting small game and live on butcher's meat like normal people. Perhaps raise some chickens and ask Salem Cope to slaughter and dress them—that was not a job that should be left for tenderhearted Madeleine, either.

Jayne smiled as she listened to Maddie's cheerful voice run on, chattering and laughing about her day. It hadn't been that long since Maddie had been a frail, mute, white-faced creature who knew not a word of English and was too frightened to speak French. She felt better about her decision to bring them all home. Whatever the inconveniences of their life in Pennsylvania, it had to be better than leaving them behind in France.

The door slammed, and the children thundered into the house: Henri and Jean-Luc, in tandem as usual, fighting over the gun; Hildegarde right behind them, clasping two dead rabbits to her chest, heedless of the blood dripping down her dress. Jayne immediately looked around for the baby, and was relieved to see her sleeping peacefully in a basket in the pantry

"Jonny! What have I told you?" Jayne said. "The gun must always be treated with respect. Show me that it's unloaded. Then put it in the closet at once. No hunting for you tomorrow."

Jean-Luc scowled, but he looked at the knife in Jayne's hands and decided not to protest.

"Put the gun away like a good boy," she said, "and I'll let you skin the rabbits and hang them in the smoke-house.

"And the rest of you—get out to the pump and wash your hands and faces at once. There are new clothes in those boxes from the deliveryman, but you can't see them until you're clean!"

I've got a job, she thought triumphantly, as she cleaned the fish. *Glory hallelujah—and never let it be said that higher education doesn't improve a young lady's prospects in life!*

CHAPTER FOUR

DAZZLE PAINT

Why are we here?" Jayne said, as she followed Rocco up the stairs of a downtown hotel that had seen better days. "And why can't we at least use the elevator?" she added.

"You know the house doc Max mentioned?" Rocco said. "This is where he keeps office hours. And Max said he didn't want anybody to see us on the way in."

"I'm not sick," Jayne said suspiciously. She'd been driving with Rocco for weeks now, and this was the first time they'd ever been summoned to a bedside consultation. Yes, she was armed. But she still found the juxtaposition of "Max" and "hotel room" profoundly disturbing.

"Don't flatter yourself, Miss Taylor," Rocco said. "It's about Duffy. He's the guy Max assigned to my run—the one I would have been driving if you hadn't come along."

He shot Jayne a resentful look.

"The doc called Max this morning, said there's some kind of a problem with Duffy. And Max wants we should see it for ourselves."

Rocco pushed the stairwell door open, and they stepped out into the carpeted hallway. He rapped out "shave and a haircut" on the door to the nearest suite.

The first thing to greet them was the business end of Max's pistol.

"Put it away, boss, it's just us," Rocco said.

Hoff's face was shiny with nervous perspiration as he waved them in.

Jayne stepped past him to survey the room. It held only the usual hotel furniture—chipped dresser with mirror, a couple of chairs, and a bed. The man bent over the bed wasn't wearing a white coat, but he did have a stethoscope, which he was applying to a bandaged form sprawled on the bed. She guessed he must be the house doc, and the patient, presumably, was Duffy.

The doctor shook his head as he folded the stethoscope and put it back in his bag.

Hoff lounged in the doorframe, a safe distance from the patient.

"See that?" he said. "Even the doc here don't know. Is that what I pay you for, Doc? To tell me 'Your guess is as good as mine'?"

Jayne saw the doctor's lips tighten under Hoff's needling.

"I'm paid to tend gunshot wounds and DTs, dispense drugs and keep my mouth shut," the doctor said. "I've never seen anything like this."

Jayne stepped closer to see for herself. All of a sudden she knew how Hoff felt. It seemed oppressively hot in the room, and her skin prickled. Duffy's injuries were eerily familiar. Gauze bandages covered the right side of his chest and his right arm. Both hands were wrapped, but the right seemed more swollen. Where the skin showed, it was reddened and shiny, as if from a severe sunburn. Blisters showed at the edge of the bandaged area, and the hair was falling from his patchy-looking scalp.

"I'd have someone stay with him," the doctor said in carefully neutral tones. "For his own protection."

"You mean to make sure he don't try to run away," Hoff said.

"Well, yes. He seems a little out of his head. I think this is an injury of some kind, not a contagious disease, but I can't be sure. And if it is contagious, you wouldn't want it to be traced back to you."

"You got that right," Hoff said. "I'll get someone in here to watch him."

"Good. Give him plenty of liquids. Keep those dressings clean. I'm leaving some medication for the pain. Make sure the man you leave in charge is reliable."

"You mean, so he won't hustle the dope? I get your drift."

"Yes. That's important. You want the patient to get the full dose, so he stays quiet. And stays put. After what happened with the influenza, you could be looking at a lynch mob if people get the idea you've brought in a new epidemic along with the whiskey. Keep him under. I'll be back tomorrow to see how he's doing."

He waited for Hoff to step aside so he could leave.

"Boss, what are we doing here?" Rocco said. He, too, stayed as far from the bed as he could get.

"I wanted yez to see what happened to Duffy," Hoff said. "Because you're taking over his route."

"Boss!" Rocco protested. "We're just getting in good with the customers from the brewery run."

Jayne's attention strayed from the argument to the figure on the bed. She'd never brought herself to ask Maddie exactly what had happened before the bombing of the convent. At first, Madeleine had seemed too fragile to face those memories, and later, when she'd returned to a happy life, Jayne hadn't wanted to risk bringing back the darkness. Now Duffy showed similar injuries. Maybe—if Duffy lived—she could finally learn what the German had done.

"Forget about the brewery run," Hoff said. "That's peanuts compared to this one. Special shipment, special price. No screwups. You wind up like that one, I'll dump you in the river. Like I shoulda done with him." He jerked his head contemptuously toward the figure on the bed—and noticed Jayne bent over Duffy, staring.

Hoff turned his bad temper on her.

"Hey, get away from there," he said. "Didn't you hear what the doc said? That could be contagious. This is no time to play nursie."

"I've seen worse," Jayne said curtly. But she moved away from the bed and washed her hands thoroughly in the corner sink.

"Okay, now shake a leg," Hoff said, showing them the door. "You've got a pickup to make."

"Where the devil are we going?" Jayne said. An evening mist rose as the darkness closed in. She could barely see the road ahead.

Rocco slouched in the passenger seat. His tommy gun lay on the floor by his feet, stuffed into a shopping bag with a jacket laid over the top. He pulled a greasy waxed-paper packet out of the shopping bag and unwrapped the paper carefully, scrutinizing the contents. It smelled like a ham sandwich with mustard.

"Rancocas Creek," he said, before biting into the sandwich.

"I gotta admit, this has turned out to be a sweet deal," he added indistinctly, around a mouthful of rye bread and ham. "You driving, I mean. I'll be having my caviar while you carry on with your duties. Maybe a nap after."

Jayne stomped on the pedal, causing the truck to lurch. The sandwich muffled Rocco's curse as he wiped mustard off his shirt.

"Why?" Jayne said.

He shrugged. "You know the drill. Boss sends us out to make a pickup. That's all I know."

"No, I mean why did he pull us off the brewery route?"

"Guess Max finally got tired of busting my head for that little mistake I made in the alley," Rocco said. "He had Duffy replace me on the specialty deliveries, to punish me for screwing up. Now it looks like Duffy screwed up worse."

"Specialty? What's special about it?" Jayne said.

"Well, you gotta figure it's coming up the Delaware. So chances are this is the real stuff, old whiskey and vintages from Europe, maybe Canada. Anyway, it's the deluxe article, not homemade rotgut like our usual cargo. Somebody must have ordered this special."

"So we're meeting a boat?"

"That's my bet."

There was something wrong with Rocco tonight, Jayne thought. He was far too agreeable. He never talked this much, or responded so obligingly to questions. He was trying to cover something up. She wondered what he knew that he wasn't telling her.

"Duffy was burned," she said abruptly. "Not ordinary thermal burns, though. Did you ever see anything like that before?"

He glanced over at her.

"Gas?" he said. "Is that what you're thinking?"

"It could have been," she said. "I've seen mustard-gas burns, and I'll bet you have too. That quack doctor has never been to the front. He wouldn't know."

"What's your point?" he said warily.

"Well, I don't think it's gas," she said. "With burns that extensive, he would have had to inhale. But when I went over there, I didn't hear his lungs gurgling. He was breathing all right."

"So?"

He'd gone back to his usual taciturn manner, she thought. She must be on the right track.

"So, it's not gas. Or not any kind of gas we know about. But this special cargo could be something other than whiskey."

"Such as?"

"Such as illegal munitions, and don't give me the dunce act, Mr. Smith. You're a good deal quicker on the uptake than you care to admit. Goldberg's army surplus has been doing a brisk trade in tommy guns and bullet-proof vests. Who's to say they'd be unwilling to sell more potent arms as well?"

"What's it to you?" Rocco said. "A package is a package. I don't ask what's inside. And the day you start asking, you're out of my truck, for good."

He was right. Jayne had to back off. She didn't dare start showing scruples now, even if she felt them. But the best defense was a good offense. She might back off, but she wasn't going to back down.

"'My truck'?" she retorted. "Since when? It looks to me as if I'm driving, and that makes it my truck as far as I'm concerned. And I'll drive any damn thing I'm paid to drive, but I want to know what it is. Especially after what happened to Duffy! And if you don't like it, *you* can get out of *my* truck!"

"Okay, okay," Rocco said. "Don't get your knickers in a twist. I get your point."

He downed the last of his sandwich and wiped his mouth.

"So, did you ever see anything like that before? I saw you looking." His sideways glance was piercing, curious. Apparently he'd noticed her interest in the bandaged man.

"Yes," she said, striving to keep her tone casual. "I saw burns like those on a civilian in 1917. We wondered if it was a new kind of weapon. But nothing ever came of it. Now I wonder."

"Did he die?"

"Who?"

"The civilian."

"Oh—no," Jayne said. "She was sick for a few weeks, but she got better."

"Well, all right then," Rocco said. "We'll just watch our step, not pull any stoppers out or open any boxes. We'll be fine."

Jayne didn't mention seeing the German on the docks. She'd put the incident out of her mind, convinced it had been her imagination, nothing more. Now she felt uneasy again.

"Turn here," Rocco said.

The truck bumped over a one-lane bridge. A couple of miles later, the road dwindled to a rutted two-track, and then dove into the woods. Jayne slowed to a crawl and rolled her window down. It was pitch black in the trees. She could smell the water and hear the sound of it, somewhere off to the left.

"Hold up. I'll get the lantern and wave you in to the boat launch," Rocco said. Jayne noted that he'd been here before. She pulled up and let the motor idle while Rocco fussed with the lantern.

Suddenly she saw a light, off to the left. That wasn't Rocco's lantern. He was still crouched by the right bumper. And the light was pale, unearthly, nothing like the yellow flame of a kerosene lantern. The light came closer, wavering.

In a spasm of cold terror, Jayne saw that it had a shape—a vaguely human outline, seeming to float above the ground. She heard the soft whoosh as Rocco finally got the lantern lit. He swore as he, too, saw the light. He staggered forward into the dark, holding the lantern ahead of him like a weapon.

"Stay put." His disembodied voice came back to her.

She scrabbled under the seat for her gun and climbed out of the truck. She flanked Rocco on the left, hoping they could trap whatever it was between them and divide its attention.

She could hear the creature moaning. She froze behind a tree as it blundered past, arms raised in a pleading gesture. It was human. She heard its feet thud against the ground, though she couldn't see them. From the waist up, it glowed in the dark with a pale green light. The right arm and hand shone most brightly. Every finger was clearly outlined. The face was dimmer, mottled, but not too dim to show the features—swollen to a doughy sketch of a face, with puffed lips and eyes that were dark dimples. Jayne shrank from it, but in horror, not in fear.

She heard a rustling in the woods—behind her, coming up from the river. Not Rocco. She could still see the lantern light on her right. She held her breath, straining to hear. There was a rattle, a chattering sound, with the rhythms of speech, but in no language she'd ever heard. Not bootleggers. Not gunrunners. The hair rose on the back of her neck. She dropped flat in the ferns and brush as a flash like horizontal lightning shot out from behind her and crackled around the glowing man. He burned with cold blue fire, some force holding him up for seconds that seemed like eternity, before the light went out, leaving Jayne so dazzled she could see nothing.

She could still hear, though: the thud as what was left of the burning man hit the ground, the crash of breaking glass as Rocco dropped the lantern. Then there was light again as the spilled kerosene caught and flared up in the damp brush. The flames backlit Rocco as he crawled toward the body on the ground.

"McCracken?" he said. "Mac? Is that you? Oh God—"

Jayne noticed that his voice broke, and he sounded completely unlike the stony-faced hood he had been playing. She also noticed that he was perfectly outlined as a target.

"Rocco! Hit the bushes!" she screamed. She rolled over onto her back and fired into the brush behind her, waist-high. She couldn't see a target, but one of the slugs hit something and whined off, leaving behind a brief blue crackle and a smell of ozone.

She rolled and scrambled away as fast as she could, as the blue lightning struck the place where she'd been and the ferns exploded into a brief burst of sparks. Footsteps thumped through the brush toward her. If she moved, she'd give her location away. If she stayed put, they'd find her and sweep her with that blue fire. She tried to remember how many shots she had left.

The stutter of a tommy gun exploded into the night. Twigs and leaves rained down on her. Under cover of the deafening noise, she dove deeper into the woods. When the sound died away, she found herself nose to the ground, hugging the biggest tree trunk she'd been able to find. She raised her head just in time to hit the dirt again as a retaliatory lightning bolt speared past her and hit the truck. Blue fire sizzled, setting the paint aflame.

Two sets of feet shuffled past her as she held her breath. But they weren't hunting her. As they moved into the light of the burning truck, they cast shadows like human beings. They wore human clothes. But something about them made Jayne shudder with a fear she'd never felt around any human being. They moved with a stiff, shambling gait. One of them carried something cradled in its arm. It had to be the lightning gun. It raised the device and aimed it toward the truck again.

Where was Rocco? The flames blinded Jayne to all around them. He had to be in the darkness somewhere— under the back of the truck, probably, but if so, the heat would soon drive him out of hiding to be fried by the unearthly weapon.

Jayne edged sideways to get a clear shot at the lightning gunner. Something inside made her hesitate for just a moment before pulling the trigger.

Just keep your head down and let them go after Rocco, that voice inside said. *Why should you stick out your neck for him? He's nothing but a two-bit hood. He wouldn't take a chance for you.*

But at that moment she knew she'd try to protect even Boo Boo Hoff from these two strangers. Everything about them made her blood run cold. They might look human, but they were *wrong*. Even a two-bit hood deserved better than to fry like a bug on a hot stove.

She squeezed off the shot. Then another. Then the hammer clicked on an empty chamber. Damn.

The gunner staggered under the impact of the shots, but there was no blood. Instead he *wavered*, shimmered, as if he were melting. He collapsed like a bundle of sticks. The other figure snatched up the gun and fired another bolt at the truck. The engine caught fire and exploded. The truck listed as the tires burst into flame, and crashed sideways like an elephant rolling over.

Jayne caught the muzzle flash from the corner of her eye just before the tommy gun fired again. She could have cheered. Rocco had gotten away before the truck became a trap.

The man with the gun stumbled, and something that glittered in the light sprayed out as he ran across Rocco's line of fire. He must have been hit. But he didn't go down. He kept running. He turned his head right and left, and the firelight gave Jayne one glimpse of his features. It was the German.

Shock tore a cry from her, but he didn't pause. He threw away the gun as he dashed with a weird, stilted gait, like a puppet on strings, into the woods and disappeared.

Jayne stared at her useless gun. She'd left the spare ammunition in her purse. In the truck.

Out of the roadside darkness, Rocco came limping, his face sooty and grim.

"Jayne," he called hoarsely.

She hesitated. He still held the tommy gun, muzzle up and ready. Was he calling her so he could eliminate the only witness?

"Jayne! Are you all right?"

"Yes. I'm here."

She picked herself up, brushing off cobwebs and dirt. Fleetingly she thought of her clothes. Kensie would kill her for sure this time, if Rocco didn't, and Maddie would help.

"Thank God," Rocco said, another expression that seemed oddly out of character. He hadn't shot her. Not yet, anyway. Kensie might still get her chance.

"Here." He threw her the purse. "Reload."

He limped over to the place where the original gunner had fallen, and kicked at something in the grass.

"Holy—" he said. "Taylor! Will you get over here and look at this?"

Jayne felt better now that she was armed again. She approached warily.

What lay on the ground looked at first like a bundle of clothing wrapped around a pile of sticks. It took time for her mind to give meaning to the outlines revealed by flickering firelight. The sticks weren't wood. They were a body—just not a human body. Long limbs, hard and shiny like those of an insect, lay twisted inside the fabric of normal trousers and stockings. The torso was an ovoid casing roughly the size of an artillery shell. It was shiny and smooth, except where bullets had smashed it and green foam oozed out around bulges of internal stuff that looked like spoiled pudding full of maggots.

Jayne felt sick. She tried to ignore the sound of Rocco retching into the bushes. *Lucky I didn't get half that sandwich*, she thought, and then was sorry. Swallowing hard, she forced herself to look at the thing's head. It had something like eyes and a mouth, with a cluster of pits and lumps instead of a nose. Half-skull, half-insect, with that disconcerting metallic sheen—that was all she had time to see before the remains started to smolder and then suddenly flared up in a burst of white sparks.

Jayne jumped back. The body burned with a hard, intense flame, until there was nothing left but a scorched pit in the earth and a few lumps of carbonized rubber from the shoe soles.

"What in the hell?" Rocco breathed. The fire in the truck was burning low, and it was hard to see. He walked in zigzag patterns, kicking in the grass till he found the lightning gun. Jayne saw him bend down to it, and heard his exclamation of pain as he snatched his hand away.

"Ouch! Damn! It's still hot as blazes."

He tried to take his coat off, but fumbled as he shifted the tommy gun from hand to hand.

"Get this off me," he said.

Jayne held the coat so he could shrug out of it. She felt him wince as he pulled his arm free of the sleeve.

"You're hurt," she said.

"It's nothing," he said. "A little burn, that's all."

He wrapped the coat around the weapon so he could pick it up and carry it closer to the firelight.

She bent over the strange gun with him. It had a section resembling a stock attached to a muzzle-like cylinder, but the cylinder seemed solid, not a hollow tube. Between the muzzle and the stock was a metallic pod that must have held the firing mechanism. Unfortunately, it had been struck and pierced by bullets from Rocco's gun. It had become a twisted piece of junk. Bringing his hurt hand awkwardly into play, Rocco tilted the shattered pod toward the light, and a fine-grained, glittering powder spilled out over his fingers and chest.

"Come out of the light," Jayne said. "I need to see something."

She dragged Rocco away from the truck into the shadow of the trees. His fingers glowed eerily.

"Jeez!" He lifted his hands to stare at them. The powder sifted down like fairy dust.

"Drop it," Jayne gasped. "Drop it now!"

She shook his arm, thinking he'd be unwilling to let go of this solitary piece of evidence. But he obeyed her instantly. Then she saw why. The metal had heated up to a dull red glow. Rocco's coat smoked and burst into flame.

He tried to stamp out the fire, but in vain. Jayne pulled him back before he could set fire to his trousers as well.

"Come with me," she said urgently. "We have to get to the river. You have to wash that off."

He tried to resist.

"Now!" she said. "Do you want to end up like Duffy, or what's-his-name there—your friend?"

He stumbled after her to the riverbank.

"Scrub it off," she said, scooping handfuls of sand from the riverbed. "You have to get it off."

He hissed with pain and pulled his arm away.

"What's wrong?" She tried to see, but it was too dark.

"They must have winged me with that zap gun," he said. "It stings. Feels like a burn. Nothing broken, though."

"I'm sorry," Jayne said, "but we have to get that dust off you."

More gently, she dipped his arm into the flowing water.

"What is this stuff?" he said. "How do you know about it?"

"I told you," she said. "I saw it in France. Something like it, anyway. I don't know what it is, exactly. It's something like radium. It burns without fire. If you keep it near you long enough, it will burn you too. Maybe a scientist could understand it. I don't. I just know it's poison."

"Death dust," Rocco muttered. "McCracken—he was a good joe. He was—" He clenched his jaw on the rest of the sentence.

Luminous swirls of dust floated away and vanished downstream. Finally the last grain was gone, and Rocco's hands were dark and cold. Jayne stood up, and extended a hand to help him rise.

"Come on," she said. "We need to go for help. And figure out what to tell Max, on the way."

"We aren't going to tell Max anything," Rocco said. "I'm going to pick up what I came for. It's still out there."

"Don't be ridiculous," Jayne said. "We won't do any such thing. You need to see the doctor, now. Max is just going to have to understand that something went badly wrong. The customer will have to make lemonade. It happens."

Rocco did not reply. Jayne thought he was going to be obstinate, but he slumped back against a tree.

"Wrap this hand for me, wouldja?"

"With what?" Jayne grumbled. "You managed to get your coat burned up. And your truck burned up."

She rummaged in her handbag. Thank goodness her mother had taught her never to go out without a handkerchief. And thank goodness she'd chosen to bring a capacious bandanna, instead.

She tore the remnants of his scorched sleeve away, and dressed the burn.

"Now let's get going."

He took her hand, but he didn't rise. She became uncomfortable and tried to tug her hand out of his grasp, but he was too strong. A thrill of alarm went through her.

"Taylor, you've been a good little soldier," he said. "I gotta give you that."

Jayne wondered if he was becoming delirious.

"But now it's time to walk away," he continued. "Go home, tell Max I fell in the river and I'm dead as far as you know. Tell him I went nuts. Hell, I don't care, tell him any damn thing you want. But walk away. You don't need to be involved in this."

"I can't walk away while you have a death grip on my wrist," she pointed out. "And you're not going anywhere without help. I've seen shock, Mr. Smith, and I believe you've got it. I don't believe a second-rate hood would go to these extremes for a case or two of imported liquor. Why don't you try telling me what's really at stake here? Perhaps I could be of assistance."

"Just a beef between mobs," he said. "Like when Lucky's torpedoes shot at me in the alley."

"I don't believe that," she said. "Max wouldn't trust you enough to put you in charge if that were true. He'd pick Iggy or one of his other pals. He likes you because you're smart, not because you're loyal."

Relatively smart, she amended privately.

His eyes caught a brief glint of moonlight as he glanced up at her. She couldn't tell what he was thinking. It was too dark.

"Miss Taylor, you're not a bad joe, for a jane," he said. "But you made it clear you were in this for the money. So how do I know you won't sell me out, if I tell you the truth?"

"You don't have much choice right now," Jayne said. "Whatever you've got planned, you're going to need help. So maybe you'd better figure out how to make it worth my while."

"Worth your while," he repeated. He sounded bitter. "Okay, *cutie pie*, how does a federal pardon sound?"

"I haven't been convicted of anything, that I know of."

"Oh, you will be—as soon as I testify."

"Testify?"

She reached instinctively for her gun, but the handbag was on the ground where she'd left it. Rocco grunted with pain when she wrenched at his hurt hand, but his grip didn't waver. And he still held the tommy gun tucked under his other arm, muzzle pointed in her direction.

She tried to kick him anyway.

"Let me go, you lousy stoolie!"

"I'm a federal agent."

Jayne froze, although inside she felt as if she were scrambling to keep her feet under her. She was disconcerted and furious. How dare he lie to her? At the same time, she felt a curious sense of vindication.

"I knew it!" she cried triumphantly. "I knew your name wasn't 'Rocco.' And you dyed your hair, didn't you?"

"It showed?" he said uncertainly. Jayne felt she had scored a point and disconcerted him, in turn.

"Only to a woman's discerning eye," she said smugly. "I doubt that Max noticed."

"Well, it hardly matters now, does it?" he growled. "The point is that I've been under cover for the Bureau of Investigation on a matter of national security. I'm going to send every last one of Boo Boo's boys up the river when I get out of here, and you're going with them unless you want to give me a hand. If you help me, I'll do my best to leave you out of it."

"Oh yeah? Well, what if I turn you in, instead? What if I walk away the way you originally said, and tell Max you were a stoolie? Better yet, what if I bump you off first?"

She saw another glint of light. He'd moved the gun barrel. The sound of something sliding along the ground told her that he was using it to drag her handbag toward himself. She made a futile grab for it. The gun barrel swung back and nudged her rudely in the ribs. There was a chuckle in the darkness.

"Hard to do, when I have your gun."

"Don't you dare poke me with that thing," she hissed.

"Don't waste my time," he said. "Are you in or out?"

"I can ditch you in the dark," she said. "You can't hang on to me all the time."

"Okay! Okay! I promise you immunity right off the bat. Plus five hundred bucks if we get out of this alive. Will that do it for you, Miss In This For The Money?"

Five hundred dollars, she thought. The driving job was over, for sure. She figured Max would have fired them even if Rocco hadn't turned out to be a plant. She'd need the money to tide Maddie and the kids over until she could come up with something else.

"I'll shake on that," she said.

"Ow! Go easy on the arm!"

"But you need to tell me what's going on."

"I'll fill you in on the boat," Rocco said. He pulled himself upright and finally let go of her hand.

"Boat?"

"Yeah, our objective is anchored out in the river. Know anything about handling boats?"

"Sure, I know boats," she lied briskly.

Well, she'd been out in a canoe, anyway. And occasionally sailed a masted dinghy. She knew a *little* something about boats.

She stumbled after him along the shore, to a muddy cut in the bank, where a rough incline formed a boat landing. Moonlight suffused the mist, and they could see a little. A rowboat fitted with an outboard motor sat beached on the shore.

Rocco ushered Jayne into the bow and started up the motor. They moved forward into the wall of mist, and the shore disappeared from sight.

The current pulled them along faster. Jayne guessed they had reached the mouth of the creek and were gliding out into the Delaware.

"What are we looking for?" Jayne said. "And how are we supposed to find it in this soup?"

Rocco pulled out a compass.

"I have the heading," he said. "Keep a lookout for a pair of lights, red over white. There's a barge."

You're never going to find it, Jayne thought.

"I don't know what it is," Rocco said. "We pick up cargo and transfer it to a third party. Same basic process as the bootlegging. But the Bureau is concerned that smuggling of a more dangerous nature was going on under cover of run-of-the-mill criminal activity."

"Secret weapons?" Jayne said.

"We don't know. Mac and I could have hijacked a sample weeks ago, but we needed to find out who was the ultimate receiver of the materials. We spent months wangling a place on this route. Then you came flouncing in and busted up our setup."

"Well, excuse me for breathing," Jayne said. "Are you sure that compass works? It feels to me as if we're going around in circles. I know enough about boats to know we'd be smarter not to be out here on a night like this."

She was startled when she saw dots of light twinkling through the fog.

"Lights to starboard," she said.

Rocco cut the motor and the boat coasted toward the barge that loomed ahead. He kicked the handbag along the bottom of the boat toward Jayne.

"Get out the gat," he whispered. "Stay sharp and follow my lead."

Jayne tied up the boat and followed Rocco up a rope ladder onto the barge.

"Who goes there?" someone growled.

"Boo Boo sent me," Rocco said.

A short, tough-looking man came out of the deckhouse.

"What happened to Nino and Mac?" he said, looking Jayne up and down with a little too much relish.

"Nino and Mac had a little accident," Rocco said. "We're the replacements."

Jayne tapped the muzzle of her gun against her boot top and glared back at the short man with an expression she hoped would seem tough and disdainful. She knew her hair was bedraggled and her dress soaked through. That didn't excuse his staring.

"I don't know yez," the man said.

"I brought my friends Mr. Grant and Mr. Jackson," Rocco said. "That's all you need to know." He pulled a wad of cash out of his boot top.

"Okay," the short man said. "Once I got the cash, Boo Boo is your headache."

"Not so fast," Rocco said, holding the money just out of his reach. "Load us up first."

"Nino and Mac loaded their own," the man complained.

"Do you see them around here?" Rocco said, giving them a hard stare. "Me and my partner don't do hard labor. I pay cash when received. And it ain't received till it's in the boat."

"Moe! Get out here!" the man shouted. A bigger thug emerged from the deckhouse. Grumbling, the two of them rolled a half-dozen canisters across the deck, bundled them one by one into a sling, and winched them down into the boat.

"What's with the hoist?" Rocco said. "Don't you have the muscle to do it yourself?"

"You try it," the short man snarled. "They're heavy. Heaviest booze I ever lifted. I'd like to try it in a glass. Yez could break an elbow!"

Jayne took care climbing back into the boat and casting off. The weight of the new cargo had sunk it almost to the gunwale. She expected to return quickly to shore, but instead Rocco steered in a direction she was almost sure would lead them downriver, toward the sea. They were riding with the ebb tide, and picked up speed rapidly. Mist still clung to the water's surface. The sound of wavelets curling over and slapping into each other made a white noise that covered the soft burr of their engine. It also masked any sounds of anchor chains rattling or propellers churning that might have helped them pinpoint the position of bigger ships that could run them down. A foghorn blared intermittently in the distance.

Jayne stationed herself as a lookout, perched on the bow. She clutched an oar in one hand, on the slim chance that she might be able to fend them off from an unexpected obstacle. She thought furiously as she peered into the mist.

She'd seen the German again. She knew she wasn't hallucinating this time. And after what she'd seen, she couldn't believe that he was involved in anything as simple as smuggled liquor. She knew she was in over her head. Bootlegging was an innocent child's game compared to arms smuggling. If someone was really trying to import deadly unknown weapons, Jayne could not be a part of that, for any price. Yet how could she get out of it? She was in an overloaded boat and couldn't see land in any direction. She wondered if it would be best to play dumb until they returned to land, or to turn the gun on Rocco now and take the helm. Either way, she'd be risking the wrath of Boo Boo Hoff and his whole operation.

"Taylor," Rocco said. Something in his voice made her turn around. She looked straight down the muzzle of his tommy gun. Apparently he'd seen a similar dilemma, but he'd made his decision first.

"Hands up," he said. She had a brief flashback to her first meeting with the German—but Rocco was coldly sane and armed with a machine gun. Her gun had been high and dry on the seat in the middle of the boat. Now it had disappeared. There was no chance she could disarm Rocco. She raised her hands.

"Now keep 'em up and listen carefully," he said. "The plans have changed, see? Mac was my partner. He got me the location for the drop. We were going to work it together and bust up their game. Now I'm going to get the mugs who did this to him. I need you to back me up, help me get on board their ship or whatever they've got. After that, you're on your own. Turn the boat around, get to shore, tell Max I'm dead. Tell him whatever you want. But don't interfere till I get there, or I'll have to shoot you. Understand?"

"Believe me, I don't want to interfere," Jayne said. "All I want is to get out of this racket now. I signed up to drive trucks. I don't want any part of *this*."

It wasn't hard to sound sincere, with the gun in her face and her clammy wet clothes making her shiver till her teeth chattered. She knew she'd feel a lot warmer if she had a tight grip on the butt of her Mauser.

"Scout's honor, I won't try to stop you," she said. "Now you might want to give me back my gun. Two of us armed is better than one if there's any trouble."

He grinned.

"Nice try, Taylor. No gun for you till we get there. I'll leave it in the boat when I go. You can have it back then."

But he did lower his own weapon.

"Show's over—get back to your lookout," he said, with a jerk of his chin toward the fog ahead.

Jayne stretched low over the bow, trying to see below the curls of fog. She shivered in the chill, damp air. She thought she heard a different sound in the waves ahead—a hollow *thunk-thunk*, like water impacting metal. Waves against a hull? She turned her head back and forth, trying to get a direction.

"A little to starboard, I think," she said. "That would be to your right."

She got a glimpse of white through the dark gray mist. Was it a random whitecap, or a boat hull catching a stray moonbeam?

"Stay on this heading," she said. "There it is!"

Now she could see something big in their path—big enough to be an oceangoing yacht.

Rocco cut the engine and let their little boat coast alongside. No crew members walked the deserted deck. No one hailed them. The only sound was the chuckle of water against the hull.

"How are you planning to get on board?" Jayne said.

"I don't know. Mac was supposed to pass me a signal to use, but he didn't have the chance."

The yacht's sides gleamed shiny and smooth, bare of any lines or ladders.

"Here, take the tiller," Rocco said. "Get me in close to the stern. I'll go up the anchor cable."

He slung his gun over his shoulder and changed places with Jayne. The boat rocked dangerously, shipping a splash or two of water.

"Stay down!" Jayne said. "Keep the center of gravity low, or you'll have us both in the drink."

Rocco crouched in the bow, ready to leap for the cable, as Jayne steered in under the side. But before he could make a grab for the chain, the boat collided with something. More water cascaded over the side. Rocco sat down suddenly, as Jayne dropped the tiller and threw her weight to the side in a desperate attempt to keep the boat from swamping.

There were no life preservers, she noticed. *What's the first rule of boating? Never go out without a life preserver*, she thought crossly. She could see herself and six shiny canisters of something sinking to the bottom of the bay.

But not just yet. The gunwales were still above water.

"What the hell are you doing?" Rocco said. "I thought you said you knew about boats."

He dragged himself up to a seat. Jayne saw that he was soaking wet, too.

"I know plenty about boats," she hissed. "If I didn't, we'd be under water by now. We hit something. Something invisible."

She reached gingerly over the gunwale and felt along the side. It suddenly occurred to her that they might have struck an underwater obstacle that might have holed the boat. But the water didn't seem to be rising.

Then her hand struck against a smooth surface—but it wasn't under water. It was right next to the boat. Her hand kept moving. She could feel the surface, but she couldn't see it.

"It *is* invisible," she whispered, as the hair rose on the back of her neck.

"What are you talking about?" Rocco said. He started to scramble back toward her again. Of course—he couldn't see anything either. He could only see her waving her hand in the air and talking nonsense.

"Stop right there!" she ordered. He actually stopped. "Put your hand over the side. Right about where mine is. What do you feel?"

"Holy—"

She didn't need an answer. She could tell by the look on his face that he'd hit the same wall of strangeness.

Whatever she was touching, it was solid and it was fixed in one place. It curved on top. She could rest her arm across the curved segment, and hold the boat in place that way. She pulled tentatively, and they moved sideways along whatever the strange surface was. Rocco got the idea, and pushed against the surface from where he sat. The boat bobbed along until Jayne felt the invisible surface begin to taper down toward the water. She pushed the boat around its tip to the other side. Now they were between the object and the yacht's side.

But it wasn't a yacht anymore. Rocco's jaw dropped. The shining white surface had changed to dull silver. The sharp lines of a seagoing craft with deck and masts had changed to a rounded, streamlined pod shape on stilts above the water. The stilts ended in floats that sat atop the water. It was one of those floats they'd been feeling their way around. And the craft had wings.

"Holy Mother of God," Rocco said devoutly. "It's a monoplane."

"It's a seaplane," Jayne said. "These are pontoons. But—how?"

She unshipped an oar and backpaddled, out past the end of the pontoon. The outlines of the seaplane melted into the mist, to be replaced by the image of the yacht. The pontoon vanished. But when she struck out with the oar, she felt it thump the shape that wasn't there. Quickly, she paddled back in that direction. When they were on the far side of the pontoon again, the seaplane came back into view.

"When you get close enough, you can see it," she said.

"Yeah. It's like dazzle paint," Rocco said. "I saw this in the war. They tried to paint the troop ships so they'd blend in with the water, be hard for U-boats to see, like fish blend in so you can't see them. Or paint up tanks and such so they'd blend with the underbrush."

"Did it work?'

"Damned if I know!" he said, shaking his head. "I guess it helped. If they got close enough, they'd spot you anyway. But this—this is ridiculous. Who are these people?"

"That's what I'd like to know," Jayne muttered. It was easy to call this a seaplane, but that didn't describe it adequately. It was nothing like the planes Jayne had seen before, with their clumsy wires and rivets, canvas and paint. The fuselage was completely smooth, streamlined, and opaque. It had an unearthly grace, as if designed to sail a rarer element than wind or waves.

"It's like the airships of Helium," she said.

"What do you mean, helium?" Rocco said. "This is no zeppelin."

"I mean, like the airships of the *city* of Helium—on the planet Mars. In Edgar Rice Burroughs's stories. I would have expected you to know of him. He writes adventure stories of other worlds. Just the kind of thing boys like to read about."

"I don't have time to read magazines," Rocco said.

Jayne felt sure he wasn't telling the whole truth. She'd seen some luridly colored recreational reading stuffed under the back of the truck seat.

"H. G. Wells, then. Invaders from other worlds."

She was prepared to needle Rocco until he admitted knowledge of airships and Martians, but her own words sent a chill down her spine and dried her mouth.

An invasion from beyond the Rhine was frightening enough. What if the smugglers had crossed a true no-man's-land, a border where no human had ever set foot?

"Heads up," Rocco said. "I guess they finally heard us."

The stern end of the fuselage opened up—the surface pulling back soundlessly somehow—and a ramp extended itself from the opening.

"Do you still want to get on board?" Jayne asked.

Rocco pulled the sling of his tommy gun around to the front again, and nodded. Jayne paddled them over to the ramp. Before Rocco could edge over the side, a crew member emerged at the top of the ramp. He was tall, muffled in a long overcoat and wide-brimmed hat that couldn't conceal his skeletal thinness. The hat brim shadowed his eyes, and a long scarf muffled his nose and jaw.

He stopped at the top of the ramp and stared at them. Jayne felt that prickle of *wrongness* again.

He spoke.

"Where . . . kk . . . Nino . . . kk . . . andt Mackkk?"

The voice was tinny and scratchy, full of clicks and static, like a bad telephone connection.

"They had a little accident," Rocco said. Jayne could tell by how loud his voice sounded that he was scared too. "We're the replacements. I have your cargo."

The figure on the ramp seemed to consider this, staying utterly motionless for long seconds.

"You load . . . kk . . . can . . . kk," he ordered, in the same tinny voice.

Rocco knelt in the bottom of the boat and strained to get his arms around one of the canisters. It was wet and slippery, and he couldn't lift it to the side without rocking the boat dangerously.

Jayne bent to help him, but he shook his head.

"Once I get on board, take off," he whispered. "Get ready to move fast."

Rocco heaved the canister into his arms, and looked helplessly up at the ramp.

"Could I get some help here?" he said plaintively. "It's too heavy."

The thin figure made a "tch" sound—for the first time sounding fully human—and came down the ramp with the same jerky motion Jayne had seen in the German. He bent over and grasped the canister. Up close, his spidery limbs were even more evident. Jayne didn't expect him to be able to budge the heavy container, but was startled to see him lift it with the ease of an ant grasping a crumb. He straightened up as if on springs and carried his burden up the ramp.

Rocco stared after him.

"I was gonna, you know—" he said, making a chopping gesture. "But—how does he move so fast?"

With a massive effort, he lurched to his feet with another container, and stepped out of the boat onto the ramp.

"Go!" he said.

Instead, Jayne crawled out of the boat and followed Rocco onto the ramp.

The creature—having come this close to him, Jayne simply couldn't think of him as a man—emerged from the doorway and brushed past them, on the way to retrieve another container.

"Hurr-rrry," he said. "KKQuickly!"

He bent over the boat again.

Rocco hurled the container he carried at the stooping figure. It struck his shoulder, knocking him flat on the ramp. He dropped the barrel he had just been lifting from the boat. The heavy cylinder struck the gunwale, pushing its edge under the surface. The next wave gushed in, filling the boat. For a moment it floated just below the surface. Then it rolled over and sank out of sight.

The creature gathered his long limbs under him and sprang erect, like a grasshopper. He gave a high-pitched screech, but Jayne thought it was for loss of the cargo, not for any injury. He bounded up the ramp, seeking to gain the doorway, but Rocco stuck the barrel of his gun between the creature's legs and brought him down again. This time Rocco landed on top of him, holding him down by pressing the gun barrel across his neck. Spindly arms and legs flailed like the legs of a half-crushed spider.

"Get him!" Rocco yelled. "Tie his hands!"

Jayne looked around wildly. The rowboat's painter had gone down with it. There was no rope in sight. She was about to start tearing up her dress when she saw the belt on the stranger's trench coat. She yanked it loose, dodging the thrashing limbs, then caught the wrists—or where the wrists should be—one at a time and wound the belt around them.

As soon as the job was done, she dropped the creature's arms and scrambled away, shuddering. Beneath long sleeves and gloves, those limbs had the same cold, bony texture she'd last felt on the body of a dead German, who had risen to haunt her.

The creature had gone limp when he felt himself confined.

"Come here," Rocco panted. "Help me get him inside."

"What happened to 'take off'?" Jayne said. "I liked that one a lot better."

"That one went down with the boat," Rocco said.

Jayne swallowed her fear and picked up the creature's legs, holding them by the cuffs of the long, floppy trousers. Rocco lifted the bound arms. Together they dragged the stranger up the ramp and through the open doorway.

Jayne stared at the interior of the fuselage. She saw dials, like the gauges on a dashboard, but in bewildering complexity, and lights that glowed, and flat, mirrorlike insets covered with moving shapes. If this was a control panel, she couldn't see where the controls were. There were no levers, pedals, or wheels—only a row of odd-shaped knobs clustered below the dials.

While she and Rocco stared at the lights, the creature suddenly bent its head back at an impossibly sharp angle and uttered a shrill whistle and a volley of clicks that sounded like Morse code at double speed. Jayne felt the floor push upward against her feet, and looked back at the door just in time to see the opening close up behind them.

The creature whistled again, and it felt as if the floor suddenly went sideways. Jayne fell and slid into what had been the wall, with Rocco on top of her. The creature kicked off its shoes—hurling them in Rocco's direction as it did so—and clawlike appendages appeared where its feet should have been. It shot out one long leg and seized a bracket on the wall in its claws. The other foot stretched to the control panel, and one talon pecked the row of knobs. The aircraft steadied, but the floor did not level, and the feeling of pressure didn't go away. Jayne knew they were still accelerating.

She pushed herself away from the wall, struggling to get up. Her damp skirts had wrapped themselves around her legs as she rolled over. She kicked out, and felt the fabric rip.

This is the last time, she thought, *the very last time I'm going to work in a skirt.*

"Where'd you put my gun?" she said.

Rocco groaned.

"If you let my gun go down with the boat, I'm going to kill you with my bare hands," she said.

The creature still clung to its toehold on the wall. Its other foot slipped from the control panel, and it scrabbled for a better purchase.

"Gun . . . pocket," Rocco managed. Blood sheeted down over his face from a cut on his head.

Jayne stretched to get her hand into his coat pocket. Her hand closed over something hard and cold, and she pulled it out. And cursed. It wasn't the Mauser. It was a jar of mustard. Wrong pocket.

Stepping on Rocco's shoulder for leverage, Jayne clawed her way up the tilted floor. She got one hand on the console, and with the other she smashed the jar against the creature's face, right between the faceted, spiderlike eyes. Something cracked like a hard-boiled egg, and for a moment she felt grim triumph. Then she realized that the substance oozing over her fist was only mustard. The jar had cracked, not the creature's skull. She smashed the broken jar into the green, skull-like carapace again. Sharp splinters gouged her palm, and she winced and cried out.

The creature screamed and lost its grip on the bracket. It rolled on the floor, smashing its head against walls and furnishings in a vain attempt to dislodge the sticky yellow substance that evidently stung it beyond bearing.

After an avalanche of clicks and whistles, it dropped back into English again.

"Whh . . . wwatt-tterrr kkk!" it rasped pathetically. "Bitte bitte bitte!"

The convulsive jerking of its thin limbs made Jayne feel sick. She'd seen gassed men gurgle and writhe that way.

It's not a man, she told herself. *It's some kind of monster.*

But she couldn't watch. She ripped off the flounce at the hem of her skirt. It was already torn, and the thin fabric parted easily.

"Water, where?" she demanded. Her cut hand left stains on the cloth, and the floor was splashed with Rocco's blood. They all needed water.

Rocco had managed to pull himself upright and find the tommy gun, which had slid to the other end of the fuselage. He used the barrel as a lever to pin down the creature's legs so the taloned feet could not kick out at him. The creature could no longer move, and couldn't point out to Jayne where to find the water.

She crawled back toward the place where they had entered. The fuselage was surprisingly roomy. It was more like a yacht than any aircraft she'd seen. The bulkheads contained racks that could have been used as bunks. Between the racks there was what looked like a cupboard door. It was exactly what it looked like. Thank goodness, an ordinary door with a completely ordinary latch. She pushed the latch sideways, and the door opened.

The first thing she saw was something like a child's sandbox—a rectangular container full of a grainy yellow substance. Next to it was a shallow basin with a spigot just above it. She turned the tap, and clear liquid came out. Warily, she held the strip of cloth under the tap and sniffed the moisture first, then touched her tongue to the wet cloth. It was water—unadulterated, as far as she could tell.

She soaked the rag and hurried back with it. Rocco had re-tied the creature, using one end of the belt for its hands this time, and the other end for its feet, completely immobilizing it. Carefully, Jayne wiped the mustard away from its sensing organs and squeezed water over them to wash away any residue. She picked a few shards of glass from the rigid surface of its face. Definitely a carapace, she thought. Not skin.

"Ttt . . . tanks sks," the creature fizzled.

"Gag it," Rocco said.

Jayne examined the face dubiously.

"I don't think I can without choking it to death," she said. "I think the part where it whistles is these three holes above the jaws, and if I plug those up, it'll suffocate."

"Nnottt, do n'ttttt!" the creature confirmed, chittering anxiously.

"Is there a reason I should care?" Rocco said. He pressed one hand to his head, where the blood was still flowing.

Jayne suffered a pang as she realized that he was still bleeding while she tended the creature. "Your head!" she said. "Keep an eye on him—I'll get you more water."

She couldn't use the stained remnants of the rag. She had to rip another section from her skirt. This time it wasn't as easy. Her skirt was in tatters, exposing most of her legs. For the first time, she wished she had one of the long, multilayered skirts of her mother's generation. A muslin petticoat would be good, too, she thought. The Jazz Age was useless when it came to making bandages.

She wished for a container, too, but had no time to search. She just soaked the fabric until it was sopping wet and hurried back to Rocco. The aircraft seemed to be flying level now, which helped.

She wrapped his cut tightly to stop the bleeding, and cleaned him up as best she could with the cloth she had left. She wished for a blanket, or a cup of tea, or anything to make him more comfortable, but there was nothing in sight. She found her handbag where it had fallen, under the console. She removed her gun and put the bag under Rocco's head to serve as a pillow.

She saw his eyes widen as his gaze traveled up her bare legs. She felt naked. She glared furiously, daring him to say a word, but he looked away first.

"You!" he shouted at the creature. "Where are we going?"

Jayne felt a chill go through her. She hadn't had time until that moment to consider the fact that they were still trapped inside an object that was flying through the air at an unknown speed.

The creature did not respond.

Jayne leaned as close as she dared.

"Where?" she repeated urgently. She didn't know how much it understood. She moved her hands in a swooping motion like an airplane. "Where?"

The creature clicked. She saw its jaws moving, more like the mandibles of an insect than a human mouth.

"Neee," it shrilled. "Nee . . . pppon . . . kk."

It jerked out a brief burst of clicks. Jayne couldn't tell what it meant. It could have been an expression of pain. But she had a horrible feeling that it was laughing.

"Nee-pon?" Rocco said. "What the hell? What does that mean?"

"I think it said 'Nippon,'" Jayne said. "It's what the Japanese call themselves. It thinks we're going to Japan."

The creature's eyes dulled and it stilled. Jayne pushed its sticklike leg, but it didn't respond.

"Is it dead?" Rocco said.

"I don't think so," Jayne said. "But it's unconscious or something."

Rocco laughed painfully.

"One bug, no mustard," he said. "Plenty of ketchup, though. All over my shirt. Who'd have thought."

Then he passed out too.

CHAPTER FIVE

ISLAND OF EXILE

Jayne picked her way around the two sprawled bodies to the console. She was being carried farther and farther from Madeleine and the children, on a mission that wasn't her problem. She wanted to know how to turn this thing around.

She wasn't afraid they'd crash. The plane stayed in steady, level flight. Occasional flutters of that elevator feeling in her stomach were the only reminder that they were in the air, rising or sinking with its currents.

"So what does that tell me?" she muttered. "I guess that either someone's driving—but I can't see them—or the machine drives itself."

She examined the slotted ridges on the console. It looked as if they'd been built so a creature like the one lying tied up on the floor could insert a taloned digit into the slot and somehow control the machine. It looked as if a bobby pin would work as well as a talon—but random meddling didn't seem like the best idea. Especially when she had no idea where they really were. She left the controls alone for the time being.

She found a wire basket bolted to the console. It held a thick stack of maps. They looked like ordinary maps; some of them had publisher's annotations in fine print at the edges. But they'd been drawn over with a thick, scarlet ink, subtly changing outlines of natural features, or marking certain points with symbols Jayne couldn't read.

Jayne felt a sense of growing dread. They'd *corrected* the maps. That meant . . . that meant they must have overflown the landscape repeatedly. Looking down from the sky. Watching us.

And who were *they*? Not the Germans. The Germans had lost the war.

She flipped rapidly through the maps. They didn't cover the whole earth. Just segments of the northern United States, Canada, then the Bering Sea, the coast of Siberia . . . she flipped to the final map: the western coastline of Japan.

She wasn't seasick; the plane held steady in the air. But she was seized with a sickening need to see out of this metal cylinder littered with damaged bodies.

Why had they built a plane without windows? How could they have mapped the earth without seeing it? Light was coming from somewhere, but she couldn't see an opening to the outside. A soft white glow emanated from glassy strips mounted around the top arc of the fuselage. She reached up cautiously to touch the strips, and found them cool to the touch. So it wasn't any kind of electric light she was familiar with—but it must come from a power source other than the sun. And it must be automatic, because no one had switched it on. She had no control over that either.

She slammed her hands against the blank, curved wall next to the console in frustration. She wanted toggles, latches, switches, any comprehensible way to open this sardine can and let herself out.

Instead, she found a thing like a tiny, blinking red eye. She recoiled from it, glancing wildly around the cylinder where she was trapped. Were they watching her, even now? Who *were* they?

She dared to brush her hand back and forth across the winking gaze of the eye. Fine—if they were watching her, let them know she knew it.

She waited for a response. Instead, silently as a wink, the wall in front of her opened wide and she was staring out into empty air. Clouds rushed past. But there was no rush of wind in her face. Holding to the seat by the console with one hand, she reached out cautiously. She could still feel a smooth, hard surface between her and the sweeping skyscape. It was another false appearance. More dazzle.

She brushed her hand again over the eye. This time it spoke to her in a brief susurrus of slurred clicks. And the picture changed again. She was still looking *out*, but what she saw was *down*. Vertigo seized her, and she had to close her eyes.

When she looked again, the earth below was still moving past. It didn't go as fast as the clouds, but it moved, at a steady, majestic pace. Steadily and irrevocably, they were leaving Jayne's known world behind. It was too strange to be frightening.

She'd always liked leafing through atlases, so the passing scene below had a distant familiarity: rows of green wrinkles on a slant, like a tablecloth pulled askew by a careless child. And in the middle, a thick blue rivulet, as if the same child had knocked over a pitcher and water had run across the center of the table.

That was the Susquehanna. The ridges were passing by—Blue Mountain, Allegheny. She couldn't see the coastline to the east. They had already left Philadelphia far behind.

A groan from behind her pulled her attention back into the small, enclosed space. Rocco sat up slowly. He'd developed a big goose egg where his head was cut, and that side of his face was puffy. Blood had soaked through and dried on the bandage Jayne had made for him—dark rusty stains blotching the cheery meadow flowers of what had once been a ruffly summer dress.

"Cold," he complained. "And thirsty. Is our little pal still down for the count?"

"Yes, I'm afraid he won't be much help."

"You could close the window," he said, shivering.

"It's not a real window. It's more like a movie screen, or something. But it does show our position. We're still over the U.S.A., but we're heading for Japan, all right."

He struggled to his feet, eager to see.

"If we had parachutes . . ."

"Sure, let me know if you find any," Jayne said. "Anyway, it doesn't open."

She rapped her knuckles against the window, to show him.

"I'm cold too," she said. "Check out these controls. See if you can make anything of them, while I forage."

The bunk racks in the back were bare, but a storage area under the bunk held a stack of garments, presumably meant to help the strange pilot conceal himself when the plane touched down. The first thing she pulled out was a military uniform, boots, puttees . . . neither American, French, German, nor British. Possibly Japanese.

She held up the trousers. They looked far too big, but she was ready to roll them up, tuck them in, or make do somehow. Anything was better than spending the rest of the trip freezing, with Rocco looking up what was left of her skirt.

Another urgent problem had to be dealt with first. No cupboard she opened seemed to contain a water closet or even a chamber pot. A man might have used the drain in the basin under the water tap, but she couldn't see how that would work for her, even if the thought had been less distasteful. The box of sand next to the tap seemed the only possible alternative, so she made the best of it.

She returned to the problem of finding something to wear. She reached into the darkness under the bunk. She thought she could see a shadow there, possibly a blanket. When she touched it, she snatched her hand back. It had a soft, yielding feel, like something alive. But the thing didn't leap toward her. It wasn't alive. She forced herself to try again.

This time she kept a grip on it and pulled it out far enough to see. It wasn't skin after all—just leather. The weight of it startled her. She could hardly lift it. She turned the bag upside down, and the contents slid onto the floor in a shimmering, clinking heap. Jayne gasped.

I found a bag of gold, she thought. *This is like a fairy tale!*

She glanced instinctively toward the front of the cabin, to see if Rocco had observed her. He had his back to her, staring at the window.

She picked up one of the flat, oval coins and looked at it closely, rubbing her fingers over its buttery golden sheen. It was stamped with floral shapes at both ends of the oval, and Japanese characters in the middle—to designate its value, she assumed.

Swiftly, covetously, she scooped the gold pieces back into the bag.

"Hey, what's taking so long back there?" Rocco called.

"I'm dressing, so please keep your back turned!" she said.

She rummaged hastily in the locker. At the bottom of the stack, she found a blue coat and trousers more her size than the uniform—though they had a complicated waist-tie arrangement that took some figuring out. She pulled them on. The heavy cotton was warmer than the remnants of Kensie's summer dress. She slung the bag of gold beneath the jacket. It was heavy, but she thought she could manage to carry it this way, undetected.

She took the uniform coat back to the main cabin and draped it over Rocco's shoulders.

"Best I could do," she said. "They don't seem to have packed blankets. If you want a drink, you'll have to go back and get it out of the tap. I couldn't find a cup either."

"Did you find the . . . uh . . . " Rocco stared at the console, and Jayne was pretty sure the tips of his ears were turning pink. His moments of unexpected delicacy puzzled her.

"I suggest you use the sandbox. I haven't seen a pet kitty around here, but I tried it and nothing bad happened. It seems to be all they've provided for us."

While he was in the back of the cabin, she kept her eyes scrupulously front, and tried to think logically about the gold instead of dreaming about all she could do with it. It would mean so much to the kids and to Madeleine. She could send Maddie to teachers' college, make the old house a place of ease and comfort, get the farm in working order again. Even complete her own interrupted studies and get a decent job, one she wouldn't be ashamed to tell the children about.

But she'd have to get it safely home first—and that meant keeping it a secret from Rocco. Her mistrust of him resurfaced.

She'd thought he was a bootlegger. Now he claimed to be a federal agent, posing as a bootlegger to stop potentially dangerous shipments of unspecified war matériel. Was that the truth? Or was he in fact a bootlegger, merely posing as an agent to gain access to smuggled goods of greater value than second-rate rum and rotgut whiskey? Who could really be trusted around so much gold?

She heard splashing and spluttering. Rocco, or whatever his real name was, finally returned with his damped hair finger-combed into submission, his face somewhat cleaner. He carried a small tin box.

"You missed this," he said, offering it to her.

It held round white balls that looked like boiled quail eggs. Jayne picked one up. It felt like a boiled egg, too—slightly damp and rubbery. But when she pulled it apart, it was white all the way through.

"This is no yolk," she said. She giggled, and much to her surprise, Rocco snorted and then laughed out loud.

"But seriously, is it edible?" she said, when he'd stopped chuckling. She sniffed it. The bland, sweetish smell reminded her of rice pudding.

"One way to find out," Rocco said. He popped one of the spheres into his mouth, munched, and shrugged.

"Beats an empty stomach."

Jayne took one and chewed. It was rubbery but not distasteful.

"It's not the kind of thing I would have expected *him* to eat," Jayne said, pointing with her foot to the comatose creature on the floor. "With those clawed feet, and the teeth or mandibles, or whatever they are, in his mouth, I'd have figured him for a carnivore.

"And I wouldn't think the German would eat dough balls, either. Noodles, yes; potatoes, yes—but just plain dough, I don't think that's a German thing."

She'd been thinking out loud. She realized how much she'd given away only when Rocco put the box down and gave her his full attention.

"You know these mugs," he said. It wasn't a question. His eyes were cold, and Jayne was looking down the barrel of the tommy gun again.

"Oh, for—" she said. "I don't know them! How could I know a creature like that? I've never seen such a thing in my life.

"I *recognized* one of them, that's all. The one who ran away into the woods. The first time I saw him, he was wearing a German uniform. I saw him again on the dock when I returned to New York City. I know it's the same person, but how or why that could be, I have no more idea than you do."

The gun barrel didn't waver.

"You're not telling me the whole story," Rocco said.

"No, I'm not! Because up until a couple of hours ago, I thought you were in cahoots with Boo Boo Hoff! You haven't exactly been upright and forthcoming with me, either!"

They glared at each other for a tense moment. Then he made a face and lowered the gun. He patted his pockets.

"Mind if I smoke?" he said. "I guess it's time for those war stories."

"Yes, I do mind!" Jayne snapped. "We're in an airplane, for goodness' sake, even if I can't see any gas tanks. And don't you think we should focus on how to get *out* of here?"

"We're not getting out of here," Rocco said flatly.

"And what makes you so sure?"

"I did some flying in the war," he said. "Jennies, Camels, this and that. I took a Camel up to twenty thousand feet once."

"I'm impressed—but what does that have to do with the price of eggs?"

"You can't stay up there for more than a couple of minutes," he said. "The air's too thin. If that really is the ground we're seeing in the magic window, I'd say we're above thirty thousand feet right now. Explains why the window is sealed."

"Why?"

"Don't you get it?" he said impatiently. "They've increased the air pressure in here. The cabin must be sealed, airtight. If we *could* open a window, we'd die. We wouldn't be able to breathe. I don't know if we could use a parachute from this height. It's never been done."

"I guess it's a moot point, since we have neither a parachute nor a window," Jayne said. "But don't we have to come down to refuel at some point?"

"If this were a normal aircraft, I'd say yes."

He roamed restlessly back to the window and rested his forehead against the surface that wasn't glass.

"If," he said. "But it obviously isn't. I've been trying to calculate our airspeed based on apparent distance covered, checked against these maps."

He ran a hand through his hair in frustration.

"I thought I was doing something wrong, because it just doesn't make sense. But if the numbers don't lie, we're cruising faster and higher than any bird I've ever heard of."

"So, how fast would that be?" Jayne said.

Rocco shook his head. "It just can't be," he said.

"Mr. Smith!" Jayne said. "A number, if you please!"

"One thousand six hundred miles per hour," Rocco blurted.

"Is—is that fast?" Jayne said.

"Only twice the speed of sound. Give or take," Rocco said. "Which isn't possible. But we seem to be doing it."

"How long would it take to get to Japan at this speed?" Jayne said.

"Maybe four hours," Rocco said.

Jayne stumbled across the cabin to join him at the window.

"*Mon dieu*," she said faintly. "But—Japan is the other side of the world."

Nothing in the window looked familiar anymore. Glints of blue showed under a gathering cloud cover. Could it be one of the Great Lakes? Jayne had never been west of Pittsburgh. She'd never been on the top side of the clouds, for that matter.

There had to be some way to stop this. She had to get home to Maddie and the kids. Maddie wouldn't know what had happened to her. They'd think she was dead. She could only hope that Madeleine wouldn't be too scared to think of calling Kensie or Clementine Cope.

"*Damn* it," she whispered.

Rocco's lip curled.

"What's the matter, Miss Taylor?" he said. "Getting the wind up now? You should have thought of that before you decided to play with the big boys." He laughed. "I can tell you, this is a walk in the park compared to dealing with Boo Boo and his friends all day every day. I'm feeling no pain. I'm just going to take a nice nap until we arrive in Japan."

"I'm not afraid of anything," Jayne said defiantly. "But I have responsibilities at home. Something you might not know anything about."

"You said you had no family," Rocco said. "What responsibilities could you possibly have?"

"I said I had no parents. I have family. I have five children!" Jayne said. She was too worried and angry to care about keeping secrets any longer.

It was worth it to see the look on Rocco's face. He was stunned. Jayne had never before seen a man's jaw literally drop.

"You . . . how did you . . ." he said.

"Oh, for heaven's sake. I adopted them. In France. What did you think? Two sets of twins and a spare? Or did you assume I'd started at age fifteen?"

A deep red flush spread over Rocco's cheeks.

"I didn't think— I mean, I— Dammit!"

"What's it to you, anyway?" Jayne said. "You have a strange sense of propriety. You associate with the scum of the earth, you shoot people, and all that just to stop the average working man from having a beer or two at the end of the day. Yet you're shocked that I might have a child."

It stung to see Rocco constantly judging her. Even though there was no reason for her to care what he thought.

He glared at her. That had made him mad again.

"'A beer or two at the end of the day'?" he quoted. "You have no idea what you're talking about. I guess you've never seen a man so drunk he couldn't see to beat his wife. Talk about kids! You haven't seen what happens to the kids when their dad drinks his paycheck away before he even gets home on Friday night."

"And you have?"

"Doesn't matter if I have or not," he growled. "It's the law, and I'm here to uphold the law. I don't make light of it for *money*."

"Well, I wouldn't make light of it either," she flashed, "but the law makes light of me. I have the same responsibilities as a man, but according to the law, I don't have to be treated the same or paid the same. When you needed my help back there, you didn't give me a job. First you threatened me, then you gave me a payoff. And now you want to preach to me."

"Who's taking care of all those kids, anyway, while you're out playing Ma Barker?" he said.

Changing the subject! Jayne thought. *Typical!*

She told him about Maddie, poor Maddie whom she had left alone again. That was what got to Jayne the most. She tried to tell herself that Maddie would be fine. She'd call Clemmie and Salem. She'd call Kensie. They'd help. Jayne bit her lip furiously. For heaven's sake, she was *not* going to blubber in front of Rocco. Her eyes watered, and she blinked hard.

"Aw, for crying out loud," Rocco said. He patted her awkwardly on the shoulder.

"I had a little sister," he said. "She had two or three kids by the time she was your age. No fancy college for her. Kids barefoot, cupboards bare—I guess I might have done one or two things that weren't strictly on the up-and-up, back then."

The mere hint of sympathy softened Jayne up completely. She sniffed noisily. Rocco searched his pockets, but they both knew there were no more clean hankies.

Rocco harrumphed loudly.

"But I'd have expected a college girl like you to know better—someone with your advantages."

Jayne glared at him, secretly grateful to be pulled back from the brink of tears.

"It's complicated," she managed. "Anyway, it's partly your fault!"

"How's that?" he said indignantly.

"If you'd been a yegg like Boo Boo or Iggy, there's no way I'd still be driving with you. You set me a bad example by being a halfway decent guy."

She could see him working hard not to smile, but he was obviously pleased with even a backhanded compliment.

"And by *lying* to me," she accused, wiping that smile right off his face. "All that guff about you being just another torpedo. And by the way, could you please stop making me call you Rocco Smith. It's so phony it's just embarrassing."

He hesitated, as if finding it hard to break his cover, even now.

"Oh what the hell," he said. "We'll be lucky to survive the landing, anyway. You're right—it's not Smith. It's Cameron. Special Agent Grant Cameron. And what about you?"

"It's Jayne Taylor," she said. "Just what I told you."

She hated to admit that it hadn't even occurred to her to lie about her name. Obviously she was an amateur.

"Well, listen, Miss Taylor—if we get through this, I really will put you up for a bonus."

"Big of you," Jayne grumbled. But she grasped the hand he held out to her and shook on it.

"We're gonna have to stick together out there," Cameron said. "I don't know much about Japan. I sure don't know the language. One thing I do know is, they've got gangs just like we do, and some crime bosses who could put Boo Boo in the shade."

"But they fought against the Germans in the war," Jayne said. "Why would they be receiving smuggled goods from the Germans now?"

"Yeah, sure they joined in against the Germans," Cameron said. "The war was their chance to grab German colonies in the Pacific. They got what they wanted out of that deal. That doesn't mean they're friendly to Western interests. Before the war, it was the Germans who stood between them and domination of the Pacific. Now it's us."

"You keep saying 'them,' as if you can speak of a whole nation," Jayne said. "Who's in charge? Don't they have a constitution?"

"Look, I'm an agent of the U.S. government," Cameron said, "not some kind of professor. So maybe some of them are wonderful peace-loving little Woodrow Wilsons. That's not my concern. It's my job to deal with the rest of them. There are plenty of gangsters over there, in and out of government. Plenty of military bosses who can't wait for the next war. Plenty of crooked business-men waiting to buy trouble. Yeah, just like over here," he finished with surprising bitterness.

"You know a lot about history, for a torpedo," Jayne said.

He shrugged. "Tell you what my goal in life is—I want to make good on this job and move to the West Coast di-vision. Sunny California, ocean breezes, get the hell away from coal smoke and cold winters and high society. So it pays me to know about the Pacific. That's where I want to go."

"Well, that creature said we were going to Japan," Jayne said. "He didn't say where, though. I found a stack of maps while you were sleeping. We could take a look and try to figure out where we're going to land. If it's a Japanese version of Philadelphia, like Tokyo or whatever other cities they've got, then maybe we could contact the police, or at least somebody who speaks English."

She flipped to the last map in the stack. Cameron pored over it, puzzled. The final map showed an island, but it wasn't Japan.

"Turn back a few pages," he said.

The map sequence zeroed in—the northern coast of Siberia, the Kamchatkan peninsula, a few more islands, and then the trapezoid of Hokkaido, with Honshu just below. And there, just off the northeast coast of Honshu, was a tiny blip—an hourglass, a butterfly, a zigzag. That was it. She squinted at the map.

"It says—Sado Island," she said. She turned back the page. The final map was a blown-up version of that blip.

Even the large-scale map didn't show much: twin mountain peaks, with a saddle between them, a lake near the northern bay, a sprinkling of towns around the coast, nothing much in the middle.

"There's nothing here," she said. "Why are we going there?"

Cameron shrugged. "We need more information," he said.

She wondered if he was just stalling, if maybe he already knew.

While he searched the cabin again for additional printed material, Jayne perched in the pilot's seat, fidgeting with frustration and discomfort. None of the fittings seemed to have been designed for human use. The markings on the control panel looked more like ideograms than letters, but she didn't think they were Japanese.

"Look, some of them are red," she said. "What do you think that means? Does it mean 'danger,' as it would in English?"

Cameron grunted in a preoccupied fashion.

Jayne gave the little markings names in her own mind, so they'd be easier to remember.

"Running man, fish, two-headed lizard, salad fork," she said aloud.

"What are you—nuts?" Cameron said.

She jumped out of the chair and paced the floor. Once on her feet, she could feel the small dips and quivers that told her the plane was in motion. Her eyes roved, searching for any nooks and crannies, any information she might have missed. She stopped and stamped her foot against the floor.

Cylindrical fuselage. Flat floor. That meant half the space must be below her feet.

"Agent Cameron!" she said. "The cargo! Where did they put it?"

He was quick. He understood what she meant right away. They leapt simultaneously toward the back of the cabin, getting in each other's way.

Of course there had to be a cargo space! Where else had the insect creature put the containers Cameron had brought him? Jayne hunted for more of those markings, and found them, plain as day, marking a hatch beneath the starboard bunk: head of celery, salad fork, and lizard, all in red. She wondered if that meant "Cargo" or "Open here" or "Danger—don't touch!"

But how could they open the hatch?

Cameron clawed at the edges with his fingers and swore. There were little raised knobs at the edge, just like the ones on the control console, but the knobs didn't move. Each knob was marked with a deep slit, sized for a talon, not a human finger.

Jayne reached into her disheveled hair and found a bobby pin still clinging there. She held it up.

Cameron wasn't slow. He realized instantly what this simple tool could do to the controls. His eyes lit up.

"Give me that!" he said, making a grab for it. Jayne stepped back, and he tripped over the body of the creature.

"Stop acting like a three-year-old at a birthday party," she said.

"Fine, then, *please* give me that. Just give it to me *now* so I can find out how to fly this thing before it's too late." By the end of the sentence, his voice had risen and he was flushed with anger.

He pointed to the window.

"Look there," he said. "We're descending!"

The surface crawling past was pure blue from edge to edge, but now Jayne could see wrinkles passing through the silken blue—mighty waves, though from here, they still seemed no wider than a hair.

"We're close," Cameron said. "I saw the Sakhalins down there. And the first few islands of the Chishima. We have to land. What if the critter never wakes up? How do we disengage the autopilot? If I don't learn to fly this thing, we could die up here."

"I want to know what we're transporting first," Jayne insisted. "If we're carrying some kind of poison dust, it might be better if we never landed. Or if we crash-landed in the ocean, and let all of it go to the bottom."

Cameron's color faded. He stopped trying to wrest the pin away from her.

"Okay, then," he said. "Let's get down there and find out—in a hurry."

Jayne slipped the bobby pin into the slot and wiggled it gently. She felt it catch on something, and a section of the floor slid open.

Jayne lay down on her stomach and stuck her head into the opening. Light didn't penetrate very far. She didn't want to touch anything she couldn't identify. Directly below the opening, she could see the barrels she and Cameron had delivered, tumbled sideways in the cargo hold. They rocked to and fro a little as the aircraft yawed. Behind them, she could just see the shadowy bulk of more cargo.

Jayne remembered how heavy those containers had been. If there were enough of them to fill the hold, she thought, the engines must be incredibly powerful to lift that weight.

Cameron pushed past her, lowered himself through the opening and dropped.

"Hey! How are you going to get out?" Jayne called.

He didn't bother to answer. She stuck the bobby pin into her hair and dropped down after him.

It was still pretty dark down there. The light that filtered down from the hatch showed a tight stack of containers like the ones they'd hauled off the barge. Cameron pushed his way between the stacks into the darkness under the wing, cursing softly as he barked his shins on something.

Jayne paused where she could still see and ran her hands around the rim of one barrel, seeking a way to open it, but it was sealed tight. She wished for a chisel and hammer.

She wondered if it held treasure or death. She thought guiltily of the bag of gold slung across her back. What would it be like to possess a whole barrel of coins—not just modest security, but riches beyond measure? And if Jayne Taylor would turn pirate for one bag of gold, what would a man like Cameron do for a whole shipload?

She heard Cameron pounding on something.

"Taylor!" he called. "Give me a hand, will you? This one's different."

Jayne felt her way to his side. Her outstretched hand met a cylindrical object that felt more like an ordinary steel drum. It stood about waist-high. She pushed at it experimentally. It was too heavy to budge. The rough surface flaked under her touch, and when she rubbed her fingers together, they felt powdery. She sniffed them cautiously and smelled rust.

Cameron fumbled in his pocket. She heard the scratch of a match, and then the tiny light illuminated the top of the drum. As she'd thought, it was rusty. The lid sat crooked, and was dented as if it had been hammered down. It was stenciled with Roman letters, not Japanese, but they were so scratched and faded she couldn't read them before the match went out.

Cameron had rolled one of the smaller canisters into this corner.

"Help me lift this," he said. "I think I can get the top off."

"Do you think this is really a good idea?" Jayne panted, as she hefted her end of the canister.

"Got a better one?" Cameron said.

Jayne felt the container lifted out of her arms as he raised it above the oil drum and brought it down with a crash.

Jayne couldn't see what happened next. She heard a tinny popping sound—perhaps the lid breaking loose—and a whoosh of air went past her face.

"I think that did it," Cameron said triumphantly. She heard him strike another match.

And then—then she was horizontal, unable to move because pain radiated from so many places she couldn't tell where she was hurt. There was a hissing, roaring sound in her ears, and when she finally got her eyes open, she had to close them again, because instead of darkness, there was too much light.

"What happened?" she tried to say. What came out was no better than a whimper. "I can't move!"

She tried to remember what happened. She had a vague memory of being shoved backward with tremendous force, smashing into something—yes, that was it. Her head—that was the part that hurt. And her leg. And her wrist. And her back. . . . She was struggling to get up, but not moving.

Oh, God, did I break my back? Am I paralyzed?

She rolled sideways and felt something give. She had one arm free. She opened her eyes again, and figured out that she'd been temporarily pinned down by a fallen stack of canisters. She must have bumped into them as she fell.

Suddenly everything snapped back into focus. She was in the cargo hold, just a few feet from the barrel they'd tried to open. It was open all right. It was wide open and spewing a huge jet of flame that had already heated the air in the hold so hot that sweat trickled into Jayne's eyes.

A dark shadow passed between her and the fire, and she struggled into a sitting position to see around it. It was Cameron—holding the uniform coat in front of his face, weaving back and forth as if he was trying to decide where to attack and smother the flames.

Paint on the barrels next to the one they'd opened was blistering and bubbling now. If their contents were flammable too, they'd go up at any minute.

Jayne found her voice.

"For the love of mercy, let's get out of here!" she cried.

"The fire—" he said hoarsely.

"It's too big! It's out of control!"

When she gasped in air, it hurt her lungs.

Cameron looked from her to the flames. Then he hurdled the fallen canisters, picked her up in his arms, and hoisted her awkwardly toward the open hatch before she could protest.

Jayne tried to resist.

"How are you going to get out?" she said. "I can't pull you up!"

"I'll climb," he panted. "Hurry up!"

She got her arms over the edge, Cameron gave her a tremendous and undignified shove to the rear, and she sprawled onto the cabin floor, feet still dangling over the hole. She righted herself and clutched at Cameron's sleeves as he sprang upward, kicking away the barrel he was balanced on. Together they heaved and scrambled, and rolled safely over onto the floor, just as flames began to lick up around the edge of the hatch. Jayne scrabbled frantically until she found the bobby pin, and jiggled the control button. The hatch slid closed.

"That's not going to hold it for more than a few minutes," Cameron said. "We'll be grilled like crappies at a fish fry."

"Ditching in the ocean would be better than that," Jayne said. "Can you get this thing down?"

Cameron seized the bobby pin from her hand and bent over the controls. The plane yawed violently, and a shrill, intolerable whistling sounded. Cursing, Cameron snatched the bobby pin back and crouched with hands over his ears.

"Dammit!" he shouted over the noise of the alarm. "That hold should be airtight. No oxygen—the fire should go out."

"But it isn't," Jayne said. Obviously. A hot acrid smell was seeping into the cabin.

"We have to wake *him* up," Jayne shouted.

The alarm had already roused the insect creature. He writhed and banged his head against the floor, making muffled, urgent sounds.

Jayne and Cameron moved as one to undo the creature's bonds. As soon as he was free, the creature lunged for the controls, high-pitched squeals and chitterings unreeling behind him.

The little craft dropped precipitously toward the ocean, shuddering and sideslipping. The creature held himself steady, bracing his spidery legs and grasping with his clawed feet. Jayne and Cameron were shaken from side to side of the cabin.

The creature wasn't talking to himself anymore. A second voice answered him. Yet Jayne saw no one. A ground-to-air telephone? Without wires? Unfortunately, the voice was that of another insect creature, so she couldn't understand a word it said. She hoped it was giving their pilot good advice. The floor felt uncomfortably warm.

Jayne's ears popped as if she were on a fast-moving elevator. She felt a cold draft go through the craft, as if its seal had been breached somewhere. It was an uncanny feeling, like the opposite of a wind blowing—as if air were being sucked away from the cabin. The plane lurched violently upward, and then nosed over into a steep dive.

Jayne slid along the floor and ended up helplessly entangled with Cameron.

"Before anything else goes wrong," she said loudly into his ear, "tell me what happened in the hold. What *was* that?"

"I—uh—I don't know. The lid came off, I lit the match to see what was in there, and it blew up in my face."

"Gasoline?" Jayne suggested.

"No. I'd have smelled that. I'm not such a dope I'd light a match in a room full of gasoline barrels."

"So you didn't expect to find anything?" she said, watching his face closely—or as closely as she could while the plane pitched and bucked, no longer skimming smoothly along. Cameron's expression was a little hard to read, because the front part of his hair and most of his eyebrows had been singed off, his face was sunburn-red on one side and smudged with soot all over.

"Like, oh, *gold* for instance?" she added meaningfully.

She saw his eyes widen before he could cover his surprise.

"Don't look so shocked," she said. "And don't prevaricate! There isn't time. It was something valuable, obviously, and something heavy. And I'm on your side—supposedly."

"Okay, okay—the higher-ups did think the Germans might be smuggling gold out of Europe," he said rapidly.

"So they wouldn't have to use it to pay war reparations. But Mac—" He paused. She could see that the death of his partner was still a bitter pill. "Mac didn't think it was gold. He thought it was weapons. After what happened to him—I was thinking he might be right."

Jayne bit her tongue to avoid screaming "You idiot." He thought the barrel might contain contraband weapons, and he'd still smashed the top off? It could have been gas; they'd be dead now. They might be dead already.

But screaming at him wasn't going to put the plane back on course. It banked to the right, and then slewed round to bank sharply in the opposite direction, like a small boat changing tacks. Jayne lost her balance and collided with Cameron again.

"Oof!" he said. But he rolled to cushion her from impact with the wall and pulled her firmly against him. He was trying to shelter her.

That was sweet, she thought. But what she really wanted was to see out. The creature had done something to the window. It no longer showed a clear view of the ground below. Instead it was split into several portions. Two showed graphs and symbols, rapidly changing, and one showed ghostly green shadow forms that might have represented landmasses.

If that was the ground, Jayne thought, then the plane was in trouble. Because the ground was tall and spiky, and it was coming up way too—

She hit a wall again, and this time the wall was dead black and everything went dark.

She woke up in a hurry when she did wake up. The image of that wall of fire she'd seen the last time she was knocked out sprang back into her mind, and she screamed again. Or tried to. In fact she squeaked like a trapped mouse. And coughed. And realized that cold water was dribbling over her chin.

When she struggled to get up, she sloshed and floundered. They must have ditched in the sea, she thought.

"Cameron!" she choked out. But there was no answer. She was furious. He'd abandoned ship without her.

She pushed the wet hair out of her eyes. It looked as if she was the one who'd abandoned ship. She didn't know how she'd left the plane, but she had. And then she'd fallen face-first into water and mud. It wasn't deep, fortunately. It certainly wasn't the ocean. She scraped mud from her face, kneeling chest-deep in the water, and looked around.

The sun had gone down, but the light had not quite faded. She was in the middle of a wide, flat space between looming dark shapes she guessed were mountains. Their peaks were hidden by rolling cloud banks.

The plane had nosedived into the flat lake or swamp or whatever it was she was in, and still stuck there like a child's toy, one wing up, one wing down. The wing that was pinioned in the mud was streaked with soot, and its smooth silvery surface had cracked and bubbled. Jayne stared at it dumbly for a minute, and then remembered that she was trying to find out where she was.

Perhaps more important, where was Cameron?

The plain around her wasn't mud-colored. Little leaves, like blades of grass, sprang up from the water at regular intervals, carpeting the whole flat surface with brilliant green. Except for a broad swath cut by the plane as it ploughed into the water, and the smaller wallow she'd created.

And the crooked line of bent stalks and disturbed muck that led away from the plane. Someone else had started from this spot and left tracks.

Jayne struggled to her feet and waded doggedly toward the horizon, following that trail.

CHAPTER 6

UNDER GOLD MOUNTAIN

Jayne sloshed through the mud. She could hear sucking sounds as she pulled her feet free at each step, and she was afraid she'd lose her shoes. Then she realized she was already barefoot. She'd left her shoes behind somewhere in the flooded plane. She hoped she wouldn't step on something sharp—or slithery. The path ahead got darker. She could only find her way because the open water where the green sprouts had been smashed down picked up more light than the vegetation around it.

She felt strangely lighter than she had been. She felt for the bag of gold she'd slung tightly against her shoulder. It wasn't there.

But I'm going to need new shoes, she thought fuzzily. *And how will I pay for them?*

There had been new shoes in the bag, for her and for the kids. New shoes and a truck of their very own, and bicycles and birthday parties, and college later on. Everything they'd dreamed of for the future.

She wanted Maddie and the children very badly right now. She wished she were at home in the kitchen with Hildegarde sitting on her lap. Instead, she was lost, and now she'd lost the money too.

Cameron had said they'd have to stick together. Jayne slogged onward with grim determination. She was going to find him, and she was going to find the way home, and if he'd taken her bag of gold, she was going to take it out of his hide.

She bumped into solid earth at last, and was almost too tired to pull herself up onto dry land. A path ran along beside the water, but it was too dark to see tracks. She turned toward the mountains. At least they provided a visible objective. When she had gone a hundred yards in that direction, the path started to rise, and she thought she saw lights ahead, up on the mountainside.

Jayne's pace slowed as the slope became steeper. She wondered if there was any point in continuing. She had no way of knowing if Cameron had come this way. The ache where she'd banged her head for the second time grew with every step.

By keeping her eyes fixed on the ground directly in front of her feet, she could just make out the path in the gathering gloom. A fork in the road gave her a good excuse to stop and lean against a tree for support. Now which way should she choose? The right-hand fork seemed to follow a gentler slope, toward the hillside where she thought she'd seen the lights. The left-hand way ascended into the shadow of the mountain and vanished into a tumble of boulders.

Definitely not that way, she thought.

And then the faint moonlight picked out a gleam of something shining against the packed earth of the left-hand path. She limped a few steps uphill and stooped to touch the object.

It was hard, smooth, and oval. She held it up to the moon and watched the cool silver light strike out warm golden sparks. Someone had dropped a gold coin in her path. It had to be Cameron.

Had he tried to leave a trail? Or had he dropped it by accident?

If she found another one, Jayne thought, she would know.

It took an effort of will to turn and pursue the path upward, into the darker night beneath the trees. She was already so tired.

Soon it was so dark that she had to feel her way along, hands brushing against the overhanging branches. She stubbed her bare toes against roots and rocks.

Finally, the trees ended. She could see a wedge of starry sky ahead, between two dark slabs of rock. The path ran up into a stony slope. She leaned against a big boulder, fighting vertigo. How could she find the trail in the dark? Maybe it would be better to curl up under a tree here, and wait for dawn.

But as she peered ahead, she caught a faint metallic gleam among the gray stones. She groaned, but she knew she had to go on uphill and reach that tantalizing point of light.

As soon as Jayne touched it, she recognized the feel of polished metal. It was another coin.

If I find just one more, she thought wearily, *then I'll know for sure he was trying to leave a trail. If these were meant to be clues, that means he was being held captive. It means he needed help. It means—it means he needed* my *help. He was depending on me to come and get him. Because he knew these coins were mine. He knew he could count on me to come and take them back.*

119

Her legs were so tired now that they stiffened up at the briefest halt. She forced herself onward. The path continued toward what looked like an impenetrable wall, a dead end. As she scanned the shadows, she caught another glint of light at the edge of her vision. She paused and checked again. Yes, it was there—a ghostly dot that picked up the pale gleam of moonlight. Stumbling, tripping, sometimes using both hands and feet to feel her way, she reached the base of the cliff. Cameron had dropped another coin.

Jayne looked up from her find. A cold draft blew from the cliff face toward her. She rose from her crouched position and leaned against the wall, stretching out her arms, and shuffled sideways. Her groping hand moved over the rough rock and suddenly thrust out into emptiness. There was an opening here. The path led to a cave mouth. That was where they'd taken Cameron.

Her heart sank. How could she follow him in there? The opening was so dark it looked like a gap into total nothingness. She had no way to make a light. Inside, there'd be no stray light, however dim, to catch on a gold piece, however shiny. This time she really had to wait for morning.

But morning might be too late.

She took a step into the blackness, then another, keeping one hand pressed against the rock wall, desperately testing the ground with her bare toes. The starlit night behind her seemed sweet and bright compared with the utter darkness ahead.

Briefly, she considered going back, trying to find help. On this remote island, what were the chances she'd find someone who understood English and would believe her story? More likely she'd be locked up immediately as a foreigner and a madwoman.

I have to keep going, Jayne told herself. *I've got to find Cameron and find out what he knows, or I'll never get out of here.*

She felt her way forward, gripping rock with toes and fingers. For a little while, she could look back and see a grayish patch in the darkness that marked the entrance, but soon the tunnel curved and even that was gone. She thought, too late, that she should have cut a stick to tap ahead of her, but she didn't dare go back. She wasn't sure she'd have the courage to enter this blackness again.

If I keep my right hand on the wall and never take it off, she thought, *then I can always find my way back just by turning around and going back the same way. So I can't be lost. Even though I have no idea where I am.*

"I thought it was warmer underground," Jayne grumbled out loud, and was startled to hear her own voice echoing back off the walls. In fact, the farther into the mountain she went, the colder and damper she felt. Moisture trickled over her fingers as she hugged the wall. At times, she thought she heard water running somewhere within the rocks, but she couldn't be sure that it was a real sound, and not just her imagination.

Her ears were proved right as she continued. The trickles of moisture became rivulets, and the floor grew slippery and wet. She splashed into occasional puddles that came more and more frequently until she was wading ankle deep in ice-cold water. The gurgling and splashing sounds disoriented her even more than the darkness. She couldn't tell where the water was coming from. It seemed to be all around her.

And then she started hearing voices. At first she thought again that her ears were playing tricks on her. But gradually the noises became louder—human voices, combined with rhythmic tapping sounds. Jayne still couldn't see anything—but it gave her courage to splash forward through the deepening water.

She slowed down even more, afraid that at any minute she would step into deeper water and be sucked under. And then, from the corner of her eye, she thought she saw a light. She closed her eyes, shuffling forward for ten more steps before she opened them again. And there it was, clearer this time. Far above her head, there was a flicker of yellow light.

That must mean that the roof of the tunnel had arched up into a lofty cave. Just as Jayne figured that out, her hand slipped off the wall into space. She froze. If she took one more step away from the wall, she could be swept away and drowned in the dark, or lost with nothing to hold on to. But the light drew her irresistibly.

Testing each foothold, she edged out into the cave. The water was knee-deep and rising. She could feel the current tugging at her tired legs. Soon it lapped against her thighs, and she had to inch forward, keeping her feet widely planted to fight the pull.

Her foot slipped into a sudden depression in the floor. She tripped and felt her head go under, from dark air to dark water. She lost contact with the ground for a terrifying moment and was tumbled along in a directionless void.

She kicked and flailed. Her lungs were ready to burst when one hand smacked against a solid surface. There was nothing to hold on to. Her fingers scraped along rough rock, frantically clawing for a grip, until her nails sank into something more malleable than the rock face. Her fist closed around wood. The current nearly yanked her away from her hold, but she hung on, straining upstream until she got a grip with the other hand as well.

Jayne clung there for a minute, struggling to fill her lungs with air. She stretched her legs downward, but couldn't touch bottom. The water must be deepest right next to the cave wall. When she'd caught her breath, she forced herself to let go with one hand, to explore what she was holding on to.

It felt like a ladder—or what had once been one. She was clinging to a wooden crosspiece, bolted into the wall. The bolts felt rough, as if they'd rusted, and they grated loosely in their sockets if she tugged on the wood too hard. There was another rung above that one. Possibly they went all the way up, to the light. Unfortunately, there was only one way to find out. Gritting her teeth, she got a grip on the second rung, and began to climb.

She counted the rungs, but lost count when she came to a spot where one rung was missing, and the next cracked under her foot as she hooked her toes over it, leaving her swinging by her fingers for a few desperate heartbeats. She was directly beneath the light source now, and couldn't see it anymore. She climbed in pitch darkness. She was no longer thinking about finding Cameron. All she cared about was escaping from the cave.

The rungs ended. Jayne slapped the rock with one hand, still hanging on with the other. Her muscles quivered from the climb. She couldn't hold on much longer. Above her head, the rock curved smoothly inward—possibly toward a horizontal surface. But there was nothing to hold on to.

She couldn't go back. Pressing herself into the wall like a limpet, she moved her foot to the next rung and pushed upward. She half-lay on a smooth surface, her torso precariously supported, ready to slide off the minute her balance wavered.

Now she had one foot on the topmost rung. She took a deep breath and pushed herself upward again. Her palms slid over worn rock. Still there was nothing to hold on to. With a gasp of relief, she felt her fingers slip over some kind of stone threshold. She pulled with all her remaining strength, and lay full-length on an almost flat, almost dry floor.

Jayne pressed her cheek to the gritty surface for a minute, in silent gratitude. Then she blinked in surprise. She could see again. She had reached the light.

She raised her head. The first thing she saw was a pair of stocky legs, clad in trousers rolled up to midcalf, and ending in feet shod in straw slippers. As her gaze traveled upward, she saw two hands nonchalantly clasping a musket.

Jayne held her breath, amazed that the guard hadn't detected her yet. Then she realized that the noise she'd been hearing came from up ahead, as well. She could hear hammers and other metallic noises, and the confused echoes of human voices bouncing back and forth in a confined area. The soft scraping of her climb could easily have been buried in all that.

But how would she get past him now? Jayne moved forward without thinking. She crawled between his legs and seized him by the ankles as she did, neatly upending him. He let out a startled cry, not nearly as loud as she would have expected, and then she heard the sharp crack of his head meeting the floor. She scrambled around to face him, but he lay motionless. She kicked his musket over the edge, just in case he woke up angry. His bare toes stuck up, sandals temptingly askew. She snatched them off and wincingly pulled them onto her own lacerated feet.

Pressing flat against the floor, Jayne turned to see what he'd been guarding. At first, she couldn't see anything but the light. It flooded her eyes. She felt ridiculously happy just because she could see again. Then the scene cleared. The light came from burning torches, whose smoke stung her nose as it thickened the damp cave air. Light glinted off raw rock surfaces and off the sweating bodies of workers who crowded the big cave.

It looked like a giant anthill, a mass of random motion, but in a minute it started to make sense to Jayne. She had apparently broken into a mine, by knocking down a guard who'd been posted to keep people from breaking *out*.

Some of the workers plied picks and chisels against the walls, some of them trudged to and fro with baskets of broken rock balanced on their heads, and here and there she could see an overseer with some kind of clipboard, watching over it all and making check marks. The basket carriers appeared and disappeared through exits to somewhere, and the upper levels of the cave were dotted with openings to other galleries, accessed by ladders like the one she'd just climbed. Perhaps they'd tried to mine the lower levels, and been chased out by rising water.

Jayne heard a muffled groan from the guard behind her, and decided she'd better take off before he woke up. She slid down a set of rough steps into the bustle of the torchlit cavern.

The workers inside wore garments pretty much like hers, so she was not immediately conspicuous—especially now that the once-fresh blue fabric was ripped, wet, and muddy. Her hair was dark and straight like theirs. But she needed something to hide her face.

Glancing around, she saw a corner where half a dozen miners were evidently taking a shift break. Most of them lay prone, heads pillowed on their arms. One of them bent over a handful of cooked rice, wrapped in a bit of cloth. He didn't even look up as Jayne slowly ambled over, hugging the wall.

Headgear, baskets, and sandals had been dropped in a pile when the workers paused to rest. Jayne snatched up a turban of rags with some kind of straw headpiece topping it, and a carrying basket. She squashed the turban down over her forehead, pulling one end of the rag loose and drawing it across her face. She fiddled with the little straw potholder that apparently went on top. She couldn't figure out what it might be for, but it had strings attached, so she tied them under her chin. Now she looked pretty much like everyone else. Assuming the hunched position of an experienced miner, she trotted toward the basket-carriers' queue and fell in at the end, eyes on the ground. She hoped to leave the room and stay out of trouble long enough to orient herself, and figure out where Cameron and the insect creature might fit into all of this.

She hadn't reckoned with how tired her legs were going to be. She trotted for what seemed like miles, underground, keeping her head down so she saw nothing but the muscular, slightly bandy calves of the man ahead of her. She formed an impression of his life and personality, based on those bulging calf muscles, and decided that she didn't like him at all.

At the end of the trip, those legs unexpectedly dropped into a kneeling position. Jayne followed suit, as the whole line of workers shuffled on their knees through a low arch and down a ramp into a new gallery. It was very hot, and dust from the digging swirled in the foul air. Jayne smothered a spasm of coughing as she held her basket out to be shoveled full of broken rock. She shoved the basket ahead of her up the ramp, and then watched covertly to see how the others swung their burdens up to balance them on their heads. The little straw doily and the rags beneath were quite inadequate as a cushion against the sharp edges of the rocks pressing down against her skull.

She hurried forward to catch up with the rest of the line—but her legs were heavy as lead. And running back and forth with a basket on her head wouldn't get her any closer to finding Cameron. She turned awkwardly to see if the next contingent was in sight behind her. No one was visible yet. It was time to get off this path.

Jayne checked out each gallery that branched away, hoping for a route where she might disappear, but they were all crowded with busy miners. When she finally found an unused outlet, she almost missed it, because it was dark and dusty, and the opening was blocked by a chunk of roughly carved stone.

She paused to examine the image. It had manlike limbs, brandishing a staff in one hand and a fan-shaped object in the other. The face scowled fiercely and featured a nose so long and sharp it gave the image a birdlike, goblinish expression. Crude characters were chiseled into the stone beneath the image. Jayne couldn't read them, but taken as a whole the carving certainly gave off a "Keep Out!" aura.

She squeezed past the stone and kept going until she was out of sight from the path but could still see dimly by the light that filtered through. She let the basket slide to the ground, eased her cramped muscles as best she could, and tried to think.

Jayne didn't believe that Cameron would have come to this level of the mine. It was crawling with Japanese workers and officials. Unless all of them were in on the secret—which seemed unlikely—a weird insectoid creature with a Western prisoner in tow would have created an uproar. Yet they were all calmly going about their business. The most logical conclusion was that nothing unusual had happened here. Therefore, the creature must have taken Cameron somewhere else.

Mines didn't go *up*, Jayne reasoned. If you wanted to go somewhere else in a mine, the only direction to look in was down. She must have missed a turning or something when she'd been in the lower tunnels. There must have been a route that didn't end in the water. So the logical thing to do now was to try to find her way back to that level.

Jayne sighed. *Oh, how I hate logic,* she thought. *All that climbing, and now I have to go* back.

The deserted gallery sloped downward, toward the interior of the mountain, and she followed it. Within minutes, she was cursing herself for having neglected to find a torch. Again, she thought of going back, but she wasn't sure how to steal a light without calling attention to herself and being exposed as an intruder. Strangely, there was still enough light for her to find her way, and she decided to continue at least until it was too dark to see.

The passage narrowed and the roof grew lower until she had to creep on her hands and knees. Claustrophobia caught at her throat.

"All right, I'll crawl, but that's as far as I'll go," she said severely, as if to an importunate friend. "If I have to get down on my belly, I'm leaving. Cameron wouldn't do it, either. He's not that skinny!"

The tightest squeeze came at a point where two slabs of rock seemed to have tilted sideways, held up only by leaning drunkenly against each other. Jayne guessed the passage would narrow to nothing beyond that, and she'd have a good reason to turn around. But instead, she pushed her way through the rough arch, and found herself in a gallery where she could stand up.

She could see where the light had been coming from. The gallery ended in a rough rock wall with a big dark hole in it. Broken pick handles, rags, an empty basket, and other debris lay at the foot of the wall, showing where miners had once worked and had apparently given up. But fresh torches still burned in brackets on the wall, flickering slightly in a cold draft that blew from the dark opening.

Someone must be using this place, Jayne thought.

The wall bore characters scrawled in soot or charcoal, mingled with caricatures whose nature made her think they'd been created by bored or disgruntled miners. Superimposed on them, a big, bold painting of the same beak-nosed warrior gave off the same message: Go away!

But if everyone is supposed to go away, Jayne wondered, *why do they keep the lights on?*

She went as close to the dark opening as she dared and peered in. She could feel dank, cold air blowing up into her face from somewhere far below. She had a horrible sinking feeling that there was going to be another ladder here, and she'd have to climb down it, in the dark. Her knees trembled at the very thought. For the first time, it occurred to her that she'd bitten off more than she could chew.

She glared defiantly into the darkness.

"I'm fine!" she said. "I can do this!"

Just to prove it, she flopped down onto the floor and felt inside the opening. As far down as she could reach, there was no ladder.

"Well, that's a relief," she said. But to her own surprise, she was disappointed. Now what?

She brushed her hand over the rock again, and frowned. There was something strange about this. The sides of the shaft felt unnaturally smooth and even.

Jayne lifted one of the torches down and held it inside the opening. Above floor level, the light flickered on rough, natural rock, but down below, it gleamed off polished walls, cut straight and vertical.

Jayne moved the torch around the edges of the opening. Recessed behind the edge, where they couldn't be seen from outside, she found a row of bumps with a familiar shape—control knobs like those in the airplane.

She stuck the torch back on the wall and searched frantically for something to activate the controls. She didn't need to run her fingers through her tangled hair to know that her hairpins were long gone. At some cost to her already grimy and broken fingernails, she tore loose a sliver of bamboo from the rim of the discarded basket, and toggled the innards of the control knobs.

Nothing happened. She leaned her head into the shaft and peered down. She saw nothing, but thought she heard a faint hum far below. A puff of displaced air struck her face, and she pulled back just in time to avoid being struck by the device that rose from below.

It looked like the skeleton of an elevator: a square platform that just fit the dimensions of the shaft, with a pole at each corner and a bar at head height. Inset lights, like the ones in the plane, marked the edges of the platform.

It couldn't be an elevator, Jayne thought. Nothing held it up—no cables, no cranks, no motor.

She stuck the splinter into her hair for safekeeping, took a deep breath, and stepped onto the platform. It paused for a moment, then shot smoothly downward at a speed that made her stomach jump. She nearly fell against the wall that seemed to fly past, but caught herself by catching at the bar above her head.

The platform barely slowed before coming to a halt, stopping as suddenly as it had started. Jayne had expected subterranean darkness. Instead, she saw light ahead—as bright and white as daylight. She stepped out into the light, and froze.

She found herself in a huge cavern, with a smooth, flat floor. The strange tubes of white light were all around her. The flat, surreal illumination nearly blinded her after the dim torches of the mine. But she could see well enough to feel that she had been transported into another world, centuries away from a mine worked by half-naked men with little tools of wood and iron.

Gleaming metal tanks and tubing lined the cavern, dwarfing the human-sized figures that moved around them, intent on mysterious tasks. Jayne stared open-mouthed. She felt out of place and exposed, like a small, muddy frog that had hopped into the middle of a polished china platter. She scanned the room for a hiding place, but she couldn't even see a shadow. Even the workers wore spotless white from head to foot.

She had no choice. She ducked back into the elevator and jabbed at the controls until the platform slid into the darkness again. She'd assumed this was the bottom level, and that she'd go up, back to the mine. Instead, she could feel that the platform was sinking again. After just a few seconds, it stopped at another lighted opening.

This time, the corridor outside was rough, natural rock, more like the mines above. The light was dim, too, leaving plenty of shadowed spots. Altogether, it looked like a much easier place for someone dressed as a miner to pass unnoticed. Jayne felt hope rise again. This looked much more like the kind of area where Cameron might be hidden.

She stepped boldly out into the corridor.

The light was dim, the air dank and foul, but it was no longer silent. She could hear something—a murmuring undercurrent that became more and more disturbing as it grew clearer. The meaning was universal even though she couldn't understand the specific words: low moans, laments, and pleas for help.

She felt her way stealthily along the corridor. It wasn't really a corridor—not a rectangular hallway with flat sides, something built and squared off by human hands. It was more a crack in the earth, where the walls were tilted slabs of stone. Other ways and chambers led off it.

Turning toward the sounds, she emerged into a bigger room, with an arched roof that sloped down to the floor on all sides.

This was the source of the sounds. There were bodies lying on the cave floor. They were wrapped in rags and bandages, and so huddled and twisted together that it was hard to be sure they were human, at first. Her skin felt clammy with cold sweat. She knew the war was over, but her mind plunged her back into the chaos of bombed villages and field hospitals, where she'd heard that sound before and seen the same rows of pain-racked bodies.

Even the smell—God, the smell was the same: raw, fresh blood mingled with the sour stench of infection and unwashed flesh.

She leaned against the wall, feeling faint, and then, with infinite gratitude, she felt the forced calm of long practice settling over her. She could deal with this. She could classify, analyze, and react appropriately. The panic was still there, underneath, but it would not rule her.

She crept to the first of the straw pallets where the injured workers lay, and turned back the rags that covered the nearest man. The skin of his hands and arms was discolored and puffy, as if it had been scorched. Raw, unhealed lesions marked his shoulders and back. Jayne remembered the miners she had seen in the tunnels where gold was processed, carrying their heavy loads. These did not seem like injuries from ordinary mining. Perhaps something this man had carried had scarred his skin. Perhaps his burden had contained a poison that kept the wound from healing.

If these men had come in contact with what Agent Cameron had called death dust, then maybe she was on the right track. Maybe Cameron's captors had been here.

Now that she was here, she had to fight down the urge to flee at once. She knew she was far out of her depth here. She looked around the room for another exit. What she saw instead was the source of the light by which she'd been seeing all along—more opaque white light strips, like the ones in the plane. The logical conclusion was that insect creatures had been here.

She heard a scrabbling noise at the entrance. She had nowhere else to go. She flung herself down at the end of the row of pallets, and pulled a stinking, ragged blanket over herself. Pinching her nose shut to keep from gagging on the smell, she pushed the folds of cloth aside and strained to see.

Four or five creatures swarmed into the room, moving with herky-jerky speed and vigor. This was the first time Jayne had seen them acting freely, when they believed they were safe and unobserved. They chittered rapidly to each other. If they'd been closer to human, Jayne would have interpreted their mood as happy and cheerful.

She held her breath as they skittered down the rows of pallets, scratching and prodding at the bodies lying there. The humans who were still conscious pulled away from them, struck feebly at the probing limbs, or curled up defensively. One man didn't move at all. The creatures clustered around him. A claw flashed and rose again, dripping darkly. Its owner popped the claw into its mouth, between the grinding mandibles, and noisily sucked it clean. There was a little explosion of chatter and touching of claws within the group. Then they dragged the body across the floor by an arm, head flopping, and disappeared with it. Jayne heard choked sobs from the pallet next to her.

Half-choked with terror and rage, she threw off the blanket and jumped to her feet. She ran to the entrance. Caution reasserted itself in time to make her pause and look both ways before running after the creatures. A dark trail smeared the floor, marking their passage, but she didn't see them. At the end of the corridor, however, near the elevator shaft, a guard passed by. He disappeared into the shadows, but after she had watched for a few more minutes, he returned. She'd missed him by pure luck.

She might be able to sneak past him again, and escape, but she hadn't found Cameron yet. And she had found half a dozen sick men in danger of death. She looked back at them with a sinking feeling. It would be nearly impossible to smuggle them out of here with her. The only decision that made any sense was to leave now, and not wait for Cameron or the miners. But she'd seen the fate that waited for them. She shuddered. The creatures must be very sure those men were never getting out alive, if they showed themselves so openly. If they spotted Jayne, they'd certainly never let her go, either. She was dooming herself—but she simply couldn't leave them here without a fight.

She crept back to the prisoners, patients, or whatever they were. The first step was to wake them up and see if they were strong enough to be any help. If they couldn't walk, they obviously weren't going anywhere. In that case, she'd have to come back with help.

She was about to speak to the first man when she was startled by another monstrous apparition. "Apparition" was the right word, for this being seemed to materialize from the solid rock wall. He was clad all in black, so his limbs and body were barely visible in the dim light. His face was a grotesque, porcelain white mask with a ferocious, down-turned snarl of a mouth, and a nose so curved and sharp that it resembled the beak of a huge bird of prey. Bristling, bushy dark hair sprang from this goblin face. Unearthly as it was, the face seemed familiar.

She remembered—this was what had been carved on the warning stone that she'd ignored.

Tall and thin, the intruder sprang away from the wall in birdlike hops. He moved across the room without speaking to any of the miners.

The man Jayne was trying to speak to buried his face in his hands again, moaning some word that sounded like "ten-goo."

"What?" Jayne said. She shook his shoulder. "What is it?"

"*Tengu, tengu,*" the man said. She didn't know if "tengu" was the goblin-like being, or if it only meant "I'm scared" or "Go away."

"Well, you shouldn't be scared of it," Jayne said. She knew he couldn't understand her, but perhaps he'd understand the tone of voice. Anyway, the words were for herself as much as for him. "The insect creatures are real, and they are scary. But you can't assume that was a supernatural being. Just because it looked as if he walked through a wall . . ."

She walked over to the wall on the far side of the cavern. The rock there was tortured, twisted, and split. Powerful forces must live beneath this mountain. She bent down under the loom of the wall and ran her fingers over the rock. It seemed impenetrable, but when she leaned her body against it, she felt a breath, as if the rock had exhaled. Behind one lumpy protrusion, there was a crack. It was big enough for a tall man to slip through. The *tengu* being must have emerged from this opening. In the dim light, in his dark robes, it would have seemed that he'd appeared out of nothing.

She turned sideways and squeezed through the crack. Her heart beat hard, and she felt half-suffocated already, just because it was dark. She didn't know if she could go this way, with no idea how it would end, with the possibility of being trapped permanently. But she'd be just as trapped if she went back into that terrible foul-smelling room where the insect creatures ruled.

Jayne squeezed around another angle, and there was light. Another proof that the *tengu* was really human: he'd left a dim lantern burning low on the floor of the tunnel, where it couldn't be seen. Presumably he'd used it to guide him, and would take it up again for the return journey. Which meant this path must be safe. Or at least safe for the *tengu*—and where a man could go, Jayne thought she might venture.

Filled with relief, she picked up the lantern and returned to the cavern. The man she'd been talking to was sitting up, watching, with an expression that seemed both amazed and terrified.

"Ahhh!" he breathed when she reappeared. He tried to bow to her, but she grabbed his arm and pulled him up.

"Never mind that. I'm not a spirit. Just get going, will you? Tell the others to come. And quickly! Before *they* come back."

She pointed to the door and placed her hands in the praying-mantis position, then wigwagged with fingers to her head, to indicate antennae. The man seemed to understand. He nodded rapidly, crawled to his companions, and spoke to them in a low, hurried voice.

The others stumbled to their feet, some holding on to others for support but all energized by the prospect of escape. Jayne handed the lantern to the first man and motioned for him to go.

She wanted to take one final look around to see if there were any traces of Cameron. Now that she knew how to get out, she didn't want to leave without him. She moved stealthily—or what she thought was stealthily enough—toward the entrance of the cavern, intending to make a quick dash up and down the corridor to see where any further branches might lead.

She found herself face-to-face with the insect-creature guard. He clacked his mandibles at her, and she saw the gleaming, toothlike ridges inside. She fumbled in the front of her jacket for the Mauser, but the serrated forearm jerked up faster than she could find the gun. It clubbed her across the forehead like a baseball bat.

When she came to, it took her a minute to realize that she had been unconscious. Then, in a panic, she tried to jump up, but couldn't. Instead, she very slowly opened her eyes. It was still very dark, and dim, and ghostly. She wondered if something was wrong with her eyes. Surely it couldn't be night always, from now on.

Something pale moved into her field of vision. It was the grinning goblin face again. The goblin was squatting next to her, practically in her face.

"Tell them the *tengu* sent you," it said, in perfectly good English. "Just say that—'*tengu*.' They'll understand. The *tengu* can be helpful at times, but they are tricky creatures. Don't cross my path again."

He leapt away, with wild goblin strides.

Jayne tried to sit up, and groaned. Where on earth was she?

Her vision seemed to be improving. She looked up and saw pale clouds. So she was outside, and it was nearly dawn. She felt joy, but it was drowned in a wave of sorrow. She was outside, but Cameron was still lost. The *tengu* had kidnapped her before she could find him. And that meant she was still lost, too.

She pushed herself up on one elbow and looked around. She lay atop a big, flat rock, in a little gully enclosed by scrubby trees growing up its sides and nearly meeting overhead. It was like being in a house without a roof.

Over to her right, there was a wooden structure that looked like a tiny, ramshackle hut. A piece of wood with Japanese characters on it had been nailed up next to an old, rusty-looking bell. Under the bell, on a cracked piece of slate, there was a pile of food, like an offering to some small, minor deity.

Her stomach growled, and she started to drag herself toward the hut. Before she reached it, she heard a rustling in the undergrowth. After all she'd seen, she froze in fear, groping for her gun again. What was it this time? Another monster?

Jayne laughed weakly when a fat-cheeked, furry head, with bright dark eyes and a mask like a raccoon's, appeared instead. The animal was the size of a big raccoon, or a small dog, and it was indeed an animal, intent on its own natural business, with no thought of gold or poisonous weapons.

It sniffed briefly, gave Jayne a shrewd glance, and apparently decided she was harmless. It trotted over to the pile of offerings, picked up a tiny pink cake delicately in its paws, and gobbled it up. It gobbled two more, strewing fragments around, took a drink from the creek that flowed at the bottom of the gully, and scampered off into the woods again.

Jayne supposed she should try to do the same, but she was very cold, and she still ached all over. She pulled herself to her feet and limped slowly downhill, supporting herself by grasping at saplings. At the mouth of the gully, she came to a gate made of cedar wood—just two uprights and a crossbar, weather-beaten and leaning at a precarious angle. A few feet farther on, she came to another. Dozens of gates lined the path, in ghostly invitation to some other realm, but it led nowhere except to more woods.

The gates ended, but the path wound along, ever more steeply downhill, through thickets of maple trees and wild cherry. The sun rose, and the woods shone with a dewy golden sheen. Yet down below her feet, somewhere, the horror was still going on. She felt sick and dizzy.

Her stumbling feet gathered momentum as the path grew steeper, until she was nearly falling, barely catching herself at each step. Turning a corner, she almost collided with a small band of travelers. She tried to stop, tripped, and fell down, rolling to a stop at their feet.

Pain and vertigo slammed through her head. She curled protectively on the path, hearing an outburst of startled shrieks and exclamations above her—high-pitched voices, like twittering birds. They must be children, or women, she thought.

"Sorry—I meant no harm," she croaked. "Does anyone speak English? English? Français? Anyone?"

More twitterings. They must be speaking Japanese, because not one syllable made any sense to her. She remembered what her assailant had said.

"*Tengu?*" she said, without much hope. "The *tengu* sent me?"

A shocked pause, then an even louder burst of exclamations. The words produced a result. Someone knelt beside her and smoothed her hair back gently.

"Oh-ohhhhh," a voice said. It sounded like concern, if such things translated.

"*Tengu, tengu!*" someone said. She sounded excited, maybe even impressed.

"Yes, *tengu!*" Jayne repeated more confidently.

Footsteps whispered away. Jayne lay still. At least they hadn't tried to hurt her. Then a louder tread returned. A lower voice, speaking briefly and deferentially. They'd brought a man.

The man bent over her and tried to pull her to her feet. For a moment, she was upright, seeing lamplight and a cluster of round, pale faces like little moons. To her shock and rage, she knew she was about to faint, and there was nothing she could do about it.

CHAPTER SEVEN

THE MINER'S BIRD
SINGS UNDERGROUND

The plane might be some kind of miracle ship from another planet, but Cameron had flown enough hours to recognize a flat spin when he was in one, and to know it wasn't good. The ground came up fast and hard.

The next thing he knew, he surged up blindly into darkness, coughing his guts out. His head had been under water. He thrashed around and slowly figured out where he was—stuck somewhere in the front end of an airship that was half full of water.

He panicked for a minute, thinking that they'd ditched in the ocean and he was going down with the ship. But they were stationary. The water was shallow. When he stopped gasping for air and looked around, he could see a lighter patch above him where the cargo door at the back of the plane had popped open.

And then he felt sick from more than muddy water, because he remembered that Taylor had been in here with him, and he couldn't find her. He floundered around in the water, terrified he'd find her all limp and sodden, that she'd drowned while he'd been passed out. He couldn't find her body. He felt all around the cabin, round and round, bumping his head on corners of things he couldn't see, before he was satisfied that she really wasn't there.

And then he got mad. Good and mad. She must have bailed on him. She'd left him to drown. Some partner! He knew you couldn't trust a broad.

Aw, what was he saying? Something bad could have happened to her, too. He just didn't want to think it. What he should be thinking about was how to get the hell out of here and look around for her.

His hand hit something that felt like skin, and he jumped like a girl. It was slick and soft. He had to force himself to reach out and grab it.

But it wasn't skin, it was a leather bag, full of something that weighted it down under the water. He dragged it toward him. He'd recognize that chinking sound anywhere. That was the sound of money. Cold cash! Simoleons!

A good thing to have in a foreign country. He pulled out a handful and stuffed them into his pocket. Okay, that was plenty. Time to go.

And then he'd remembered that one of those bugs had been in there with him. He'd thought maybe the bug had taken Taylor away, and he'd got lucky and been left behind. That was a sickener, all right—enough to make a man upchuck, only he didn't have time. He had to get out of here before the bugs came back.

At that moment, he heard something scratching around in the wreckage, and a grasp that felt like metal pincers closed around his arm. He struggled; but it was no more use than a grasshopper's struggles when a boy catches one by a hind leg. And he could hear that un-godly cackling and crackling, as if the bug was laughing at him, just the way Cameron had laughed at the grasshopper trying to hop, when he'd been a boy.

They dragged him out of there, and he couldn't even move. They had him pinioned by his arms and legs. They jerked him along through the mud, hurting every bone in his bruised body.

When they got outside, he opened his mouth to yell for Jayne Taylor, and shut it again, grunting with pain as an-other jolt made him bite his tongue. He wasn't gonna yell out her name. If she was out there, she'd best stay hid-den. If the bugs didn't know she was there, they wouldn't find out from him.

He just hoped to God and the Blessed Mother that if Taylor was out there, she'd hightail it to the nearest American consul and bring in the cavalry. Not do some-thing stupid like follow him on her own.

He guessed she hadn't liked him much. He hoped she'd do the decent thing and make pickup on him any-way. Because this hurt a lot, and he was plenty scared. Worse than he'd ever been.

They came up out of the water and onto dry land, and the bugs let his feet drop to the ground. They shifted their grip on his arms, and while they were moving him he got one hand into his pocket and grabbed a few coins. He let one fall on the path. Of course there was no way Taylor would know that was his, but she'd talked about gold. Maybe she'd put two and two together. Cameron hoped so.

A couple more pieces slipped from his hands as they rousted him along on an endless, painful hike. Then they were underground. Cameron was hanging on by a thread at that point. He drifted in and out of thinking he'd been captured by the Boche, but then he'd hear that insectoid chattering and feel their hard claws chafing against his skin, and realize it was worse than that.

Deep, deep underground somewhere, so far down Cameron wasn't sure it was for real and not just his confused and aching head, they threw him in a cell. God! How had he come so far to be locked up in the pokey? It stank, and the floor was hard. He lay there and shivered, but they wouldn't let him sleep. They mocked with those horrible rasping mouths, and rattled the bars with their talons.

Until finally, finally, a human shape came out of the shadows.

Cameron dragged himself up to the bars to see.

"I want to see the American consul," he rasped. "I'm a very important government operative. Take me to them. They'll pay you. Big reward. Big money. Savvy?"

Cameron heard laughter. It was the kind of laughter that made him sick inside and killed every last shred of hope. He'd heard Iggy laugh like that when he stuffed a stray kitten into a rain barrel.

The figure stepped forward into the dim light. Dead eyes, cropped hair, gray soldier's coat. It was the German they'd shot at on the banks of Rancocas Creek. He might look like a human, but he wasn't.

"So, you are a government agent," the German said. "How very interesting. No, I do not think we will trade you to the American consul."

"You may as well let me go," Cameron said. "I won't tell you anything."

What a bunch of mahooey, he thought. Still, he might as well say it. Everybody said it, at least once. God knows what he'd say later.

"Oh, a tough guy, I see," the German said, his precise, accented diction mocking the slang phrases. "You will not, how is it you say, *sing*?

144

"This is understandable. The miner's bird sings underground. He does not know if it is day or night. I do not ask you to sing. But soon you will sing of your own accord. You will beg me to listen to you."

"Look, what is this all about?" Cameron said. "Can we skip the big act and cut to the chase? What do you want from me?"

"My masters, the Herrenkaefer, want you to make yourself useful," the German said. "Your stupid interference has been costly to them. I have suggested a way you could be useful."

"Yeah, what's that?" Cameron said.

"Before you can be useful, you must learn to estimate your value more correctly," the German said. "You must learn exactly what it's worth to be an agent of the U.S. government, here under Kinzan Mountain."

He turned and spoke to the bugs. They opened the cell and dragged Cameron out. He could have sworn there was nothing he hated worse than being locked up. He'd been so wrong.

They took him even deeper down, where it was darker and hotter. It smelled like the trenches there. It smelled like death. They pushed him into a cage. Oh well, that wasn't so bad, he told himself. At least there were bars between him and them.

And then they hoisted the cage into the air. It swayed and rocked, and the bars on the bottom were spaced just close enough that he couldn't fall through, but not close enough to give him any place to rest without discomfort.

He looked down and saw his cellmates. They were sick, scrawny prisoners, so twisted and stinking with illness or torture, or whatever had brought them here, that they hardly looked human to him.

And that's where he stayed—not for days, for there were no days. Just an endless eternal night of bad dreams. He had a good view of everything that happened to the other prisoners, and none of it was good.

And though it was a nightmare, and he couldn't wake up, he wasn't asleep. They wouldn't let him sleep. He couldn't pass out for more than a few minutes before his cramped position brought him back to consciousness to twist and writhe in a vain search for comfort. If he ever did stay under for longer than that, the bugs would come and spin his cage, snapping their mandibles at him and laughing as he got dizzy enough to retch, even though he'd had nothing to eat.

He started to sing, all right.

"Tell me what you want from me!" he shouted, in a voice he didn't recognize. "Just tell me what the hell you want!"

But they weren't human.

The German wouldn't tell him either. He appeared in the nightmare sometimes, and Cameron cursed him wildly, because at least the German could understand the words.

"How are we feeling today, Mr. Government Agent?" the German said, in his dead, mechanical voice, when Cameron had called him every vile name he could summon.

"Go to hell," Cameron said wearily, at last.

He was sorry he'd said that, because the German laughed again.

"I've been there," the German said. "Like many tourist spots, it is overrated. There is nothing to see in hell that cannot be found much closer to home."

Jayne Taylor, Cameron thought. *Jayne Taylor*. It was the one thought he kept separate from the nightmare. *Jayne Taylor, where the hell are you now?*

Chapter Eight

TANUKI TRICKS

Jayne regained consciousness slowly. She could sense warm light through closed eyelids, and she rested comfortably on a soft surface. Deft hands pressed something cool against her forehead.

"How do you feel now? Does your head hurt?" someone said. The voice, too, was soft and comfortable, a woman's voice.

For a blissful moment, Jayne thought she was back in France, that Madame was by her bedside, and all the rest had been just a bad dream.

But when she opened her eyes, the person tending her was a complete stranger. Instead of Madame's carefully coiffed gray hair, she saw a head shaved bare. Instead of Madame's faded blue eyes and distinctly Gallic nose, Jayne saw a smooth, serene face with dark eyes set flat beneath painted brows. The stranger wore a severely cut robe of several layers of somber colors, wrapped with a broad sash. The robe concealed the body underneath.

Jayne would not have known if this was a man or a woman, if it hadn't been for the voice and the small, delicate fingers that touched her face.

"You speak English?" Jayne said.

The smooth face smiled charmingly, without revealing any teeth.

"*Non, mais je parle Français,*" the woman said.

"Oh, thank God," Jayne said. "I understand you very well. Please tell me where I am."

"This is the—oh, how do you say it?—the convent of nuns at the temple Daijo-ji. Near the town of Aikawa. You do know you are on Sado Island, yes? You know you are now in Nihon?"

Jayne frowned. "Yes, I know this is Sado Island."

"So you know where you are," the bald woman said. "Do you remember who you are?"

"Of course," Jayne said indignantly. "My name is Jayne. Jayne Taylor."

She was about to add "And I'm an American citizen!" when she suddenly remembered that she didn't know who her friends were in this situation. She didn't know yet what information she should give out, and what she should withhold.

"Mademoiselle Jayne," the other woman said, pronouncing her name with surprising accuracy. Perhaps there were similar sounds in her native tongue. "You may call me Lady Ko."

Jayne struggled to sit up. The bald woman slipped a bolster behind her back to support her. Jayne looked down at herself. She was wearing some kind of cotton bath wrap. She looked at her hands. They were much cleaner than she remembered.

"You've been very kind," she said. Something about Lady Ko impelled her to try to be polite. "But I need my clothes. I can't stay here."

"Why can you not?" Lady Ko said. "You are my guest. I invite you to stay."

"I have urgent business," Jayne said. "I must go."

"Why so much hurry?" Lady Ko said. "You are already right here."

For a minute, Jayne suspected she was in an asylum.

"Is this some kind of hospital?" she said suspiciously.

"Indeed yes. Here we find a cure for the fevers of the mind."

"I'm not sick," Jayne protested. "Where are my clothes?"

"You don't remember what happened before you came here?" Lady Ko said.

"No," Jayne said. She was determined now not to give them any information.

"Then perhaps you are sick," Lady Ko said. She rose and opened a wooden chest placed against the wall. She took out a flat object and knelt again at the bedside, offering it to Jayne.

It was a mirror. Jayne looked at her own reflection and gasped. Her face was bruised and swollen. She had a big lump on her head. It was black and blue and felt sore to the touch. As she raised her hand to touch it, she could see in the mirror that her hand, too, had been bruised. She felt along her arms and found more sore places, and as she moved her legs experimentally beneath the covers, she could feel that they were bruised as well. Every muscle ached.

"What happened to me?" she gasped.

"If you do not know, I cannot tell you," Lady Ko said.

Jayne tried to remember, but the moments before the plane crashed were lost to her. She must have been tossed about the cabin before she lost consciousness. And she had run into other things quite a few times since then.

"My ladies told me that you said *'tengu'* to them," Lady Ko said. "Did you see a *tengu?*"

"I don't know," Jayne said. "What is a *tengu?*"

Lady Ko laughed again in that secretive way, putting her hand gracefully over her lips.

"Some people say it is just a story," she said. "They say it is something simple people believe in, like lucky charms."

"A superstition?" Jayne said.

"Yes, just that."

"Then how could I see one?"

"But you said the name," Lady Ko said. "You must have seen something."

"I don't know what I saw," Jayne said. "It was like a face. It had a long nose. But it seemed to me like a man."

Lady Ko went to the chest again, and brought out a book of soft, folded pages, bound together with silken cord on one edge. She turned the pages and handed Jayne the open book.

The paper felt thicker and softer than ordinary paper. A picture was printed in colored inks—a creature with limbs akimbo, brandishing a staff. Its scowling, ruddy face was fringed with bristly beard and featured a long, bulbous nose.

"Like that! Just like that!" Jayne said.

Lady Ko folded up the book and put it away.

"That is a *tengu*," she said. "*Tengu* can appear in many forms. Sometimes they take the form of a man. Often they take the form of a wandering monk.

"What did the *tengu* say to you?" Lady Ko said. "And where did you meet him?"

"I don't know," Jayne said vaguely. That was essentially true. She'd been lost at the time, and she didn't know the names of any of these places. She wasn't really lying to her host. "I was lost on the mountain."

"Hmm." Apparently skepticism, like the smile, was a universal human expression. Although the bald woman's smooth face remained as charmingly enigmatic as ever, Jayne had the distinct feeling that Lady Ko was not buying her feigned ignorance.

"When those who speak can place no trust in words, human speech becomes like the chirping of insects," Lady Ko said.

"I don't think that translates well into French," Jayne muttered, but a chill went down her back as she thought of the insect creature, and wondered how much this woman knew about him and his kind.

"Please, I really need my clothes," Jayne said. "I have urgent business. I was brought here against my will. I mean no harm to anyone. I only want to leave."

Lady Ko's expression softened just a bit.

"I understand," she said. "I, too, came here against my will. You are free to go. The choice is yours. But I can tell you that if I return your clothes to you, and you wander the mountain dressed as a common laborer, the authorities will think you have escaped from the Kinzan mine. You will soon be arrested and returned there. You truly did not know this?"

Jayne shook her head. She felt as if she'd fallen down a rabbit hole into a world where nothing made sense.

"Then you are not an escaped prisoner from the mine?"

"No," Jayne said. "I never heard of this mine until today."

Lady Ko frowned.

"Truth seems evident in your face," she said. "But when you were brought to my gates, you carried three pieces of stolen gold, just like any runaway mine thief."

Jayne tried to conceal her shock. Of course—they'd found the coins in her pocket!

"I swear I didn't steal that," she said. "It's a long story, but I found it. I didn't take it from the mines."

"Tell me this story," Lady Ko said. "I am the abbess of this convent. I have many responsibilities, but none of them are more important than hearing the truth."

"You are the mother superior?" Jayne said. "Oh, I really don't believe this. Why nuns? What have I done to bring all these nuns into my life?"

Lady Ko smiled with genuine amusement.

"This is an interesting question," she said. "Perhaps at this time you receive the benefit to work out the karma of a previous life."

"I don't want to work out my karma," Jayne said. "There is something else I need to do right now. It will make my karma very bad if I don't do it."

"Not-doing is wisdom," Lady Ko said.

"Please stop talking like a nun," Jayne said. "I don't give a rap for my soul or my karma. I just want my pants back."

"Now you remind me of my late husband," the nun said. "His family desired that he might devote his life's work to the diplomatic corps, and he carried this out with a spirit of perseverance. But he was a very impatient man."

"Please, my pants." Jayne felt as if she was about to cry, and there was no feeling she hated more. Agent Cameron could be dying at the hands of the insect creatures or their friends at this very moment. He might already be dead. She probably couldn't help him, but she had to try, even though all she wanted was to find the quickest route home. And instead, she was lying in bed being diplomatically misdirected by a bald nun.

"Are you not even curious as to what has become of your gold?" Lady Ko said.

Jayne couldn't help but answer that.

"Yes, very. And it is mine, you know, whether you believe it or not. If you're so worried about karma, you really should give it back."

This time, Lady Ko did not go to the storage chest. She rose to her feet in one fluid motion, only to cross the room and kneel again before a niche in the corner. Jayne twisted around in the bed to see what the niche contained. Her head began to throb again, but she saw a small altar.

Lady Ko bowed before the altar, as if apologizing, and then moved it aside just six inches, and lifted one of the richly polished floorboards. From the recess this revealed, she lifted something in her joined hands, and presented it to Jayne with a graceful gesture.

There was nothing in her hands but three dry brown leaves.

Jayne glanced from the leaves to the nun's face and back, too surprised to speak. Lady Ko's expression showed only mischievous delight, like a child who had played a trick.

"I see you told me the truth," she said. "Indeed, you did not steal this money. It could not have come from the mine, for it was only *tanuki* money, after all!"

Jayne wondered again if the bald woman might be a little crazy.

"All my people have seen it," Lady Ko said. "So if anyone should come here asking about stolen gold, they have seen nothing. They are simple people and believe in the *tengu*. *Tanuki* money has only the appearance of brightness. It can turn back to leaves and sticks any time. The *tengu* must have traded your gold for *tanuki* money. *Tengu* are tricky, after all."

"That's what he said," Jayne said slowly. The words came back to her. "He said, '*Tengu* sometimes do good deeds. But we are a tricky lot.'"

"And you understood him, even though you are not Japanese," Lady Ko said. "How interesting!"

Jayne flushed. So easily she had betrayed crucial information!

A bell sounded outside. Lady Ko rose to her feet and replaced the leaves beneath the altar.

"I must go now," she said. "It is time for morning meditation. The novice outside will bring you something to eat. I'll come back in an hour or two. Perhaps you will be rested and feel more like talking then."

She glided from the room, leaving Jayne to reflect, too late, that she had neither given Jayne's clothes and money back nor actually refused to do so. She had evaded the issue like a diplomat.

Fuming, Jayne decided she would search the room herself. But at the first sound of her stirring out of bed, another shaven head peeked around the corner of the screen. A younger nun, in less elaborate robes, hurried into the room and tucked her back under the quilted comforter. Then she brought in a tray that held little covered bowls and a small teapot. Her expression was so hopeful and shy that Jayne hated to refuse. The teapot scented the room with fragrant steam. Jayne nodded politely and let the young woman place the tray across her knees.

Jayne looked in vain for a spoon or fork. The golden-brown broth smelled so good that she picked up the bowl and drank from it, after looking around guiltily to see if anyone was observing her breach of manners. She hadn't eaten anything but the chewy snacks on the plane in so long. One day? Two days? She didn't know how much time had passed, but she knew she was hungry.

She gulped the rest of the soup. She uncovered the other dishes and recognized a heap of white rice in one, and noodles in another. The rest of the contents were a mystery. Most of it looked like vegetables, except for some white bits that tasted like fish. The flavors were completely foreign to her, but she was so hungry she ate it all.

They had given her only a pair of lacquered sticks to use in getting the food into her mouth. She tried various methods of piercing or picking it up, and finally put the bowls to her mouth and used the sticks to push the food toward her lips.

When the novice came back, the dishes were polished clean. The novice said something that sounded polite— but then, everything they said sounded polite, Jayne thought—and Jayne tried to respond in kind by beaming, nodding, and saying "Yummm" enthusiastically.

"Yummmm?" The girl imitated her, and fled the room in a fit of giggles.

Hunger sated, Jayne waited impatiently for Lady Ko to come back. She was determined to stay alert. But the bed felt so warm and comfortable. It suddenly occurred to her that the food could have been drugged—but she was already too drowsy to move. She fell asleep again.

The way she awakened was not polite at all. She was being poked and shaken.

"*Vite, vite, vite!*" said the persistent voice. "*Dépêchez-vous!*"

French again.

"What is it?" she said groggily. "Is it the Germans again? Are we being shelled?"

But no one answered the question. They dragged her to her feet and hustled her through a door. By the time she was fully awake, she was outside, feeling cool wet grass against her bare feet. A bevy of nuns supported her and hurried her along, through green gardens she barely glimpsed, and over stepping-stones across water that she could hear gurgling as they passed.

They came to a straw-thatched hut and pushed her inside. The nuns escaped into the garden like a flock of pigeons, leaving Jayne alone with Lady Ko.

"Here are your clothes," Lady Ko said. "Quick, put them on."

"About time," Jayne grumbled, struggling into the blue cotton trousers and jacket. The fabric smelled fresh, and felt soft and clean instead of grimy and damp. Obviously, someone had washed them for her.

Lady Ko wrapped a plain white cotton scarf around Jayne's head, drawing the end of it across her face, and then topped it with a straw hat, tying down the brim so it shaded Jayne's cheeks.

"This is very important," she said, as she worked. "You are a gardener now. You work for the temple. You are so very humble that you will not look the important visitors in the face. This is how we hide you so you will not be found. You understand?"

"What? What visitors?" Jayne mumbled through the scarf.

"Gold Mountain Mining Corporation. They control the mine. If you, a foreigner, are found here, where gold is mined, an inquiry will be made. And you will be a prisoner until they get an answer. To stay free, all you need is this." She pushed a wooden rake into Jayne's hands. "And this." She tucked a pair of pruning shears into Jayne's waistband. "Now you will rake the bushes on the far side of the pond and speak to no one. You understand?"

"Yes. Yes, I understand," Jayne said.

"And one more thing," Lady Ko said. "You are a boy now! Think—you are a boy!"

Lady Ko looked both ways out of the door of the hut, then darted like a swallow across the trim garden paths to join her ladies. Jayne gave her a good head start, then sauntered out in the other direction.

She forced herself to walk slowly, hoping she presented a casual impression. She wanted to dash across the lawn and hide her confusion in the bushes as fast as possible.

When she reached the welcome shadow of the shrubbery, she wormed her way through to the far side. She scratched lazily in the grass with the rake, gathering a few fallen leaves, while spying between the branches to see who these visitors were, who had roused the nun to such decisive action.

At first she thought a group of tall women had joined the nuns. They wore long robes that looked much the same as the nuns' garb but were more richly decorated and came in different colors. They had long hair, pulled back from their foreheads in topknots. But they walked with long, bold strides, very different from the tiny, gliding steps of the nuns. Lady Ko bowed to them, and bowed again, while they responded with curt nods.

When they turned toward the main buildings, Jayne got a better look at their faces, and realized that they were men, after all. The sound of their voices drifted across the lawn, deeper and rougher than those of the women. Three of them seemed different. They were taller than the rest, and their hair was cropped short. As they came closer, she could see that two of the tall ones were Westerners. One of them looked familiar, impossible as that seemed. With a cold shock, she recognized the face of the German.

I must be imagining this, she thought. *I'm shell-shocked. I should be in a hospital. He can't be here, halfway around the world.*

She gripped the rake to steady herself.

But I'm here, she reminded herself. *And for a good reason. So, maybe he has a reason, too. Maybe that reason has to do with the insect creatures, just like mine. And if that's true, then all of this must have started long ago. Before Cameron, before the bootlegging. It must go all the way back to the first time I saw him, to the nun who wasn't a nun, and the radium that wasn't radium.*

Strangely, although the German looked just as he always had, he no longer walked with that odd, jerky stride. Now he walked like a human. But the tall Japanese man with whom he seemed deep in conversation, though he looked human, even to the point of wearing a mustache, moved in that unnerving, twitchy fashion.

The cold, chilly feeling crept deeper into her bones.

So many things were not what they seemed, she thought. Maybe the German was not a German, either. Maybe he was something else entirely.

Though this was deeply disturbing, she felt better once she had figured it out— stronger, more confident, steadier on her feet.

Knowing what's going on always helps, she thought. *Even if what is going on seems impossible.*

She watched until the group vanished into the main building. Then she loitered along the hedgerow, always heading toward the edge of the grounds. This was her chance to flee, but now she wondered if she should stay awhile. The enigmatic Lady Ko might be friend or enemy—but she was the only person Jayne had found so far with whom she could communicate. The strangers were definitely a danger, but that might be the best reason for remaining where she could keep an eye on them. Boo Boo Hoff had once quoted a Sicilian proverb in her presence: "Keep your friends close, and your enemies closer."

If she found her way back into the mine, she wanted food, water, and a candle this time. She decided to find the kitchen first, steal a store of provisions, and then decide where to go. That sounded like a plan. Full stomachs make good decisions. And if that wasn't a Sicilian proverb, she thought, it should be.

She came out from behind the hedge and looked around to get her bearings. Smoke trickled from a nearby outbuilding. She followed her nose toward the smoke and a delicious smell of grilled fish. As she approached, a procession of maids and cooks burst from the kitchen wing, carrying trays and pots.

Jayne panicked. She ducked under the shadow of the eaves and through the first door she came to. She tripped over a pile of firewood and narrowly avoided tipping over a stack of pots. She was in a storage room next to the kitchen, temporarily safe. The room was empty, though she could hear the clatter and chatter of cooking in the next room. The scents made her mouth water.

She peered through a chink in the flimsy screen that separated the rooms, to see if there was anything edible within reach. And froze, as a large hand descended on her shoulder, and the voice of the *tengu* breathed against her ear.

"So—there you are."

CHAPTER NINE

THE TENGU'S DISCIPLE

Jayne was more than ready to scream. A shriek of tremendous feeling and volume swelled in her throat, only to be choked down again as she realized that she was surrounded by potential enemies. Instead, she whirled before the *tengu* could immobilize her, and stamped her heel down on his instep. She had forgotten that she was wearing only straw sandals. Even so, the results were gratifying.

He let go of her to utter a strangled cry, rubbing the damaged foot and hopping in place, while Jayne grabbed a stout stick of firewood and got ready to flee as soon as he moved away from the door. But he didn't move. He straightened up, poised with his weight gracefully on one foot. Jayne swiped at his leg with her stick and tried to dodge around him, but somehow the stick twisted itself from her hand and into his, as if the wind had carried it there. The *tengu* held the stick tauntingly behind him, and he was still in her way.

"Oh, no, you won't get away that easily," he said in English, pitching his voice so low it wouldn't carry into the noisy kitchen. "I have a few questions to ask you."

Jayne recognized the voice she'd heard in the darkness, but his appearance didn't match the fierce goblin face. She stared at him. He wasn't Japanese, though his short hair was raven black, not too different from theirs. His eyes were dark, too, intense and glittering—the one feature that resembled Jayne's *tengu*. His features were lean and strongly marked—high cheekbones, a narrow beak of a nose.

Afraid to take her eyes off his face for long, Jayne flicked a quick glance over the rest of him. His robe was almost as dark as Lady Ko's, but even at a glance Jayne could see that the fabric was of the finest quality, a rich pattern of birds and flowers woven into it. He wore a broad sashlike belt printed with a design of three triangles. Two swords were tucked into the sash. The sleeves of the dark robe were flung back to the elbow, and the man's arms were intimidatingly sinewy. They gave Jayne no reason to doubt that he could use that sword. A tassel swung from the sheath of the longer sword, and an ivory weight bobbed on the end of the tassel. The weight was carved into the shape of a grinning goblin-bird.

"The *tengu*," Jayne whispered.

By this time, the man had lowered his arms and stood square. His easy grin annoyed her.

"Just what is a *tengu*?" She scowled. "And why did you pretend to be one?"

"That's what they call me," he said. "'Noriyama no Tengu.' Noriyama's *tengu*." He grimaced fiercely, heightening the resemblance.

"Because of the nose," he explained. "And because none knows my origin. Because I come and go as I wish."

"But you don't look like what I saw," Jayne said.

"I was in my *tengu* guise then," he said. "I told you, *tengu* are tricky."

"And what did you do with my—" Jayne began, but he interrupted her.

"Too much to explain, here in this woodshed," he said. "You've got to stop trying to escape. I don't have time to keep rescuing you. We need a truce. Will you return with me as far as Lady Ko's study? We can talk there. I have news of your friend."

Twice now, he could have hurt her, but he hadn't—yet.

"I don't trust you as far as I could spit in a high wind," Jayne said. "But I'll follow you as far as Lady Ko's."

He reached into the richly patterned belt and brought out a flat package wrapped in a gold-embroidered wisp of silk.

"Carry this gift—so," he said, extending his hands flat and palm-up. "Stay close to me. Keep your head down, your eyes down. And remember you are a servant—a servant *boy!*"

She trotted after him, head down, watching his heels flicker in and out under the edge of his robe. Beneath it, he wore wide black trousers—like bloomers, she thought. A sword-carrying goblin in bloomers! She had to bite her tongue to suppress a laugh.

She felt self-conscious about her own appearance, and tried to keep her shoulders and hips stiff and straight. Her mother had always scolded her about taking such big steps and bouncing when she walked. It wasn't ladylike, she'd said. Now Jayne was afraid of looking too ladylike.

Voices and footsteps approached. The *tengu* stopped and stepped aside casually, but in such a way that he put Jayne behind him. He bowed, and his elbow struck her in the ribs. She decided that must be a signal for her to bow too, and anyway, she didn't want to stick up when his head was lowered, so she hastily followed suit.

She heard male voices, then laughter. Someone tried to reach past her and grab her arm. The *tengu* spoke in rapid, apparently fluent Japanese. If he had any accent, Jayne couldn't tell. After another burst of laughter, the hand on her arm loosed its hold—though not without a little squeeze that made Jayne's flesh creep.

Then she was hurrying after the *tengu*, across the raked gravel path that led to the main door. Inside, the big meditation hall stood empty. The *tengu* slipped off his sandals and kicked Jayne's ankle to make her stop and do likewise before she could set foot on the polished wooden floor. She complied reluctantly. If she had to run away, she didn't want to do it clad only in little white socks with divided toes.

"What did those people say?" she said, as they skirted the floor.

"You don't want to know," he said.

Jayne stopped. "Yes, I do—or I won't follow you another step!"

"Fine, then—they said, 'The *tengu* has a *chigo!*' Happy now?"

"I want to know what it means," Jayne insisted.

"Technically, a *chigo* is an acolyte. A protégé, if you will. It was Noriyama-sama himself who took your arm. He wanted a closer look at your face. Apparently you are good-looking—as a boy."

"Then why were they laughing?"

"To make him let go, I pleaded that I would be late for my appointment with the lady abbess. I said that I had a spiritual problem to discuss, and in return for advice, I needed to present my gift. Noriyama said the gift should be more tastefully wrapped. You see, as your protector, I should clothe you in more luxurious robes."

It took Jayne a minute to understand what he was saying. Then she stopped in her tracks again.

"Oh!" She wanted to make a break for the door at that moment, socks or no socks, but the *tengu* shoved her through Lady Ko's doorway before she could flee.

"It's me or Noriyama now," he said. "Trust me, you're better off with me."

Jayne dumped the package she'd been carrying unceremoniously onto the floor. Seething with indignation, she backed away as far as she could get.

"Oh, sit down," the *tengu* said.

The *tengu* picked up the package and handed it respectfully to Lady Ko. They exchanged a few words in Japanese, while Jayne waited resentfully.

"I suppose we'll have to use French now," the *tengu* said in that language, glancing at her. "Since that's the only language we all share. Lady Ko, it would be so convenient if you could complete your studies in English."

"Yes, I regret that I am so slow," Lady Ko said, smiling. "But I have responsibilities to my sisters here at the convent, as well. I will try."

She beckoned to Jayne.

"Mademoiselle Jayne, please sit. Let me pour you tea. I regret that there was no time to explain before officials from Gold Mountain Mining Corporation arrived here for their visit. But I assure you, Noriyama no Tengu is a friend."

"He may be your friend," Jayne said. "My friend is at the bottom of that mine shaft, to the best of my knowledge, and this person with the highly ridiculous nickname stopped me from rescuing him."

"The name fits me here, in this place," the tengu said. "But if you like it better, you can call me Frederick Barnet."

The name sounded familiar to Jayne. She was sure she'd heard it before, yet equally sure she'd never met this man. Probably it was another fake, she thought wearily. Like Rocco Smith.

"Well, Mr. Barnet," she said, "what you call yourself is less important than what you can do for me. You said you had news. I don't have time to sit and drink tea!"

"American," Barnet said to Lady Ko, as if that explained something. "But she could be right."

"Right action at the right time is a virtue," Lady Ko said.

"Right," Barnet said wryly. "The news, then."

He sank gracefully into a cross-legged position, sweeping the skirts of his robe around him as if he had worn them always.

"The *tengu* didn't come to stop you from finding Mr. Cameron," he said.

He paused and smiled wryly at Jayne's shock.

"Oh, yes, I know his name. And yours, Miss Taylor. The news of your surprising arrival has been circulating all around Noriyama's little entourage—two mysterious strangers take down a beetle and crash his plane. And then one of the strangers disappears! It was a good show, I must say—even though you hadn't the least idea what you were doing. Perhaps that makes it all the more impressive."

Jayne resented Barnet's condescending approval.

"And how do you happen to know so much about . . ." She stopped, not sure how much it was safe to say. She'd learned something from "Rocco Smith": that knowing a person's name didn't mean you knew the person, and that sometimes removing one mask only revealed another one underneath.

"About the *kamakiri-kami*?" he said. "That's what they call them here. It means the mantis spirits, or the divine mantids. I know a good deal about them. I've studied them for some time now."

"Then you can tell me," Jayne said. "You call them—mantids? What are they really? Where do they come from?"

"Forgive me, Miss Taylor," Barnet said, though without appearing terribly contrite. "There are many things I know but am not free to share. Just as I would not share your business with others, though I am fully aware of the real reasons for your journey.

"All you need to know just now is that you and Mr. Cameron are in danger here and need to leave at once."

"Which is exactly what we were trying to do," Jayne said.

"Not exactly," Barnet said. "The *tengu* had just located Mr. Cameron and was about to liberate him, when you appeared, interfered in my plan, and nearly blew my cover completely. I had to stop to rescue you. As a result, I had to leave Cameron behind."

"I didn't need rescuing," Jayne said indignantly. "I got there on my own. I was doing fine on my own."

"Until you ran into one of the beetles," Barnet said. "He gave you a pretty good knock on the head. Maybe that's why you don't remember. I had to risk my mission to get you out of there."

"So you say," Jayne said skeptically. She was tempted to put it in the vernacular and retort "sez you!"

"And what were you planning to do with us after you 'rescued' us?" she said.

"Lady Ko was going to risk her safety to hide Mr. Cameron here," Barnet said. "Just as she has now done for you. And then I planned to smuggle both of you off the island and send you to the American consul in Nagoya as soon as I could amass enough money to pay the fortune in bribes that would require."

"And who are you working for?" Jayne said. "Who is Noriyama?"

"Noriyama is the chief official representative of the Gold Mountain Mining Corporation here on Sado Island," Barnet said. "Gold Mountain Mining recently took over operation of the Kinshan gold mine on behalf of the Japanese government. I serve him as a liaison to various foreign governments. But I have . . . other responsibilities as well."

"Mr. Cameron is an agent of the United States government," Jayne said. "Why would your company hold him prisoner?"

"Because Noriyama is playing a double game," Barnet said. "And so must I, if I am to keep up with him."

"Well, *stop* playing games and tell me plainly what's going on!" Jayne said.

"I'm not at liberty to do that," Barnet said. "And you wouldn't believe me if I did. I will only say that Noriyama is dealing with some very dangerous people. It is those . . . people . . . who are holding Agent Cameron."

"And where do you come into all this?" Jayne said. "What's in it for you?"

"You wouldn't believe that, either," Barnet said. "What about you? Are you a secret agent, too?"

"I am now," Jayne said defiantly.

Barnet grinned. "As am I," he said. "But not for a national agency. My jurisdiction extends beyond national boundaries."

"The League of Nations?" Jayne said incredulously. "They have secret agents now?"

Barnet roared with laughter.

"That feeble debating society!" He wiped his eyes, still chuckling. "You're very funny, Secret Agent Taylor. You don't need to know with whom I work. It's enough to know that we mean you well, but our goals are too important to mankind to let you and Agent Cameron blunder into the midst of a very delicate operation. I want you both off this island, now. So you will stay here and stay out of Noriyama's way until I can get Cameron out of the mine. And then you will both get on the first fishing boat to Niigata and go home."

"Not a chance," Jayne said. "I'm going to find Cameron, one way or another. If I don't go with you, then I'll go on my own."

And I'm not going home until I find out what you're up to, she thought. But she decided not to say that until later. Take one machine-gun nest at a time.

Barnet stopped laughing. "You're not serious," he said.

"I am."

"I've told you," he said. "I can't waste my time looking after you. I rescued you once. I shan't do it over and over again."

"I don't know that you rescued me at all," Jayne said. "It's just as likely that you're in league with the mantid who gave me that crack on the head. I don't want any more of your 'rescuing.' If you really mean to help, then tell me what to watch out for, and I'll take care of myself. The more you conceal the truth from me, the more trouble I'll get into."

He clenched his fist on the hilt of his sword—a quite unconscious gesture, she was sure.

"I cannot *tell* you the truth," he said. "You need experience to understand it. Experience you simply do not have. As an educated young American woman, you have lived in a protected little world. You don't understand how little your life is worth out here. You aren't prepared to defend yourself."

"Oh, please!" Jayne said. She leapt to her feet, her anger boiling over.

"This all started in the war zone, in France. I learned something in France, Mr. Barnet. I learned that 'protection' is an illusion, nothing more. For all of us.

"Women and children are 'protected'? Not on the front lines, Mr. Barnet. A shell doesn't care how old you are, or whether you're male or female. Gas doesn't care.

"And afterward—there's no protection for children without parents, families without a breadwinner. Where's the protection for the delicate young woman, when there's no job for you because you're not a man? Where's the protection for the children who will grow up just in time for the next war, when someone is already out there, producing the weapons that will destroy them?

"The world changed in France, and it's not changing back. Nor will I. I won't be hidden in a closet while you determine the shape of my future."

She had been so angry she could hardly see, not able to focus on the *tengu*'s face. But gradually, she realized that something had changed in his expression. He was listening.

"You were in France?" he said, when she paused for a breath.

"Yes. I saw things there that I will never forget."

"I, too." He met her eyes, with a haunted look, as if her words had reminded him of something. There were dark marks under his eyes. He had the look of a man who hasn't been sleeping well.

She felt as if he were waiting for a password. If she knew what to say, he would accept her as an ally. But she didn't know.

So she blurted out the truth.

"I saw a man die in France. I mean—I killed him. Or thought I had. Since then I've seen him three times. Walking. The third time was just today. I saw him walk with you down that very path outside."

Oh no, what have I done now! she thought as soon as the words left her lips. *I shouldn't have told him that.*

The effect on Barnet was more dramatic than she could possibly have imagined. The blood drained from his already pale and somber face, until his dark eyes looked like a pair of black stones set in ivory.

"*You!*" he said. She could see the shock pass through him. "You saw the German." Though she thought it wasn't what he'd originally intended to say, she was amazed, in turn.

"You know about the German," she said. "Tell me. Who is he? And who is that man who was walking with him?"

Barnet wasn't looking at her anymore. He had turned his head, and a look passed from him to Lady Ko. They must have known each other for a long time, Jayne thought. Only old friends could communicate in silence like that. Lady Ko nodded.

"But—" Barnet said, and then shut up.

Somehow Jayne had said the right thing after all.

"Mademoiselle Jayne, I have decided it is best to share a secret with you," Lady Ko said. "You saved the lives of five men. You have a good heart."

"She has a foolhardy lack of discretion," Barnet interrupted. "For the sake of five miners, she may have sacrificed our carefully planned mission."

Lady Ko made a shushing motion at him.

"I'm glad they got out," Jayne said. "I didn't know what happened."

"Yes, they escaped. They came down the path from the *tanuki* shrine and scattered. If they recover, they will be taken off the island. If not, at least they will die under heaven, not imprisoned underground."

"*Tanuki* shrine?" Jayne said faintly. This was supposed to be an explanation, but it was confusing her more than ever. *Tengu, tanuki*—she'd had no time to learn a whole new language.

171

"Among our duties is to tend the *tanuki* shrine," Lady Ko said. "Maybe you saw an appearance of the *tanuki*. In their natural form, they are small and furry. They run on four legs and appreciate treats."

"I did see an animal eating rice balls," Jayne said.

Lady Ko clapped her hands as if Jayne had done something clever.

"Oh, good, you have been introduced," she said.

Barnet rolled his eyes.

"Tengu-san plays with our legends, but says he does not believe in them," Lady Ko said. "He disguises himself as the wild mountain goblin, the *tengu*, so ordinary people will fear him and say nothing of his comings and goings. He has spent many months searching out paths the *tanuki* makes through the mountains, and living in the *tanuki* shrine. I am sure he has made friends with the *tanuki*, but he won't admit it.

"So I'm glad to hear that you, too, are a friend of the *tanuki*."

"What is a *tanuki*?" Jayne said. "It looked like a raccoon to me—that's an animal we have in America. It's cute, but more of a nuisance than anything else."

"Ah, but the raccoon shape is only one of the many that a *tanuki* can take. When they put a *kuzu* leaf on their heads, they can change into many shapes. A man or woman! A monk or a nun. A pair of shoes or a boat. *Tanuki* are very, very lucky friends for those who need help. And since you have lent the *tanuki* your gold, he has left you the *kuzu* leaves as a promise to pay the favor back someday."

"Yes, now can we get on with it and skip the fairy tales?" Barnet said.

"Tengu-san is a man of science," Lady Ko said, without appearing to take offense. "He understands things differently. But we understand the same things."

She looked much sadder.

"Forgive me," Barnet said. "I realize it is difficult for you to speak of this."

"I was speaking of transformations, and appearances," Lady Ko said. "You asked about the man who walked with the one you call the German. That man has the face of my late husband."

"I don't understand," Jayne said. "Do you mean that you were once married to him?"

"No!" the nun said. "I was married once, yes. My husband was an honorable man, a diplomat. We spent many happy years together. Then he was asked by Noriyama to participate in this great secret project of theirs. A scientific project to bring power to all of Japan—power for electric lights, for factories, for warmth in winter and all the good things other nations have. My husband was a forward-thinking man. He was away often, working on this project."

She looked down.

"Until he found out the true nature of it, and refused to continue. Noriyama told him that he would help with the project in one way or another, with his consent or without. I did not know what he meant, but I was afraid. And then he disappeared. He never came back, and yet his face walks."

Jayne felt cold again, cold as ice. She remembered Madeleine crying out that the mother superior had been taken by a devil.

"The mantids have a device," Barnet said. "They have a way to make a copy of a human being and wear it. It's only an appearance, but they can put it on so they can walk among us without being seen. It doesn't hold up well to close scrutiny. If you touch them, you feel their true form. But, at a distance . . ."

"The one who wears my husband's face is the *kamakiri-kami* shogun," Lady Ko said. "I follow the way of the

Buddha and I think that I should feel compassion for him, but I do not. I feel compassion for all living things of the earth. This earth. For this one and his kind, I have no compassion. They have taken the secret halls of the *tanuki* and turned them into a place of horror. They have taken my husband's face. They must be stopped."

"I agree," Barnet said. "And the best way to stop them is for you to keep Miss Taylor here—under lock and key if necessary—until I can snag Agent Cameron. Then ship them both off the island and get back to work before it's too late."

"I'm afraid that will be impossible," Lady Ko said. "You can already see that I cannot keep Jayne here against her will. The only way for you to watch her is to take her with you."

"Which I've agreed to do," Barnet said ungraciously. "But only to get Cameron. After that, you're both out of here."

He gave Jayne a stern look.

"Do you agree?"

"Fine," Jayne said. "Whatever you say."

She wondered if it was childish to cross her fingers under cover of her baggy sleeve.

"Then let's get started," Barnet said.

Jayne scrambled to her feet. "There's just one thing . . ." she said.

Barnet's eyebrows rose. "What now?" he said.

"Well—I'm hungry!" Jayne said. "I started out to get some food from the kitchen, and then came all this nonsense, and now I'm even hungrier than ever."

Lady Ko laughed.

"You would not make a good nun, Mademoiselle Jayne," she said. "In this convent, you would have nothing to look forward to but some rice gruel after our evening meditation. Fortunately, I had prepared some refreshments for our friend in his guise as Noriyama no Tengu, a respected guest."

She handed Barnet a large white napkin, neatly folded around something heavy, and tied in an attractive knot.

"Please take these, also." She held up a tiny lacquered tray that held half a dozen small pastrylike objects.

"Thank you!" Jayne swept the sweets off the tray and tucked them into the fold where her jacket was tied across her chest.

"We'll go now," the *tengu* said. He bowed graciously, and Lady Ko bowed, and Jayne hunched her shoulders and tucked her head awkwardly, feeling like a goblin herself.

Barnet handed Jayne the napkin bundle.

"Since you are my servant, you'll have to carry this," he said. "It would not look proper for me to carry anything while you remain unburdened."

"Oh, *thank* you, master," Jayne grumbled. She fumbled in her jacket for one of the bunlike objects, and bit into it. It was filled with a sweetish goo that tasted more like baked beans than like jam. But it was food, and her mouth watered as she swallowed it in two bites. She reached for another one, and got something that felt like the egg-shaped objects she'd eaten on the airplane. This one was colored candy pink, but the bland, gummy texture was the same.

"What is this thing?" she said. "Japanese chewing gum?"

"It's *mochi*," Barnet said. "Rice cake. It has religious significance, so be respectful. For that matter, it's time for you to stop stuffing your mouth altogether. We have to leave, and people here don't move and eat at the same time."

Jayne shoved another bun in her mouth and wiped her fingers on her trousers.

"Where are we going?" she said.

"Straight through the front door," Barnet said.

It didn't look like it to Jayne. They ended up following the damn path up the mountainside again.

"Not more caves," she groaned.

Leaving the light behind and groping back into the dark felt almost like a physical pain. But there was still a hint of light from the cave mouth when Barnet turned to face the wall. He pulled a silk cord from his belt and held it up for Jayne to see. Its end was tied with an elaborate knot to a jade toggle that she had assumed was ornamental. She touched it to confirm its shape—a carved stone claw.

Barnet swept his palm across the cave wall, searching for something, and then scratched with the claw. Silent lights bloomed out of the rock, outlining symbols Jayne recognized. Salad fork, lizard, turkey track. Barnet scratched again, and Jayne felt the puff of air from below as a darker opening appeared in the darkness of the wall.

"This is where they took Cameron," she said. "And by the time I got here, they were gone—and I couldn't see the markings, so I kept on going into the mines!"

"You went down there?" Barnet said, nodding toward the total blackness to their right. "But the shaft is flooded! There's no way through!"

"Well, apparently there is," Jayne said. "Because here I am."

She expected Barnet to be impressed, but he was apparently thinking about something different.

"Interesting," he said. "The water level rises and falls. I wonder if that means anything. The elevator's here—come on."

He leaned into the shaft, grasped a metal bar, and stepped into the darkness. Jayne put her hand on the bar next to his, and felt into the darkness for the platform.

Her heart skipped a beat. No matter how far she probed with her toe, she couldn't feel anything but air.

"Wh-Where's the elevator?" she said.

Barnet laughed. "It's a disk in the middle of the shaft, about as wide as your hand. This is their second exit, mostly for emergencies. They didn't bother to build it to human specifications. Step in; you won't fall."

Jayne clung to the bar for dear life and stepped into emptiness. To her surprise, her feet were supported as if there were a floor beneath them. She couldn't feel it, but she didn't fall.

When actual rock appeared under her feet, she gasped for air. She'd been holding her breath.

"What is it?" she stammered. "Is it magic?"

Barnet snorted. "It might as well be. Just as kitchen matches would have seemed like magic to our ancestors who lived in caves like these. The only difference between us and them is that we understand that there must be a logical explanation. That doesn't get us any closer to finding it, though."

"Nonsense," Jayne said. "Once you know something can be done, *how* to do it is only a matter of time and opportunity."

Barnet glanced sharply at her.

"You could be right," he said. "But no more talk now. We're here."

And she couldn't ask where *here* was, because he was already stepping briskly out into a lighted corridor, and she could only follow, remembering to keep her eyes down.

The corridor widened out into a hive-shaped chamber. Jayne couldn't see how far up it extended. Strips of some glowing material had been fastened to the walls just above head height, and their glow obscured the top of the chamber.

Barnet hurried, almost running to the end of the chamber, and ducked into another opening. The tunnel beyond was clearly not natural in origin. The walls formed a perfect cylinder, and their surface felt slick and glassy under Jayne's fingers, as if it had been melted smooth. The tunnel twisted and crossed other burrows in a tangled labyrinth. Jayne shivered and tried to banish thoughts of giant worms or termites.

Barnet followed the curved walls without hesitation to an area where dry brown webbing festooned the walls, holding a jumble of implements and containers. The webbing looked like cargo net, but it smelled funny and had a flaky, untidy texture, like bark or peeling skin. After touching it, Jayne rubbed her hands compulsively on her trousers. They'd been fresh when she left the convent, but were rapidly acquiring a patina of dirt.

Barnet pulled a polygon made of the same papery material out of the net. Its facets were pitted with hexagonal cells, like a wasp's nest, and each cell held a small metal object. He extracted one of the objects and held it up close to his eye. Apparently there was something wrong with it, because he stuck it back in its socket and chose another. Then he took the first one back, and weighed them, one in each hand, trying to decide something. Finally he shrugged and dumped both of them into Jayne's palm.

Jayne turned each object over in her hands, dubiously. They felt slick and faintly warm. She saw chicken scratchings of some kind engraved on the back, but the symbols were too small to read, even if she had known their meaning. She did notice that each had one larger marking in red, and that they were different. The objects felt too heavy for their size—about the size and shape of her mother's cameo brooch.

"It goes on your skin, under the shirt," he said. "Next to a bone, it works best. They know I have one, but you'll have to keep yours hidden. And don't leave it in one place too long. It irritates the skin. It'll get red, like a burn."

A chill went down Jayne's back.

"Like radium," she said.

Barnet smiled in that knowing way that Jayne was already coming to hate.

"Something like that," he said, as if to a bright but naïve child.

"I don't want these," Jayne said. She tried to hand them back, but Barnet wouldn't take them.

"You'll need them," Barnet said. "If you want to know what's happening."

"Magic?" she said scornfully.

He shrugged again.

"Something like it. When they talk, you feel it in your ear. As if it carries through the bone. And you hear it in your own language. Actually, I don't know if this will even work for you. Mine translates from beetle-click into Nihongo—Japanese. But that won't help you. So I've given you a second—it has a marking for European on it. It could be English, French, German. I don't know. All you can do is try."

He pulled his robe aside to show her the badge, just below the collarbone.

She averted her eyes.

"How do you attach it?"

"Just put it next to your skin."

Jayne pressed the badge against her own collarbone. She felt a sharp stab of pain, and a click, as if something had just tapped against the bone. She gasped in fear and revulsion. Barnet caught her wrist before she could try to tear the button out of her flesh. He reached over and snapped the other one in place on the opposite side of her chest. She shivered again as his warm fingers brushed over her skin, but not from distaste.

Before she could protest, Barnet turned his head in alarm.

"Sh!" he said. He pulled her jacket over her chest and simultaneously buried his face in her hair.

"Be quiet," he hissed in her ear. "Just follow my lead."

She struggled to get out of his grasp and ended up with her face against the wall. He let go and scrambled to his feet, deliberately clumsy, so his legs bumped against her and kept her half-hidden. She peeked over her shoulder. Beyond the folds of Barnet's skirt, she saw the disturbing greenish sheen of mantid legs.

She gulped down her panic. She'd be seen! He'd recognize her! Then she realized that it might not be the same creature. There could be more of them. She felt sick.

The mantid clicked and chattered, as Barnet bowed obsequiously and repeatedly. Jayne curled tighter against the wall, in shock, as tiny metallic voices sounded in her ears, as well. She could hear the mantid chattering on, and at the same time, a chirping of something she assumed was Japanese. In the other ear—thank God, it was French again. Almost impossible to understand, with three separate voices buzzing in her head, but at least it was a thread of sanity to clutch. She breathed deeply and tried to focus on the words.

"What in-this-place do, nasty monkey-spawn? To hive-room go, Noriyama exchange-talk, go!"

It wasn't good French. It wasn't French at all, but it was marginally comprehensible, if she listened with full attention.

"Of course, Excellency, of course, immediately," the voice murmured in her ear, and she realized it was Barnet speaking—slightly less confusing this time, since she heard only his Japanese and the button-voice translating.

Barnet reached down and tugged her to her feet, towing her behind him through the tunnels and back into the hive-shaped room.

Noriyama and a group of his retainers stood at the far end of the room. Jayne recognized them by the colors of their robes. She kept her head down, terrified that the German would be among them, and might recognize her. But he wasn't there.

Noriyama barked something at Barnet, who bowed and answered in conciliatory tones, eliciting a chuckle from his boss. Jayne remembered to bow, too, just in time.

Barnet pushed her toward the wall, whispering "Kneel!"—once in Japanese, and once in French, in her ear. It was easier to understand him if she didn't look at his lips, moving in foreign syllables.

She sank down into the posture Lady Ko had adopted, sitting on her heels. It wasn't as easy as it looked.

Noriyama continued haranguing Barnet. The Japanese boss had a distinctive style of talking, Jayne thought— lots of growling with elongated vowels at the end of his sentences, and staccato consonants. The language structure might be different, but the general impression was a lot like Boo Boo Hoff. She wondered if there was some kind of universal human style for the Boss Men.

Then the meaning of his words started to sink in. He was scolding Barnet for bringing "him"—Jayne—to the council chamber.

"About time you showed up!" Noriyama blustered. "Now I see why you were dawdling. All right, he's pretty—*too* pretty, if you ask me! Fine—take him to your room and dress him in silk! But control yourself on the

job! Act like a man! It is a disgrace to your employer—
me, Noriyama!—that you are found by His Excellency in
a back room, kissing and snuggling like an infatuated
young girl!"

Jayne's ears burned. She wanted to jump up and
smash Noriyama with the butt end of his own ornamental sword hilt. But Barnet just continued to bow and utter conciliating platitudes.

"*Sara mo ki kara ochiru*," said Barnet's lips, and "Even
monkeys fall out of trees," said the voice in Jayne's ear.

What? Hearing the words wasn't quite enough, Jayne
thought, if you didn't know what they meant.

But now Noriyama's voice had become obsequious.

"Yes, Your Excellency, you see even my best men
sometimes can make mistakes."

He must be speaking to the mantid. Jayne heard a volley of clicks in return.

"Men of no interest, spawn boss," the voice in her ear
said. "Talk about mistakes."

"So—Excellency—it would seem that—in a manner of
speaking—well, possibly it would appear that one of His
Excellency's own, the honored *kamakiri-kami*—"

The voice translated for Jayne: "honored mantis-spirits."

"One of the *kamakiri* has made a mistake."

"Impossible! Impossible!" the mantid fizzed. "What
mistake?"

"Tell His Excellency, Tengu," Noriyama said.

"There was a fire in the cargo hold, aboard your
plane," Barnet said. "I have examined the plane, and it
appears the cargo is lost, and the plane damaged."

The mantid's mandibles rattled so fast that Jayne's
talk-button couldn't keep up. Consternation and outrage
were his themes.

"Sun Substance lost?" he said, when the translator
caught up with him. "No final shipment of Sun Sub-

stance, no project completion! No necessary density! Cannot do!"

Noriyama growled again.

"My noble master wishes me to remind you that our agreement was very clear," Barnet said.

"Obtain more Sun Substance! Monkey-spawn humans do it now!" said the mantid.

"I'm afraid that will be impossible, without a demonstration of good faith by the *kamakiri-kami*," Barnet said. "The noble Noriyama-sama has obtained for you everything we agreed—gold to purchase the Substance, human workers, the beneficent protection of the Emperor and the Gold Mountain Mining Corporation.

"In return, you promised to create the Divine Sun project for us. So far we have seen nothing—nothing but a big hole in the ground."

"Deny us would you?" the mantid sputtered. "Monkey-spawn would dare deny, would distrust—"

"Of course we trust completely in the abilities of Your Excellency and the *kamakiri*," Barnet said smoothly, bowing again. "But forgive us, our feeble eyes must see some glimmer of the promised light before we can provide more of the Emperor's gold."

"Without the Substance, cannot complete project! Impossible!" the mantid said. "Monkey-spawn make no demands. Monkey spawn are . . . kkk . . . ." The mantid's opinion of monkey-spawn apparently could not be translated.

"Of course, Your Excellency, you are always right. We make no demands. But if you could show us the possibilities—just a small demonstration of your power would banish all obstacles," Barnet said.

The mantid cocked its metallic head. Light gathered and flared sullenly in the multifaceted eye sockets. The creature emitted a staccato series of shrill whistles.

"Oh, Lord, not this again," Barnet said. He spoke in English, and there was no translation, so Jayne thought he must be speaking only to himself, and perhaps to her.

Jayne's legs ached fiendishly after only a few minutes in this position, but she was afraid to fidget and call attention to herself. She felt suddenly afraid, and unnaturally alert. She heard scrabbling sounds, and smelled a strange, acrid odor.

Her first thought was *Gas!* and her heart began to thump in panic. Gas in an underground cavern—they'd all die—

Barnet reached down and squeezed her shoulder so hard it hurt.

"Get a grip," he muttered. "It's nothing. Just *them*. Their way of doing business."

Barnet stood firm in a warlike pose, feet planted wide, hand on his sword hilt. Beyond him, more mantids swarmed out of the side burrow and encircled Noriyama and his retinue. Their mandibles kept up a constant clicking, and their forelimbs waved in the air, brushing against the humans and each other. The acid smell grew stronger in the enclosed space as the mantids performed their weird dance.

The boss stood up to the onslaught for a few minutes, fists clenched and eyes popping with rage. Finally, he couldn't take any more, and let out a roar of disgust and fury. He shook his fists helplessly. The mantids behaved as if he were a dog barking. They kept on probing and chittering until they had finished the process. Then they drew away into a circle of their own to confer. The humans also circled their leader, grooming his ruffled feathers.

As swiftly as they had come, the mantids departed, scurrying into the burrows with their odd, jerky movements. There was silence. Then the sound of human footsteps, slowly approaching Barnet's position.

"A decision has been reached," said a human voice. Jayne recognized that voice. It spoke bad French, French with a German accent. It was the same voice that had once threatened to kill her, in the ruins of a church in Picardy. She wanted to look, but she didn't dare.

"Tell your master that His Excellency will provide the demonstration he seeks. The Divine Sun will visit this island and demonstrate the power of the *kamakiri*. And you will place no more obstacles in our path, or the Divine Sun will touch your toy kingdom with the fire of his hand, till even the ashes are burned."

Barnet bowed. "I understand, and will convey the message."

When Jayne heard departing footsteps, she quickly stole a look. It was hard to be sure from behind, but the burly form, the wooden, military way of walking, and the close-cropped head all looked familiar. It was the German—again. He disappeared into the burrows, after the mantids.

Noriyama called Barnet to him in peremptory tones. Jayne heard loud discussion, much barking of orders, but tuned out the translation. The German was real. This time she'd seen him by daylight, heard him speak, seen him recognized by another sane human being. He was not some figment of her imagination. The world was stranger than she'd ever imagined.

She saw the marching feet of the Japanese go by, presumably headed for the elevator, but Barnet stopped in front of her.

"Oh, you and your friend have completely screwed up this operation," he muttered. "Get up! We're in a hurry now."

He dragged her back into the burrows, scrambling quickly through the maze until they broke through into a natural rock tunnel, slanting downward. The burrows were lit by the mantids' white light strips, but the old darkness waited for them inside the tunnel.

She caught at the walls, dug in her feet, and twisted her hand out of his grasp.

"No!" she said. "No more caves! No more running after you! I want to know where I'm going."

He frowned at her quizzically.

"You said you wanted to see Cameron," he said carefully, as if speaking to a slow student. "I thought you'd want to go there. And now—thanks to your interference—we don't have much time."

"There! That's just the kind of thing I mean," she said, exasperated. "You make reference. You don't explain. *Why* don't we have much time? What's going to happen?"

"I'm not sure," Barnet said. "But it's not going to be good. You heard them in there."

"I heard a lot of things I didn't understand! The Divine Sun? What are they talking about?"

Barnet held up his hand. "Just one minute," he said. "From here on, we're in *tanuki* territory. I can't tell you where we're going. It took me months to learn these tunnels. This is the *tanuki*'s road, and in here, we have to be clever like the *tanuki*."

He pulled off his rich robe and turned it inside out. The other side showed rough and dark, blending into the shadows.

"Your clothes will have to do," he said. "They're good and dirty now, anyway. That will help. Here—hold still."

He opened one of the pouches slung at his belt, dampened his fingers with moisture from the cave wall, and dipped them into the pouch. They came out smeared with black powder. He reached over and smudged the powder across her face.

She blinked and spat. It tasted like soot.

"Stop it! What are you doing?"

"Darkening your face so it won't show up like a rice ball in ashes."

He smoothed the mixture over her nose and forehead and took pains to rub it into her ears and neck. The touch of his fingers disturbed her.

"I can do it myself," she said. But he wouldn't let her pull away until he was finished.

He reached into his belt pouch, pulled out a curved object, and tied it to his head by the laces strung on each side.

He raised his head, and the mask of the *tengu* grinned at her.

"There now, the *tengu* is back," he said. "Come along, my *chigo*."

Now she understood what she'd seen before. The *tengu* was just a mask he wore, to disguise himself when he wanted to go where he shouldn't be seen. But he'd used another strange word.

"What's a *tanuki* road?" she said.

His answer came back muffled by the mask.

"Follow me and you'll see."

The roof of the tunnel came down lower and lower, until Jayne and the tall *tengu* first had to stoop, and then get down on hands and knees and crawl. The walls were no longer pure, solid rock. In places, they were made of packed earth that crumbled under Jayne's fingers and gave off a damp, musty smell. She couldn't see ahead. She had to reach out and touch the skirts of her guide's robe to reassure herself that he was still moving ahead of her.

I hate this, Jayne thought.

"Are you sure you know where we're going?" she called out.

"Completely sure," the muffled voice came back.

Moments later, she bumped into the *tengu* when he stopped moving. She saw the flash of a match, and the goblin face gleamed out, illuminated by a candle flame. She could see that they'd come to a place where two tunnels crossed, leaving a small open area big enough for the two of them to sit upright.

"Give me some of that rice cake," Barnet said.

She reached into her jacket and pulled out a couple of the leftover treats. Their rubbery texture made them durable. They were a little gritty, but otherwise intact. Barnet laid them out in the center of the open space, and then shuffled backward into the tunnel. He stuck the candle stub into a crack between stones and waited.

Jayne heard a tiny scratching sound. Barnet tapped her arm with a finger. She opened her eyes wide and stared into the darkness.

The first thing she saw was the gleam of eyes far back in the approaching tunnel. Then she heard a snuffle, followed by a chirping sound. A furry dark head and black and white body moved cautiously forward into the light. The raccoon-size creature sat up on its hind legs and sniffed the air, then reached out with clever clawed paws and seized one of the treats. It gobbled down the rice cake, popped a second into its cheek, and then scurried away down the tunnel.

Barnet pinched the candle wick between finger and thumb, and the darkness flooded back, feeling even more oppressive to Jayne after the brief respite. Jayne heard Barnet shuffling forward again, and followed him with a resigned sigh.

"Sado Island is famous for being the home of *tanuki*," Barnet said. "Lady Ko knows hundreds of stories about them. I thought they were purely imaginary, till supplies started to vanish from these tunnels. I hid and watched until I caught the thief in the act. But I didn't do anything to stop him. Lady Ko is right—all the stories say that getting on the bad side of a *tanuki* is very bad luck.

"Instead, I watched to see where he'd come from. Animals don't live down here in the dark, obviously. So that meant the *tanuki* must be digging their way, or finding their way, from the outside. According to Lady Ko's stories, people sometimes found a *tanuki* path and followed it—of course, they found grand feasting halls where they attended banquets that went on for years. That's never happened to me, but I have found some very useful tunnels. A little cramped, I grant you, but handy when you want to get around unseen. I've made sure to keep Mr. Tanuki in a good humor, too. I show my gratitude for the use of his right-of-way!"

Jayne's knees were sore and scraped from crawling when Barnet stopped and turned to the left. She heard him scratching at the wall, and a sound of rock scraping against rock. A faint light trickled into the tunnel.

Barnet turned to her and put a warning finger to his lips.

"You speak to him," he whispered. "Quietly, now. I don't see guards, but there are sure to be beetles nearby."

Jayne pressed close to the opening and peered in, expecting to see Cameron. Her eyes adjusted to the dim light. She was looking into a rock cell. She could see from this peephole in the back wall all the way to the bars on the other side, but the cell was empty.

"He's not there," she whispered.

Barnet pushed her out of the way.

"That's impossible," he muttered. "But—dammit! You're right. They've moved him. That guard I coshed— it must have alarmed them. The guard I coshed to save *your* neck."

He turned and glared at Jayne. "You've certainly messed this up in every conceivable way," he said.

"Me?" she whispered indignantly. "What about the way in which *you* meddled unconscionably with *my* plans? Cameron and I could be leaving this godforsaken island at this very moment if you hadn't interfered."

"Or you could be where he is at this very moment," Barnet said.

"Which is where, exactly?" Jayne said.

"There's only one other place where they keep prisoners," Barnet said. "If he isn't there . . . oh, my God." It sounded as if he'd just thought of something truly horrifying. This time Jayne didn't ask. She just followed Barnet as he plunged back into the *tanuki* tunnels.

After another long, stifling scramble through the darkness, they emerged into what Jayne recognized as a mantid burrow. The *tanuki* hole was an opening barely big enough to squeeze through, situated behind a clutter of crates that smelled pretty much the same as the crates behind any grocery in Philadelphia. Evidently they had once held food, but now there was nothing left but a few wilted cabbage leaves. The distaste Jayne had originally felt for the mantids' wormholes turned to relief. At least she could stand up. She brushed dirt off her bruised knees and out of her hair.

Then she was struck again by the deathly smell.

Barnet held up his hand for silence before she could say anything. Ever since they'd found the empty cell, he had been silent and driven. He'd stopped taunting and chastising her, and had moved with the speed of a desperate man, a speed she could hardly keep up with. Now he seemed frozen, afraid to step beyond the entrance to the burrow.

"What you're about to see . . ." he muttered. "You have to remember—they're not like us. This means nothing to them. You will control yourself, or you will remain here, and above all, be silent! I can't deal with hysterics. I'll rescue Cameron if I can, but I'll abandon you both rather than jeopardize my mission further. Do you understand?"

She stared at him. "No" was the obvious answer. He wasn't making any sense. He sounded on the brink of hysterics himself.

"I've already seen where they kept the sick miners," she said. "It can't be worse than that. I can handle it."

He gave her a dark and disbelieving look.

"It gets worse," he said. "A lot more have died than just those few you saw down here. The Sun Substance makes humans sick. It doesn't seem to affect the mantids in the same way. They demand more and more of it for their special project, and Noriyama gives it to them, and hides the cost of the workers. He's fudging the books for the gold mine—stealing gold to pay for more shipments to the beetles, and faking accidents to account for the lost workers."

Jayne found herself scratching at the skin around the translation button. She felt queasy, even though she knew it was only a psychological reaction.

"It's not contagious," Barnet assured her. "I've been here long enough to catch it, if it were. Noriyama's hiding the deaths to avoid suspicion about his project, that's all."

"But what is the project?" Jayne said. "What could possibly justify all this?"

Barnet's white goblin mask turned toward her with its meaningless grin.

"Power," he said. It was a chilly-sounding word. "Japan is a small, cold country, like a little boat afloat on a big ocean. Eating raw fish, building a little fire of twigs to boil a pot of rice. The *kamakiri* promised Noriyama a power like the sun itself. A rising sun to rule the seas. You don't think that's enough to justify the deaths of a few dozen miners?"

"Why don't you *tell* someone?" Jayne said.

"Whom should I tell—the prefect of Niigata? The American consul?" The *tengu*'s voice dripped with sarcasm. "The League of Nations? When you see . . . what's in this room, you'll understand why no one would believe it."

He led her through the entrance into another hive-shaped chamber. They crept along the edge of the wall, in the shadows, watching for any sign of mantid guards.

Jayne fought down a surge of claustrophobia. She felt trapped in this dark underworld of lies and confusion. Who could be trusted? She almost wished she'd stuck with Boo Boo Hoff—an ordinary man whose evil was simple and easy to understand.

"You said Cameron would be here."

The *tengu* grasped her arm.

"He is." He pointed upward with his other hand.

Jayne looked up into the shadowed dome, and gasped. Barnet's grip tightened on her arm. Only that reminder kept her from crying out.

A bamboo cage hung from the roof, suspended by a strong chain. It was the kind of cage in which a child might keep a mouse, or a cricket, till kinder parents made him let the creature go. This cage was big enough to hold a man.

Crouched in a corner, clinging to the bars in a vain attempt to find a position of some poor comfort, Grant Cameron was huddled. His head hung low. She recognized him only by his short hair, showing fair at the roots.

"Cameron!" she said, as loudly as she dared. She reached out, but even the lowest bars of the cage were beyond her reach. Cameron seemed unconscious.

She cast a panicked glance toward Barnet.

"What are they doing with him? How do we get him out?"

But Barnet had no reassurance to give. Instead, his grip on her arm tightened even more, and he scrambled for the darkest corner of the cavern, dragging her after him.

"Beetles!" he hissed. She wondered how he could tell, and then she felt the telltale clicking against her collarbone. The talk-button was picking up chatter.

Jayne had been relieved not to see any more sick humans underground. She hadn't thought anything could be worse. A group of mantids gamboled in, and she knew she'd been wrong. Like the ones she'd seen before, they dragged a corpse with them. She'd been shocked by their callous disposal of the human body they'd dragged out of the other cavern. Now she was seeing what happened next.

They dropped their burden on the ground under Cameron's cage. The mantids jostled it to and fro, making that chattering sound of horrid glee. Two of them seized an arm, tugging it back and forth between them, until the arm tore apart at the elbow. The mantid who had secured the forearm lifted the limb and gnawed it with busy mandibles, as a human would eat a chicken wing, while others bent over the rest of the corpse, and a slow river of blood streamed silently across the floor, to be pursued and lapped up.

"Still warm! Delicious!" said the demon whisper in Jayne's ear. She wanted to tear the button from her flesh and hurl the voices away from her. The only sound she heard beyond the mantids' feasting was Cameron sobbing.

"Kkk . . . hey, you!" One of the mantids hurled a leg bone at Cameron's cage. The missile cracked against the bars, and Cameron scrambled to his knees, clinging to the bamboo. "Wakkke upp! Here—a snack for you, monkkkey-spawn!"

All the creatures joined in flinging gobbets of flesh in Cameron's direction, splattering him with blood.

"Kkk—kk!" The button in Jayne's ear crackled with sounds of delight.

Cameron screamed curses back at them in a voice so hoarse and tortured that it hardly sounded human.

Barnet held Jayne down to keep her from leaping upon them in futile rage.

"Not hungry yet? Will be soon!" said the voices. "Soon pet monkey will takkke food. Nice monkey. Pettt monkkkey! Kkkk—tt!"

The mantids scrambled from the room, satiated, leaving behind a small heap of raw bones gnawed clean, and a skull casually cracked and drained of its contents. The scent of blood was heavy in the air, along with the acrid chemical traces of mantid emotion.

Jayne scrambled to her feet, her fingers clenching convulsively as she searched for the gun that wasn't there.

"I'll kill them," she snarled. "I'm going to crush them like—like bugs!"

She turned on Barnet and tried to tug the sword from his belt.

"You have weapons! If you won't kill them, I'll do it!" she said.

Barnet gripped her wrists as she struggled.

"I know what you're feeling," he panted. "But—do you want to kill a few now, at the cost of Cameron's life? Or do you want to wait just a little longer—and kill all of them?"

Jayne shuddered and choked back her nausea. It was a moment before she could speak.

"All right," she said. "We'll get C-Cameron. But after that—they have to die!" She glared at Barnet. "You knew they were doing this," she accused him. "You knew they were *eating* us. And you haven't done anything to stop it."

"What's happening here is much bigger than a few mine workers," Barnet said. He didn't even sound angry. She hadn't reached him. Something else occupied his attention—something that frightened him far more than what they'd just seen. That realization chilled Jayne's anger to icy terror. All she wanted was to get out of here, to see the sun again. But she couldn't go without Cameron. She tried to focus on that.

"H-How do we get him down?" she said. She called again: "Cameron!"

She could hardly see him. He was curled tightly into the corner of his cage, arms over his head.

"Cameron!"

This time there was a response.

"Damn you!" he sobbed. "Go away."

"Cameron! It's me, Jayne Taylor."

There was a scuffling in the cage as Cameron turned about in its tight confines.

"What—where?" he croaked. A wild-eyed face looked down at her, pressed between two bamboo bars.

Jayne realized that she was coated with soot and probably almost invisible in the dim light.

"I'm in disguise," she said in a small voice. She sounded ridiculous even to herself.

"I'm dreaming again," Cameron said. His voice broke.

"No! No, you're not," Jayne said hastily. "We really have come to rescue you. But there are creatures everywhere. Can you get out of there?"

Cameron laughed a little wildly.

"Whaddaya think—that I haven't tried?" he said. "The bars are hard as iron. They're lashed with cord, but it's too tough for my teeth."

"Get back in the corner," Barnet said.

Cameron hitched himself painfully up into a crouch again.

Barnet drew the stout-bladed knife that matched his sword. He flicked it upward. It *chunk*ed into the underside of a bamboo bar and quivered there. Cameron reached down and yanked it out, then sawed frantically at the cords that bound the nearest corner of his prison.

But before he could complete his escape, he froze, looking toward the place where the mantid burrows opened into the cavern. Then he motioned frantically to Barnet and Jayne, with one hand behind his back.

"Someone's coming!" Barnet hissed.

Jayne hit the dirt before he could push her again. They scrambled for their hiding place under the curve of the wall just as solitary human footsteps sounded on the stone floor.

"Good morning, my friend," said the flat voice of the German. He was speaking English this time. "How are you feeling? Have you been considering the benefits of the friendship of the *kamakiri*?"

"Never," Cameron coughed.

The German bent and picked up the broken skull. He gazed into its eye sockets.

"Never is a long time," he said. "Isn't it, Yorick-san?"

He contemplated a smear of blood left on his finger and then deliberately licked it off. Jayne heard Cameron retching.

"Our friends the *kamakiri* are a little boisterous at times," the German said. "But they bear you no ill will."

"They eat human flesh," Cameron choked in strangled tones. "And you're a bug like them."

"Permitting you to observe this was done to make a point, not to torment you," the German said. "You need to realize that human beings are animals who inhabit this little planet—no more, no less. It is perfectly appropriate for intelligent species to consume the flesh of dead animals. You are getting—how do you Americans put it?—

your knickers in a knot over nothing. The sooner you see this, the sooner you will have a clear understanding of your situation."

"Go to hell," Cameron said. "You're not human. They broke you. But you'll never break me."

"I believe we are closer than you think, right now," the German said. "Consider the possibility that I have never broken. That I merely saw the truth. The truth breaks fools and weaklings. The strong it makes stronger."

He tossed the skull casually to the ground.

"I appeal to you as a fellow soldier, a patriot," he said. "Thousands, millions of bones like that one now lie in the fields of Europe. You helped to put them there. Can you really find so much meaning in a single skull, here in this place? After all, that one was merely put to use after he died of natural causes. No one slit his guts with a bayonet.

"I've used the bayonet myself, and so have you, I'm sure. It was in a good cause—defense of our countries. What once was my country lies helpless now. Would you not sacrifice a few more of your fellow men to keep your country from a similar fate?"

"We fought for freedom," Cameron croaked. "You can't twist that."

"Ah, yes—freedom," the German said. "What human beings call freedom is so often another form of slavery—to ignorance, to petty tribal loyalties. Just another word to justify the shedding of blood. True freedom is found in power. America is free because it is powerful. You want America to stay free. By all means. Then you must make sure that America stands at the right hand of the new power that has come to earth. Those who will not ally with that power will be merely useful fodder—like this poor fellow."

He toed the skull with his boot.

"Wouldn't it be worth something to you to keep your America preeminent in power?"

Cameron said nothing. Jayne saw his fists clenched on the filthy fabric of his shirtfront, and knew he'd hidden the knife there. But the German seemed to find his silence satisfactory.

"I think our *kamakiri* masters may have misjudged you, Mr. Cameron," the German said. "Like me, you are not a man to be convinced by force. Perhaps you require a demonstration of the advantages. They have used the stick—it is time to show the carrot. Yes. I will see what I can do. Till my return—think good thoughts!"

As soon as the German disappeared into the shadows, Jayne flung off the concealing rags to stand under the cage. It was as far out of reach as ever. Cameron slashed furiously at the lashings.

"Get me out of here," he raved. "Get me *out!*"

"No," Barnet said. "You have to wait—he'll be back any minute. It's too late."

For once Jayne was entirely in agreement with Cameron.

"He's right," she said. "Damn your mission. Get us out of here."

"Don't you see—it's no use getting you out of the cage if I can't get you off the mountain. It's too dangerous. You must wait until I have a plan."

It was already too late. The German returned, and at his side stalked the horned mantid Barnet had called the *kamakiri* shogun.

While Jayne still stood in shock, Barnet gripped her by the hair, and bent her wrist behind her, immobilizing her. She gasped, unable to fight free or think of anything but the pain and the betrayal.

"Look what I found," Barnet said easily, as if he turned on his own kind every day. "The gardener's boy—'he' is a girl—spying on us!"

CHAPTER TEN
CONVERSATIONS WITH THE GERMAN

The German roared with laughter.

"So, it seems your little acolyte was not what you thought! Noriyama will find this funny—at least, you'd better hope he does."

Jayne blinked back tears of pain and rage. The German walked around her, taking a good look.

"Not Japanese, after all," he said. "You speak French? English?"

Jayne didn't know which answer would be safest, so she said nothing. Barnet said nothing, either. She wondered why not. If he was going to betray them, why not tell them everything?

"Perhaps she came here with that one," the German said, eyeing Cameron speculatively. "That would explain why she has found her way to this exact spot. Unless she is working with someone else, who brought her here for another reason. What do you think, Mr. Tengu?"

Jayne thought fast. The German seemed to be hinting that it was Barnet who was working with her. She could pretend that was true, and maybe get him in trouble— which would serve him right.

Before she could speak, Barnet swiveled toward Cameron, forcing her, too, in that direction.

"Why don't we ask *him*?" he said.

The mantid shogun gave an order, and the cage was slowly lowered to the ground. One of the worker beetles casually slashed the tough lashings and swung the side of the cage open. Cameron couldn't get off his knees, though. Not until one of the mantids reached in and dragged him up.

The shogun chirked at Cameron, inches from his face.

"He says, 'Do you know this woman?'" the German explained. "And do not lie."

Cameron cast a brief, desperate look at Jayne. It hurt her to see him like this. He'd suffered, she knew. And that look said that he'd suffer yet more before he'd tell them the truth. Even if there was no point.

"I don't know what you're talking about," he said hoarsely. "I never saw her before in my life."

The shogun drew the point of one talon down Cameron's face. Cameron jerked away with a stifled gasp of pain. A line of bright blood trickled down Cameron's face. The shogun sucked the talon clean, and then chattered to the German.

"He thinks you are lying," the German said. "They can taste the desperation in your blood. It makes you particularly tasty. Like fresh pepper."

He made a twisting motion with his hands. Jayne would have liked to do that to his neck.

"Stop," she heard herself say. "He's only trying to protect me. Stupidly—because I don't need his protection."

The mantid head, with its impenetrable compound eyes, swiveled in her direction.

"So you do know him?" the German said.

"Yes. We both work for the U.S. government." If the mantids tasted her blood, they wouldn't find anything wrong with that statement.

"So, perhaps you are fond of him?" the German said, suggestively.

"What? Of *him*?" Jayne said. She didn't have to feign her indignation. "Certainly not!" She did her best to put on Kensie's Main Line drawl. "Why he's . . . he's not even a gentleman."

She braced herself for the touch of the shogun's claws, but instead the mantid turned to the German again and chattered to him. The German smiled mirthlessly.

"He asks if it is not the case among humans that females defer to the male."

"You can tell him it is certainly not true in the United States of America. Women are equal to men."

Heaven help me, now I am lying, Jayne thought. *But it's the principle of the thing.*

"Leave him out of this," she said. "I'm just as fully empowered to talk to you as he is. I'm intrigued by what Mr.—uh, Mr.— "

"Just call me the Mouth," the German said. "The *kamakiri-kami* are not concerned with human names."

"I'm intrigued by what your Mouth has been saying," Jayne said. "If there could be an advantage for my country in working with you, I want to discuss that."

The mantid pinched Jayne's chin between two claws and turned her head this way and that. She watched the serrated scaly fringes along its forearms lift and separate like feathers. They seemed to be sensing organs of some kind. Jayne blinked hard.

Those are not tears, she told herself sternly. *It's just that my eyes are watering.*

The German watched her with that flat, colorless gaze. "You feel fear," he said. "This is natural."

"I'm not afraid," Jayne said. She hoped that her voice would remain steady. "It's just very . . . *strange.*"

"You get used to it," the German said. "Do you know, he can clip your head from your body with those claws. They are much stronger than we are."

"Thank you," Jayne said dryly. "That makes me feel a lot better."

Her knees felt shaky, but she told herself he couldn't see that. As long as her voice didn't shake, he wouldn't know.

The mantid chattered its jaws, presumably speaking. She watched the fingerlike protrusions within its jaws writhe and rub together.

"The shogun suggests we dispose of you," the German said. "In the past, females have not been deemed useful."

He faced the mantid and bowed.

"Allow me to suggest to Your Excellency, this female is of a different type and may warrant further consideration. I undertake to investigate her usefulness, if he allows. I suggest the human male be returned to a regular cell where he can be cleaned up. We can deal with him later."

The shogun chattered again, briefly, and its subordinates seized Cameron.

I failed, Jayne thought. *I let him down again.*

Barnet had turned on her, and Cameron must be thinking she'd done the same thing to him.

He struggled with berserk frenzy. Jayne was terrified. She was the only one who knew that what he really wanted was to get hold of the knife. She was relieved when they pinioned his hands behind his back. At least he wouldn't be able to get himself killed immediately.

She tried not to listen to his ragged protests. He wouldn't be in the cage anymore. That had to be better, she thought desperately.

"Bring her," the German said. Then she knew how Cameron had felt. Two of the soldier mantids clutched her arms in a harsh grip that felt like steel rings closing over her flesh. They dragged her along with painful negligence, not even noticing if her feet touched the ground.

When they stopped, she was in the huge bright cavern with the white machines again. It was like something out of a dream, or a nightmare, but it was real.

"I'll take her now," the German said.

The mantids locked cuffs around her wrists and linked them to a leash that they handed over to the German.

Jayne felt briefly encouraged when they left her alone with him. But even if she could have broken away, there was nowhere to run in the bare, super-clean room.

He led her across the floor and into an office on the side. She'd just spent hours in the dark, in the dirt, getting used to crawling on hands and knees through trickling damp and foul, stifling air. Now she was equally jolted by the incongruity of a room that was cleaner and more modern than anything she'd seen in Philadelphia.

But her stomach knotted in fear when she saw that the flat surface she'd taken for a desk was a table, with a padded surface and a bar across one end. The German clipped the leash to the bar.

"Oh, please, lie down," the German said, smirking. When she pulled back, he added, "That was not a request."

"You don't have to tie me up," she said. Her voice quavered. She hated that, but couldn't help it. Confinement was the one thing she truly feared. "Honestly, I'm not going anywhere."

"Shut up and do what you're told," the German said. He sounded bored and impatient. "You cannot understand this, so I'm not going to explain it to you. The restraints are necessary, as the machine requires you to remain very still."

"Machine? What machine?" Now she sounded scared, even to herself.

The German yanked on the leash and the cuffs at her wrists parted. A force like a strong magnet pulled them toward the metal bar, and they clicked into place before she could resist. He swung her feet into place, and her ankles were pinioned as well. She could feel her heartbeat accelerating like a freight train going downhill.

The German made a little "tch" of annoyance. He sounded just like the mantids. She wondered how long he'd been with them, and if he actually understood any of their language of clicks and raspings.

"So much hair," he complained. "I shall let them deal with this."

He went to the door and whistled. Soldier mantids reappeared. Jayne struggled to crane her neck enough to see what they were doing as they approached, but she couldn't see them.

She shuddered as she felt their claws moving through her hair. She shut her eyes and frantically retreated in her memory to the time when she'd gone to the salon and told them to bob her long hair. That had been frightening too. She'd been terrified of how she'd look, what her mother would say—but everything had been all right in the end. It was just a haircut, she told herself over and over again. She pictured gum-chewing, giggling female assistants instead of unearthly insects with talons.

It really did feel like a haircut. The cool brush of a blade shearing away the hair, the whisper of the cut locks falling. . . . In a blessedly short time, she heard the German ordering the mantids out again, and heard their mailed feet clicking away over the tiled floor.

Her head felt bare and tender. He placed something cold against the skin, and the chilly cap seemed to shrink itself tight to her skull. It felt as if there was nothing between the device and her flesh.

Oh, no—surely they hadn't—

"Did they shave my head?" she said.

"Yes. The hair interferes with the contacts needed by the machine."

"Oh! That is just the limit!" she said. She wasn't afraid now. She was furious. She pictured herself bald, like Lady Ko. How Cameron would have laughed at her—back in Philadelphia, before the beetles put him in a cage.

She could feel a kind of vibration that went through her skull, down her spine, and tingled in her fingers and toes. She couldn't move, but she glared at the German as he stood at the end of the table, watching something beyond her head.

"Normally we use this to make templates for delicate machine work," he said. "Fortunately, we can also use it to create a blank storage device attuned to your neural patterns. You will wear it. Over time, it will store the impressions needed to create a template of you. It's a kind of pantograph."

"Is this really necessary?" Jayne said indignantly.

"Yes. In this way, even if you fail to prove useful as an individual, your image can still be of use to the Herrenkaefer.

"We've taken few female templates in the past, because the female sphere of action has been limited. The Herrenkaefer do not really understand the human division of the sexes. Among their kind, distinctions are those of hierarchy, not of gender. When choosing humans to copy, they prefer specimens who have a better position in human hierarchy."

He made some adjustment to the device.

"I explained to the shogun that in America, females may soon achieve a greater ascendancy. If we wish to acquire American resources, you—or at least your image—could be a useful asset."

The buzzing in Jayne's skull made her head feel heavy and slow, like a gramophone record running down. She imagined the machine marking all the grooves in her brain the way a needle followed the grooves in a recording. Was that what they were doing to her? Trying to create some kind of waxen simulacrum they could replay over and over?

He'd shown no sign of recognizing her. Perhaps she'd killed only his image. At first that made her feel strangely relieved. No one had died, after all. But that wasn't true. She'd seen the blood, the broken flesh. She'd killed someone. She just didn't know anymore who it was. And that didn't make things better. It only left her wishing, in impotent frustration, that it *had* been him. She lay there hating his pale, bloodless flesh, his meaningless grin, his dead eyes. Most of all, she hated the fact that he had power over her now, because she'd been stupid.

She tried to fight off the weakness that spread over her, and the fear that came with it. It was just exhaustion, she told herself. Anyone would be tired after the day she'd had. It would be so easy to slip into sleep or unconsciousness, but she couldn't let that happen. She tried to think of a way to keep him talking.

"H-How long have you been with . . . them?" she asked. It seemed like a feeble question, but to her surprise, he responded.

"Since the early days of the war," he said remotely, eyes still fixed on controls she could not see.

"I was the first human they encountered who was allowed to live. They'd recorded an image or two. When they first came here, they realized they would be hunted down and killed by ignorant humans, so they tried to remain in hiding. When they needed to walk among men, they tried to make images of those who stumbled upon them and had to be killed. But those templates were too incomplete to survive scrutiny. It was I who persuaded them to try keeping a specimen alive long enough to capture sufficient information. And by the time they'd captured my image, they realized a living servant could be even more useful."

"Didn't you ever try to escape?" Jayne said.

The German laughed again.

"Escape? To what?" he said. "I was escaping when they found me. Escaping from the trenches where my messmates had just frozen to death. Look around you. This is the order of the future. This is the birthplace of limitless power. This is the escape route from a world where 'power' means dirty lumps of coal, dug by starving children to warm ignorant pigs like Noriyama."

She could almost see his point. She could almost see the image of a solitary, shivering soldier, stumbling across some frozen, war-torn wasteland, only to encounter a reality more terrifying than the one he fled. How much of himself would he have to give away, in the struggle to survive? How much had he already lost, to human masters equally heedless of human life?

"I've been in France," she said carefully. Since it hadn't been him she saw there, admitting her presence couldn't be too dangerous. "I saw enough to see the truth of what you're saying. Enough to know that you're right, and I'd give anything to stop that from happening in my own homeland."

That might not be quite true enough to make her blood taste sincere, but maybe the German didn't have senses as acute as those of the mantids. Maybe even the German could get lonely, over all those years. Maybe he'd see the usefulness of another human presence, and let her live, as the mantids had allowed him to stay.

"We shall see," he said. The flat tone did not reflect any of the susceptibility she'd hoped for. "Don't think you can barter your way easily into their grand project. You *will* 'give anything,' as you put it. You will pay quite dearly enough to test your sincerity. By the time you know the whole truth, you will have cast aside the identity you cling to even now. That illusion will be burned away. It is one of the many gifts of the shogun's service. Believe me, I know."

Jayne felt a chill at her very core. She didn't need to taste his blood to know he meant it.

"Others have come with similar words, and failed to stand the test. No matter; we keep their images and use them."

He shrugged. Jayne revised her guess that he must be lonely. Perhaps he'd got beyond the need for human contact.

He moved away to sit at a console. She saw his hands moving as if at a typewriter. Behind her, she could hear a whirring noise, like a lathe or a drill, but softer and more subdued. Finally, he nodded, satisfied.

He rose and moved out of her field of vision. When he came back, he released her bonds. She felt the cap slide from her head, heavy and flexible, like metal mesh, but she couldn't see where it went. She sat up, rubbing her wrists. Her arms and legs ached from the tension.

The German bent toward her and pulled the collar of her jacket aside.

He "tch"ed again as he saw the translator buttons.

"Little thief," he said. "I see you're already acquainted with the Herrenkaefer devices. Really, we must do something about Noriyama and his *tengu*-Mouth once this project is complete. They are completely unreliable."

He pressed a locket-size object, still warm from the machine that had given birth to it, against her collarbone. She flinched from the sudden sharp prick as it punched through her skin, and the click that vibrated through her bones.

"The device is custom-fitted to you," he said. "It clips into a bone so it can receive vibrations of speech, much like the devices you already wear. Perhaps you have already learned not to expect a one-to-one correspondence in translation. If not, I caution you now. Their language is complex and the concepts cannot be exactly matched with our primitive terms."

He turned her over to the mantids, who marched her back to the dark and dirty underground and threw her into a cell next to Cameron's. He was curled up in the far corner, as he had been in the cage. She stretched her hands through the bars and called to him.

"Oh, Cameron! Are you all right?"

He turned his back on her.

"Cameron, look at me! Please."

"Why should I?" he said. "I'm not even a gentleman."

"Oh, for—" she said. "You knew better than to take that seriously, didn't you?"

Obviously he hadn't. Her eyes stung with hurt. Unfair! It was so unfair for him to misjudge her so harshly.

"Well, fine. If that's how little you think of me," she said.

"How little *I* think of *you*?" he said. "You're the one who said it. You're the highbrow Main Liner. I'm just a common thug."

"It's not fair," she said furiously. "I've never treated you that way. You're the one who assumes I'm high-hatting you. I don't act superior."

"That's just it," he said. "You don't act it. But you know you think you are. *I* know you're thinking it. You're so much better than I am that you'd rather associate with the bugs and their Boche lickspittle."

Just when she really wanted to explain herself, she couldn't.

"Listen," she said, "they put some kind of a recording device on me. I don't know exactly what it records, but whatever you say—"

He turned around enough to give her a dirty look, and then his jaw dropped.

"You—what happened to your hair?"

"They—um—they had to cut it, and . . ."

She gestured toward her head. She still hadn't been able to bring herself to touch it. With a helpless wave of the hand, she burst into tears.

She felt instantly humiliated, and buried her face in her hands, but it had a gratifying effect on Cameron. He dragged himself to her side of the cell, thrust one dirty hand through the bars, and patted her shoulders.

"They shaved your head! Aw, you poor kid."

She told herself it was a good thing to cry and get it all out, and then she'd feel better. It was a strategy. Really, she probably was doing it because she couldn't help it. But whatever the reason, she sobbed loudly until she felt calmer, and then blew her nose on the much-abused shirttail of the blue jacket.

"It's all right," she sniffed. "I'm just tired. And hungry."

"I got nothing," Cameron said. "Not sure I could eat, anyway. Not after . . ."

He swallowed hard.

"No," Jayne said. She was about to add that she'd never be able to look at a ham sandwich again, but the image of pink flesh was too much for her, and she shivered in silence.

Jayne checked to see if she could slide between the bars, but her head wouldn't go through, even though it was shaved slick. She stopped trying before she became irretrievably stuck.

And after that there was nothing left to do but sleep. By tacit mutual consent they crept up into adjoining corners of their cells, backs to the bars and to each other, but taking some comfort in the presence of another human being.

CHAPTER ELEVEN

LIFE IS LIKE GOING OUT TO SEA IN A SMALL BOAT THAT IS GOING TO SINK

Mantids woke them, whistling shrilly outside just before slamming the cell doors open and dragging them
out with clawed grips that stopped just short of actually
cutting the skin. Groggy and disoriented, Jayne felt as if
she had slept only an hour or two.

The mantids stood them on their feet next to a wooden
tub full of water, and chattered loudly. Jayne's hand flew
to the button on her collarbone. As the mantids spoke,
the bone beneath the button vibrated, a tickling, buzzing
sensation like striking her funnybone. It felt excruciating,
and made her long to tear the device out of her flesh. But
at the same time, she felt the buzz inside her skull, and a
tiny voice whispered a translation in her ear.

"Monkey-spawn wash, kkk yes yesss, gett kklean," it
said.

"I understand," Jayne whispered, when she could get
over the shock. She bent and splashed the water with her

hand, in case the mantids didn't have the equivalent of the translator button.

"Thirsty," she added, looking to them for some traces of comprehension. But they showed none. She scooped up water in her hand and put it to her mouth. They said nothing. The water tasted all right, so she drank it. Cameron followed suit.

"They want us to wash," she said.

Cameron started to rinse some of the dirt and filth from his face, but at that the mantids stirred again. They tugged impatiently on the rags of his shirt.

"I think they mean more like a bath—all over," Jayne said.

She could see the dull red rise to Cameron's cheeks.

"I may not be a gentleman, but I'm not going to strip in front of a lady," he said.

"It's all right, I'll turn my back," Jayne said hastily. "They can't understand anything about human manners. It's better just to do what they say."

"You first then," he said, apparently determined to maintain his concept of chivalry under whatever adverse circumstances.

Jayne wasn't sure that would have been her preference, but she slowly removed her clothes. Cameron kept his back turned. The mantids had a disconcerting way of remaining perfectly still when they had no specific orders. Their bulging compound eyes appeared to be fixed in her direction, but it was hard to tell if they were really staring at her or not.

As she dropped her clothes, the two mantids rasped forearms and made scritching sounds that sounded all too much like human whispers and giggles. Jayne wrapped her arms around to cover herself as best she could, her bare skin feeling very soft and vulnerable. She wondered if the insect creatures found human flesh as disconcerting and disagreeable as humans found the metallic mantid carapace.

Defiantly, she made the best of a bad situation and scrubbed herself thoroughly. Then she realized she had nothing to put on but the same filthy garments. Before she could reach for them, one of the mantids stretched out a claw and drew it lazily across her stomach, testing the flesh. With a startled cry, Jayne shied away—but not too quickly to see that Cameron had turned involuntarily at the sound. He whirled again, when he realized that she had not been harmed, clapping his hands over his eyes. But she was mortified. He'd seen her bald and naked! She could only hope that he hadn't seen much.

The mantids clicked and "tch"ed, bowing and waving their forearms in a way that Jayne suspected was their way of laughing. The translator told her nothing.

One of them tossed her a bundle of cloth. She had to sort it out and put it on without advice. The undergarments seemed complicated. She hoped that she had the layers in the right order when she finished, but she had to wrap it up in a hurry, because the mantids were already prodding Cameron impatiently while she was still fiddling with the sash.

The clothing seemed to be a less luxurious version of the garments Barnet wore—wide trousers under a kimono robe that crossed over and tied. While she sat with her back turned, listening to Cameron's splashing in the tub, she smoothed down the fabric and enjoyed the feeling of clean cloth against her skin—until it occurred to her to wonder where the clothes came from, and what had happened to their last owner. She hoped devoutly they'd come from the Japanese equivalent of a Salvation Army store, rather than from a dead body.

Jayne felt faint with hunger. She thought of signing for food, but then recalled what they'd been offered earlier, and decided to wait until she saw a human being.

When Cameron cleared his throat and said "Ready," she turned to see him dressed in identical fashion. She wanted to ask if he'd somehow been able to keep the knife hidden, but couldn't figure out how to do it without giving anything away.

"You should be happy," he said. "They put men's clothes on you."

He must be feeling better, she thought. He was strong enough to be obnoxious again.

"So you hope," she said. "What if these are women's clothes? You might be wearing a dress! You'd better hope I don't tell. You'd never live that down back in Philly."

The mantids marched them back in the direction of the elevator.

"Got any idea what's going on?" Cameron asked. He was trying to sound casual, but she knew he was bluffing.

"All I know is that they were talking about that demonstration the German spoke of," Jayne said. She hoped that saying that much wouldn't be held against her if the device was recording it.

"Noriyama and the head bug got into an argument about it when I was in the room. At least, that's what Barnet told me. Noriyama wouldn't guarantee to get them any more of what they call Sun Substance until they showed him what it could do."

"What is this stuff? Any idea?" Cameron said.

"No more than you," Jayne said. "They made it sound like some kind of fuel, or maybe some kind of high explosive. Could it be both?"

"Well, if you take gasoline," Cameron said thoughtfully, "it can burn as a fuel, but under the wrong circumstances, it will explode. It's just a question of how rapid the combustion is."

His eyes brightened. "Maybe you have something there," he said. "Maybe the Germans developed a synthetic fuel source at the end of the war, and this Boche is selling it to the Japs. That could explain a lot."

But not why there are six-foot mantises involved, Jayne thought. It was so much easier for the mind to revert to what was familiar, she reflected. Even if the familiar didn't even come close to explaining the observable circumstances.

The human-shaped tunnels of the cell area connected with mantid burrows, from which they emerged into the brilliant light of what Jayne thought of as the Clean Room. Cameron was all eyes. Jayne kicked his ankle and told him to keep his head down, after hearing one of the nearby mantids hiss, "Spying—kkk—little eyesss!"

"God damn," he muttered. "Oh, sorry! But those are the biggest damn magnets I've ever seen. Where in hell do they get the power to run something like that? And what's it all for?"

"Button it," Jayne said. If he'd guessed anything crucial, she didn't want her recorder to know.

In the Clean Room, they were met by another group of four soldier mantids who walked ceremonially at the corners of some object shrouded in metallic draperies and wrapped in a golden cord tied in ornamental knots and tasseled with jade carvings. Each of this color guard of mantids rested a hand on the object, as if they were carrying it, but as far as Jayne could see, it was being levitated. She couldn't see any supports or wires. It was like a conjuring trick, except that the mantids seemed quite unaware of doing anything remarkable.

They progressed in solemn ranks to the elevator, and so finally out into the air and light again. Noriyama's henchmen had set up a whole complex of tents and seating on the cliffs overlooking Senkaku Bay. Noriyama was seated in state, in his most flamboyant robes, accompanied by Barnet and an entourage of samurai in sober, dark-colored kimonos.

"They look like a bunch of Irish widow women headed for a wake," Cameron muttered. "I hope it's not our funeral."

Silk awnings shaded Noriyama and his lesser officials from the sun, and a series of screens mitigated the stiff ocean breezes. Lacquered tables held sake, plum wine, trays of refreshments, and utensils for tea making. Elaborate wrought-iron braziers held charcoal fires to keep hot water always available.

The German marched Jayne and Cameron toward the cushioned seats set up for Noriyama and his associates, and pushed them down into a bow. As Jayne lifted her eyes, she saw, standing next to Noriyama, what appeared to be a middle-aged Japanese man, dressed in a stiff-collared, impeccably tailored Western suit.

The German steered Jayne to one side, where Barnet and two samurai stood by.

"That—is the shogun?" Jayne said to Barnet.

He nodded.

As long as the *kamakiri-kami* shogun sat still, no one could have told the image from the original. When he walked about, there was a jerky, incongruous quality to his movements that immediately set off alarms in Jayne's mind. But to an ordinary person who had never seen the mantids, he'd probably pass muster as a somewhat cold and awkward human being.

How terrible for Lady Ko, she thought, to see the image of someone she had known and loved, walking like a ghost, being used by his enemies to do things he would have hated. Jayne shivered at the thought that someday a dead-eyed, shambling version of herself might walk the streets of Philadelphia, and no one who didn't know her would even look twice.

The two mantid guards wearing dazzle buttons paced ceremoniously along with the draped object between them. Jayne could see from their covert glances at the thing that Noriyama's supporters were agitated by the progress of the mysterious device. They tried hard to maintain the customary poker face, but Jayne saw them shy away from the object as it passed, like nervous horses.

The bearers stopped before Noriyama's seat and waited while two priests from nearby shrines came forward and blessed the device. They shook sprigs of pine over it, scattering droplets of spring water. At the end of their procession came a small, demure figure, gliding with tiny steps, eyes cast down, hands tucked away in trailing sleeves. It was Lady Ko, who bowed and laid a final offering of flowers and leaves atop the silk wrappings.

As she passed by Barnet's position, she slid one hand out of her sleeve. She held a single arrow-shaped leaf, like those she'd left on the object. She shook a drop of clear water onto Barnet's sleeve, then looked up into Jayne's face and brushed her hand, too, with the leaf.

"*Tanuki* magic," she whispered in French. "Transformation and protection."

She bowed her head again and began to chant, covering up her cryptic message.

"May I be a protector to those without protection, a leader for those who journey, and a boat, a bridge, a passage for those desiring the farther shore. . . ."

It sounded like a prayer. It was still in French, so Jayne thought it must have been intended for her ears, but she didn't know what it meant.

Lady Ko was accompanied, as always, by a pair of nun attendants. As she passed, she signed to them, and one of them bowed to Barnet and offered up a familiar-looking package, tied up in a white, crisply folded napkin.

As Jayne reached for it, the German frowned suspiciously and moved toward them. Barnet quickly snatched the packet. He unfolded the top of the napkin, poked around inside, and tilted it toward the German to show him the contents—rice balls wrapped in *kuzu* leaves, bits of eel and fish in paper-thin dark green wrapping. Barnet offered the packet to the German, who waved it away with a look of disgust. Jayne wondered what he ate. He seemed contemptuous of the whole idea. She wondered if he'd been converted to the mantid diet.

Perhaps Lady Ko had tried to give them the food because she'd thought of a way to help them escape, she thought hopefully. She began to edge away toward the rear of the group, just in case. There were several options—climb down the cliff, or slip down the crest of the hill behind them and run into the woods. She just had to wait until all eyes were focused on the eagerly awaited demonstration.

But Barnet was ahead of her. He poked her in the back. "Hey, where do you think you're going?" he said. "This way—we're heading for the boat."

"But—but what possible use could we be on a boat?" she stammered. "I thought—*his* idea was that Cameron had to see this demonstration."

"Quite," Barnet said. "And the German plans to keep his eye on you every minute until the demonstration is over. He's accompanying the 'Sunflower Seed,' as I believe this device has poetically been dubbed, out to the boat on behalf of the *kamakiri-kami*, and I'm keeping an eye on things for Noriyama-sama. You'll be along for the ride."

Jayne's heart sank. They'd have no chance to escape while confined in a small boat. Obviously, that was what the German thought, too.

"And don't make any suspicious moves," Barnet said. "Or we'll have to put the leash back on."

"Sunflower Seed," she muttered scornfully, to cover her misery as she was forced to follow Barnet down the steep steps that led to the harbor. That was the biggest, fattest, most pretentious floral object she'd ever seen. She noticed that the disguised mantids didn't have to strain to carry it down the stairs. It floated down with them, as if of its own accord. The two genuine samurai brought up the rear. Jayne thought wildly of flinging herself over the edge of the steps, trying to land on the sand, running away. . . . But the rocks looked steep and sharp, and the crescent of sand below was empty and without cover of any kind.

At the edge of the sand, they piled into a small sailboat that smelled strongly of fish. The object was lowered into a wooden cradle, where it fit snugly, and the disguised mantids crouched on either side of it. To Jayne's eyes, they appeared distinctly inhuman, and she noticed that the human guards kept their distance.

Jayne and Cameron were seated on the floor, against the port gunwale, where they could watch the steersman working his oar. The German stayed in the bow, near the object, jealously watching over it. Amidships, it was somewhat crowded by the presence of a tub boat that seemed to be serving as a catchall for an assortment of gear, and possibly as a lifeboat as well.

Jayne wondered if she could jump overboard once they were under way, while the German's eyes were on the Sunflower Seed. She tried to catch Cameron's eye. But Barnet squeezed past the guards and hunkered down next to her, making private communication impossible.

Barnet pulled Jayne's robe aside, unceremoniously, to expose the recorder button embedded in her chest. He flicked it with a finger.

"So, you plan to create two new little Mouths," he said to the German. He didn't even bother to speak to Jayne.

"Or one, or none," the German said, without looking back in their direction. "Perhaps just two more shadows to walk unnoticed among men, like my own shadow. The Masters have become bolder, as the usefulness of the shadow device has become evident, and they choose more and more often to go forth and conduct their own business."

Barnet poked at Cameron's collar and got a fierce growl in return. Jayne pinned Cameron's wrist to her side before he could take a swing at the goblin warrior.

"I see you haven't even bothered to tag this one," Barnet said.

"He has been too intractable so far," the German said. "The Masters have agreed to try a new approach. Perhaps he'll see reason when they demonstrate their power. If not—" He shrugged.

"A Mouth who was a trusted government agent would be quite a trophy to bring your masters," Barnet said.

"But a shadow agent would be almost as valuable," the German said. "And possibly more trustworthy. We shall see. Stronger men have seen the light."

His expression was blank, as always, but something about it made Jayne shudder. She hated him fiercely, but she hated Barnet almost as much. He considered himself human, but he sat beside her, talking over her head as if she and Cameron were cattle.

"I don't suppose you've bothered to feed them this morning," Barnet said casually.

"It had escaped my attention," the German said. If he felt that was a mistake, he covered it well. It didn't seem to matter to him in the slightest.

"You don't take much care of your recruits," Barnet chided him. "If you plan to subjugate the human race, you have a lot to learn about proper care of your pets."

"I have not eaten," the German said, in that dead, dull tone. "They have some weeks of life still available, based on their current fat stores."

"Yes, but hardly in optimum condition," Barnet said. "They need their wits about them to make a proper evaluation of the demonstration."

Barnet opened the napkin-wrapped package, picked out a chunk of eel sushi, and chewed noisily.

"Here, eat," he said, passing the packet to Jayne. "Of course, you know, it would be a terrible breach of etiquette for lowly beings like you to snack in front of Noriyama-sama. But as he is only present in spirit at the moment, I think we might risk it. Your appearance is shockingly bad. Try to perk up. Noriyama-sama is a great lord and does not care to see his retinue in such unappetizing condition. Even the dogs have to be brushed to a high sheen for his official visits."

He nodded smugly to the German as if he'd scored a point, but the German appeared to find him and his rice cakes beneath notice.

Jayne rummaged under the rice balls to see what further delicacies might be concealed under the leaf wrappings. She froze when her fingers bumped into something hard, a shape that was definitely not food. She covered her shock by stuffing another bit of fish into her mouth with one hand, while the fingers of the other continued to trace the outline of the surprise object. She dared not look to confirm her guess, but she was almost sure it was her Mauser, its distinctive shape concealed by the woven basket and its napkin padding.

Meanwhile, Barnet reached into his neatly starched and pleated kimono front and brought out a handful of small oranges. He created a maximum of mess and distraction while peeling them, dripping juice that smelled delicious, and licking it from his fingers.

"Like one?" he said, offering a section to the German. But the German stared ahead with his graveyard expression and said nothing. Barnet shrugged and ate the last of the oranges himself.

As the German steadfastly ignored their activities, Barnet turned his head toward Jayne a fraction of an inch and gave her what looked for all the world like a wink. His eyelashes swept down and up again so fast that she couldn't be sure she'd seen it. Was he trying to tell her that nothing had changed, though all reason said otherwise? Hope, fear, betrayal—all churned inside her as she tried to keep her grip and look as if nothing had happened.

Jayne could feel Cameron's hand moving surreptitiously, under cover of her skirts and his, spread out over the planks beneath them. Was he trying to signal her in some way? It felt as if he was trying to get under her skirt. The incongruous gesture made her uncomfortable, and she wanted to wriggle away.

Instead, she slid her hand closer to his, and ran into something sharp. She snatched her fingers back, trying not to let the pain show. Cameron still had the knife. Under cover of the voluminous kimono, he was working the sharp point between the bottom boards.

She searched for a distraction to cover the activity. If Barnet wanted to get friendly again, she'd chat as much as he wanted.

"How is Noriyama going to be able to see what we're doing?" she said. "Where are we going?"

She twisted to look back over the stern. The shore already seemed far away. Noriyama and his entourage were merely a bright spot atop the cliffs, where the colored silks of his pavilion caught the sun.

"The Mouth of the Kamakiri has assured me the demonstration will be dramatic enough for everyone to see," Barnet said. "Possibly *too* dramatic. That's why we have to be a good way out. The German there has made the calculations. We're on a heading of his choice."

"It's a bomb, isn't it?" Cameron said. His busy hand momentarily stilled as he spoke. "Or a depth charge. Something like that. I recognize the shape under all the fancy wrapping paper. First time I ever saw a weapon all dolled up like a box of lady's bonbons."

The German kept his gaze fixed on the horizon, but proved he was still listening.

"Something like that," he said. His dead eyes gleamed.

"He won't see anything but a waterspout anyway, not from back there," Cameron said. "You come cheap, Heinie—sold out for a torpedo? You'll have to sell me something bigger than this to get me to sell out my country."

Jayne elbowed him in the ribs to encourage him to shut up. It seemed insane to continue provoking the German, when they had a chance to sink the boat and possibly escape. She wondered nervously how far she could swim in these skirts.

Cameron wasn't shutting up, though she could feel him digging even more energetically.

"Listen, Heinie," he said, "I know something about explosives. You can't pack enough HE into a tube that size to make a bigger bang than I've already seen."

"It will be big enough," the German said.

"Huh," Cameron said scornfully. "Is that what you're doing under the mountain? Manufacturing explosives? I can't see what all the fuss is about—just another kind of bomb. Big deal."

Jayne felt a cold tickle against her feet. Water was seeping into the boat through the damaged seam. She shook the last of the rice out of the napkin and stuffed it into her under-kimono, with the Mauser inside.

The water was deeper now. Surely Barnet must be feeling it, too. But he didn't move. The other guards were seated on thwarts. They might not notice the leak until the water was deeper. Jayne thought she could already feel a slight sluggishness in the steering, a slowing of their speed. She glanced at Cameron, wondering when they should jump.

The German bent over the object—the bomb. He beckoned to one of the mantids, who turned back the silk wrappings and apparently applied his fingers to the surface of the device. Jayne knew that in reality he was pressing his talons into the slots of one of those mantid-only control panels.

The German turned and spoke to the helmsman in Japanese. He pointed to a faint white line ahead, where spray was breaking over rocks.

"Hai," the steersman responded. He nosed the boat a little to port, and Jayne felt it roll as the wind freshened and the bow met the waves.

Cameron gave a final vicious hack at the planking. Jayne heard a crunch as something gave way. Cold water flooded in around her ankles. The sailor at the tiller shouted and stared openmouthed at the water swirling in the bottom of the boat. He let go of the steering oar and climbed over Barnet to reach the tub boat stored amidships. He started to drag it to the side.

The mantids stared at him blankly, then looked at the German for guidance. One of the human samurai jumped up to stop the sailor, but the other took hold of the tub and tried to help the sailor put it over the side. The two guards wrestled with each other until the desperate sailor was thrown overboard. His mate threw an oar overboard and leapt into the water himself. Sharing the oar, the two sailors swam for shore.

No one was bailing. The sailboat was beginning to sink by the bows, as the weight of the bomb threw it off balance.

"Jettison the bomb!" Barnet said to the German. "It's taking us down."

"Bail!" the German ordered. He demonstrated for the mantids, who began to splash furiously. The water ran from their hands, between their simulated fingers, as the true talons beneath the illusion failed to hold it.

"It's no use," Barnet said. "We're going down. Dump the bomb!"

"No!"

The German's eyes gleamed with fanatic determination.

"We will reach our destination!" he said. He splashed back to the stern and took the steering oar himself. He clouted Cameron across the shoulders in passing.

"Bail, you maggots!" he said.

A wave slightly larger than its fellows struck the bow, and the boat nosed under. It seemed to stick in the water for a moment, like an arrow arrested in flight, and then the dark water poured in. For a moment the boat hung, swamped, just beneath the surface. The white silk draping over the Sunflower Seed billowed up and then slid away.

The German cried out again in wordless rage and flung himself toward the bow. His arms went around the gleaming, shark-shaped projectile now revealed in its cradle. For an instant, it seemed he would prevail and hold the massive steel object up in the water by sheer will. Then it shot downward, his arms still wrapped around it.

Jayne stared after him with her mouth open—until salt water flowed in, choking her. She realized she was up to her neck in cold ocean water, her toes just barely touching the boards of the sinking boat. It slipped away, leaving her adrift and suddenly struggling with all her strength to stay afloat on the surface of the abyss that was hungrily tugging her down.

It wasn't the water that was tugging her down, she realized—it was her clothes. Her head went under, and she kept treading water while she struggled with the knot in her sash. By the time she pulled it loose and felt it drop away, her lungs ached. She peeled away the sleeves of her kimono like an unwelcome embrace and kicked the sodden fabric into oblivion as she shot to the surface to breathe.

It was much easier to swim now, but the icy water penetrated through the thin fabric of her undergarments to steal the feeling from her skin. She shook the wet hair out of her face and looked around for Cameron. The tub spun lightly on the waves, a few yards off, still empty. Cameron clung to the side with a one-handed grip, unable to pull himself in because the disguised mantids were trying to climb right up his body, using him as a ladder to get on board themselves. He kicked at them and yelled, but risked losing his precarious hold on the tub in the effort to dislodge them. Their combined weight would surely pull him under, but they clawed at him in panic. Jayne guessed that giant insects probably didn't float very well—she'd never given the problem any thought up till now.

She struck out for the tub, trying to catch up before Cameron was carried away by the waves. When she reached it, the struggle was still going on. She flung herself on the nearest mantid's back, and shuddered at the feel of his sticklike limbs through the fabric of his human clothing. She hung on to him, trying to choke him off Cameron. She wound her arms around his neck and kicked at him from behind. Both of their heads went under, and she was taken aback when the creature suddenly turned on her and clutched her like a life preserver. He was pushing her downward in the struggle to reach the surface—on her back, if necessary. Her mind flashed back to a picture of ants trying to cross a rivulet. They trod upon each other in a giant ball. Most would drown, but those who stayed on top would reach the other side.

That might be the mantid way, she thought furiously, but she was damned if she'd let an insect use her as a stepping-stone.

She squeezed his neck, trying to choke him into letting go. She was distracted, even in those moments of struggle, by a smooth metallic knob stuck to his thorax, where the collarbone would be in a human. Desperate to get a purchase, to inflict aversive sensation of any kind, she scraped at the knob with her nails and twisted. To her surprise and pleasure, the button popped loose in her hand. The mantid's limbs jerked, and his grip loosened just enough to give Jayne leverage for an underwater kick to the abdomen. His taloned hands scratched her neck as she kicked again, and he lost his grip on her. She backstroked up the side of an oncoming wave, and the mantid was carried out of reach.

Revealed in his insectoid form, the mantid thrashed the water with his scrawny, metallic limbs. She saw him splayed out on the surface for a moment, like a water spider, and then the waves came between them. Still clutching the dazzle button, Jayne swam toward Cameron with renewed determination.

He was still struggling with the remaining mantid. She saw him gasp for air, and then he went under as the mantid's weight pulled the side of the tub down. Just as she reached him, Barnet appeared at his side, swimming strongly, even though he was still clad in his kimono. He rode high in the water because he clasped a pair of oars in his arms, and they partly supported his weight.

As Jayne approached, he thrust one of the oars at her.

"Take this," he panted. Still holding the other in one hand, he swam to the tub. He caught hold of it on the side opposite Cameron, counterbalancing the other man's weight so the tub righted itself and Cameron emerged from the water, half-drowned. Barnet swung the oar one-handed and smacked the flat of it down on the mantid's head.

"Get his button!" he said. Jayne threw the one she'd already confiscated into the wildly rocking tub. Gritting her teeth, she reached for the mantid, who flailed in the water, trying to catch hold of her. She let him get close enough that she could feel for the protrusion on his chest. Then she used her feet for leverage as she pulled at the knob. For a moment, she was under water with the creature thrashing and scratching. Then the button popped free in her hand, and she backpaddled to get the tub between her and the mantid. Barnet boosted an exhausted Cameron over the side. Then he climbed in himself.

Only when he'd picked up the buttons and stowed his oar to his own satisfaction did he lean over the side to help her in.

"Don't drop that oar," he said. "We're going to need it."

"And what about *me?*" she said, as he hauled her into the tub. "Nice of you to decide you might need me after all."

"Oh, I knew you'd be all right," he said.

She huddled on the bottom of the tub, shivering and trying to catch her breath. He poked her with the butt end of the oar.

"Get up and paddle!" he said. "We don't want to be anywhere in the vicinity when the balloon goes up."

"Balloon?" She pulled herself up and tried to find a position from which she could get leverage for the oar. "What balloon?"

"It's an expression," Barnet said impatiently. "When the shogun's demonstration project kicks off. It's not a balloon. But it will go off with a bang."

He poked Cameron with his toe.

"Brilliant sabotage effort," he said. "Sadly, the bomb had already been armed."

Cameron groaned. Jayne paddled with renewed vigor.

The round boat bobbed toward shore with agonizing slowness. Cameron recovered enough to spell Jayne at the oar.

They were still outside the surf line when Jayne felt a strange lurch in the tub's progress, as if they were in an elevator that suddenly leapt several floors at once. She clutched at the sides of the little boat, and glanced back.

It looked as if a dome of glowing blue glass was rising out of the sea. The bubble swelled and turned white, and was pierced and lifted by a massive shaggy column like a tree trunk or a thick, brutal toadstool that sprang out of nothing in an instant. At first it was dark, and then it gleamed whiter than snow, with an unearthly light, and then it darkened again as the dome burst upward and rolled over into a mighty cloud that shadowed its stalk and spread over the sky with unbelievable speed and force.

There was a white ring skimming over the water like the spray that flies before a wind gust. But it went so fast, so—

Jayne couldn't even register the speed, the enormity of what was happening. It drowned her senses. She had no thoughts for this, no comparisons, no frame of reference. It was a curiously blank sensation, as if she'd been transported instantly into another world, one where nothing as insignificant as a single human being had any voice or standing for an opinion of these events.

Weirdly, unbelievably, the upward motion of the boat didn't stop. The boat was soaring, flying, being tossed into the air, and the whole ocean was rising with it.

The tub flipped into the air and Jayne was sent flying, tumbling. And then the sound arrived—a roar, a raging, a breaking of the sky. It didn't even register as sound. It was a blow of unspeakable force that slammed Jayne across the waves as a racquet strikes a tennis ball.

She felt herself skidding through the water, up and down, tossed and blown. And it didn't feel wet or dry, cold or hot. Vaguely, she sensed a rapid flashing of light and dark, but that was all. It was as if she'd been blown right out of her body and her senses no longer had any connection with her mind.

She regained consciousness in the midst of a sound that was still overwhelming, but on a more human scale—a rush and rumble, accompanied by choking spray and grit, and a feeling that once again she was being hurled up and forward. She was moving her arms and legs as if swimming. Her mouth was full of sand. She had to get to air, but she didn't know where it was.

She was dragged across the sand, as if a gigantic fist held her by the ankles. Another wall of water crashed down on her head. Again she was dragged, and again hurled back. A tiny spark of will reawakened within her, and she knew that she would drown if this didn't change.

The next time she touched down, she dug her fingers into the shifting sand and rolled, and gained a little ground. She kept feebly moving her arms and legs. She found herself on the sand, half-buried. A hand grabbed her—a real hand this time—by the hair and by one arm, and dragged her farther up the beach.

Suddenly things came into sharp focus again, and the focus was mostly pain. She gasped for air, and then gagged miserably, as the sand and water she'd already inhaled racked her lungs. Her skin felt as if it had been rasped off. She was stung, cut, and bruised all over, and she couldn't get her legs to work.

The hands kept dragging her, mercilessly.

"Cam-ron," she croaked.

"Haven't seen him," said Barnet's voice. "Come *on!*"

Jayne planted her feet and stood firm, pushing the tangled hair out of her eyes. Where was Cameron? The shoreline had changed. The orderly rows of boats had been piled up and tossed every which way, entangled with nets, planks, uprooted trees, all kinds of debris— like dresser drawers emptied by pillaging soldiers.

Her eyes skipped over heaps of seaweed and dead fish and lit on splintered, round-curved boards, driven deep into the sand.

"Under there," she said.

Barnet helped her as she tore feebly at the pile of wreckage. Buried underneath, with his arms still locked in a death grip around one of the boards, they found Cameron. Barnet grasped him under the shoulder, shaking him loose from the splintered wood.

"Get his other arm," Barnet said.

"He's not breathing!" Jayne said.

"No time," Barnet said. He was already dragging the heavy, waterlogged body up the shore. "The water—it'll come back."

Jayne looked back. The waterline had gone down, as if the tide were out. She looked up and saw people rushing down toward the beach.

"No! Go back, go back!" Barnet shouted, but his voice was too hoarse to carry that far. He waved them away, but they pushed past him and ran on toward the wreckage of the boats.

He looked at Jayne.

"*Sauve qui peut,*" he said, snuffling back the blood that trickled from his nostrils.

They'd dragged Cameron almost to the foot of the steps when they heard screaming behind them. Jayne turned and saw a wave sweeping toward the people clustered on the beach. It didn't seem that big at first, but it reared up as it climbed the steep beach. When it broke, the spray rose over the heads of the would-be rescuers. Jayne moved toward them, but they'd been carried away like paper boats before she could take another step. Behind them, a towering monster stood with its feet in the ocean and its shaggy, ugly head pushing against the top of the sky. It was a cloud that still rumbled and gave forth lightnings and a baleful glow that rivaled the pale, ghastly sun.

"Would you care to help me here?" Barnet said. "Or shall we just bury him now?"

Jayne tore herself away from the sight and whirled to look at Cameron. His head lolled; his lips were blue. Barnet had opened his shirt and put an ear to his chest.

"I think there's a pulse," he said. "We have to get the water out of him."

"I know how to do this," Jayne said.

She rolled Cameron over and knelt, straddling him. She ran her hands over his ribs till she reached the short ribs near the spine. Then she leaned forward, pushing down with the heels of her hands, leaning all her weight into him. A trickle of water ran from his mouth.

She kept pushing, counting cadence under her breath. It was surprisingly hard work. One wrist hurt sharply every time she leaned on it.

Barnet had offered twice to take over when Cameron finally choked and vomited more water. His breathing steadied. Jayne moved over so he could sit up. He flopped over onto his back, saw Jayne, looked down at himself, and groaned, flinging one arm protectively over his eyes.

Barnet raised one hand into the air.

"Hallelujah, he's healed," he muttered.

Jayne realized for the first time that Cameron's trousers were shredded, revealing wide swatches of pale, sinewy thigh, and that she was clad only in some kind of Japanese underwear that was now soaking wet and splotched with blood. But what did it matter? They were alive.

CHAPTER 12

KUZU LEAF AND
FIRE BALLOONS

Jayne shook Cameron's shoulder.

"Those people need help," she rasped. "We have to go back."

"Sure . . . 'm fine," he said. "Just . . . gimme a minute."

Barnet hoisted him up off the sand, and they staggered back toward the churned wreckage. Jayne had to keep stopping to cough up more sand.

Bewildered villagers lined the beach, some wailing, some stunned and silent. Jayne joined the first group she saw, pulling away masts and stays from a smashed boat to get at trapped fishermen underneath.

Barnet found a ripped length of indigo cotton, shook the sand off it, and handed it to her without looking.

She'd forgotten her state of undress again. She pulled a piece of net rope out of the tangle and belted the cloth around her middle.

"Thanks," she said absently.

There was something more urgent on her mind.

"What happened?" she said. "What in heaven's name happened? Did you see? Was it an earthquake? A tidal wave?"

"No," Barnet said, almost gently. "That was Noriyama's little demonstration. The *kamakiri* did that for him, to convince him their power was worth working for."

"'The Divine Sun will come to earth beneath the sea,'" Jayne whispered. "That's what the German said would happen."

The survivors were finding bodies now, dragging them out of the surf and the wreckage to lay them in rows on the sand. The sound of wailing grew as they rocked in helpless grief over children who had run to and fro in happy play only minutes before, young men who had set out to fish on a sunny day. What had gone wrong? No storm had been expected. This killing blow had been struck out of a blue sky.

Barnet brushed a trembling hand over his eyes.

"Thank God it was deep in the water when it went off," he said. "The sea is cruel enough. But next time— next time the Divine Sun will come to earth in fire. There's an American song, isn't there—one of your folk spirituals, or whatever they're called—'no more water, the fire next time.'"

"Next time?" Jayne stopped digging to look at him in horror.

"Yes," Barnet said. "This could happen again. Again and again—I don't know what the limits are to their power. If there are any. This material they call Sun Substance gives them that power—if they can get their claws on enough of it. They have to be stopped."

"You're about to get your chance," Cameron said. He was looking back toward the steps, where a crowd of well-dressed men was descending rapidly.

"It's Noriyama," Barnet said. "Quick—we have to get you out of here." He shoved them toward the village. "Hide in there—I'll deal with him."

The village had been built in tiers, ascending the dark cliff that swept down close to the rocky shore. The narrow, crooked lane that led up from the beach into the village street was choked with debris. It was impossible to hurry. They climbed more than walked, slipping and stumbling as their passage dislodged little avalanches of splintered boards and broken roof tiles.

The first tier of houses had been splintered and smashed. The second level of streets hung precariously over the wreckage. The little town looked like a birthday cake that had been dropped and smashed. The people who had been inside, working, sleeping, or cooking, were trapped like fish in a tangled net. As Jayne forced her way up, she could hear faint cries for help sounding from all directions, lonely as seabirds' calls.

The first layer of damage was sodden with seawater, but the debris that had fallen from above was dry as kindling. Jayne smelled the first smoke just as Noriyama's men set foot in the lower village. She dodged around a corner to get out of their line of sight, and found her way blocked by two little boys who were crying and tugging at a cedar roof timber bigger than both of them put together.

They turned to Jayne and Cameron for help, but then saw their strange foreign faces. They stared for a minute, and then just turned away, as if they couldn't assimilate one more bizarre intrusion. Jayne heard a moan from somewhere beneath the fallen roof. Noriyama's men must be hot on their heels, but she couldn't see them yet.

"Come on, we have to help these kids," she said.

"We don't have time," Cameron protested.

Jayne grasped the end of the log and heaved. It moved just a fraction.

"Come on—one more person and we could shift it!"

Cameron eyed her and the timber.

"Well, if you have to do it," he said resignedly, "that's not the way."

He dragged a fence post from the other side of the street and worked it beneath the log.

"You need leverage," he said. "Here—you kids—get over here!"

He motioned to the children, but they drew back in fear.

"They probably think we're some kind of monsters," Jayne said. "If I only knew some words—"

She waved and smiled at the boys, and then, moved by an inspiration, pointed to herself and Cameron.

"*Tengu*," she said. Their eyes got even bigger. The older of the two said something that sounded like a question.

"Yes, *tengu*!" Jayne said. Then she took the older one by the shoulders and moved him over to Cameron's side of the log. She pushed down on the fence-post lever, and beckoned him to do the same. He joined in—tentatively, and then with enthusiasm when he saw the log start to rise. He called his brother to help.

Cameron burrowed into the wreckage, flinging tiles in all directions.

"Keep it just there," he called back. "I think I've got her!"

His head disappeared under a shutter that had jammed crossways beneath the log, creating a niche he could reach into.

"Get ready to push down hard." His voice emerged from somewhere below street level. "Okay, now!"

Jayne flung all her weight onto the lever. The log groaned and slewed sideways. The whole pile of splintered timbers slid sideways and collapsed on itself just as Cameron scrambled out, dragging a body.

Jayne saw the blood spotting the woman's apron and was afraid for a minute—but then the woman sat up and shrieked, reaching out to the children with both arms. Blood matted her hair, but she sobbed with joy as they ran to her.

A puff of smoke rose from what had been her kitchen, followed by a gay banner of flames that danced over the shingles.

"Ma'am," Cameron said politely. "Ma'am, you really need to clear the street. There's a fire hazard here."

"Goodbye now," Jayne added, tugging Cameron's arm to run. Noriyama's men appeared at the end of the street, and shouted, pointing at them. But their path was blocked by the family reunion, too. As Jayne found another set of steps and headed up, she heard a childish treble behind her squeaking excitedly, *"Tengu, tengu!"*

Dodging curtains of smoke, they ran through a maze of streets, searching for a way up to the next level. They ran down an alley that seemed clear of debris, only to find it blocked at the far end by hefty black-clad samurai. They doubled back through someone's garden, over a steep terrace and into the next street. But as they did, the smoke-shrouded house ahead of them slid down with a crash and a roar, bursting into a wall of flame. They were trapped again.

Jayne wiped her stinging eyes and tried to see which way to run. She winced from a gust of hot air.

An arm shot out from behind the cracked foundation of the house and yanked her aside.

It was Barnet.

He reached out for Cameron just as a charred cedar shingle, whirled down from a nearby roof by the hot wind, struck Cameron a glancing blow across the head.

Barnet caught Cameron's shoulders, and Jayne seized his ankles. Together they dragged him neatly into the temporary shelter of the wall.

"What are you doing?" Barnet hissed. "Noriyama's right behind you."

"We ran into a situation that took precedence," Jayne said. "There's got to be another way out of this."

"Yes—magic!" Barnet said. "Unless you can fly, it's either fry or surrender."

Magic. That rang a bell somewhere in Jayne's oxygen-starved brain.

"The *kuzu* leaf!" she said.

"What?"

"Lady Ko sprinkled us with the *kuzu* leaf," Jayne explained.

"And this helps us how?"

"Lady Ko sprinkled us with the *kuzu* leaf. She told me that's the leaf *tanuki* put on their heads when they're going to transform into another shape."

"And so . . . what?"

"And so, give me back those dazzle buttons, Mr. Tengu! You of all people should understand about transformations!"

She tugged at the recorder, still firmly attached to her chest after all she'd been through. It hurt.

"I can't get this off," she said. "Would you help me?"

She shut her eyes and dug her fists into the dirt as Barnet pulled at the button—first gingerly, then forcefully. There was an audible snap and a feeling like a tooth being pulled, and it popped free. A trickle of blood oozed down her chest. Tears ran down the inside of her nose and tickled—but she was not crying.

"Thanks," she sniffed. "Now, give me the other ones. Quick!"

She looked dubiously at them. They'd both been embedded in whatever mantids had instead of flesh. Mercifully, there were no visible remnants. They'd had a good wash in salt water. Gritting her teeth, she picked one at random and tried to slip it back into the hole pierced by the one she'd just removed. The device had a mind of its own. Placed over exposed flesh, it came to life and stirred in her hand, righting itself and extending a blunt metal stem that crunched down into the bone. Her stomach lurched queasily as the device attached itself.

Barnet looked worse. He turned white and clapped his hand over his mouth.

"What?" Jayne said, proud of herself for maintaining her composure better than he had. "It's not so bad. Really."

"But you—you—" Barnet waved a hand, speechlessly, encompassing her total appearance. Jayne was annoyed. She knew she was a bedraggled, barely clothed wreck. This seemed a strange time to make such a fuss over it.

She glanced down at herself, and was struck as dumb as Barnet.

"Merciful heavens! I'm a man!"

For once in her life, she really wanted a mirror, and time to look into it. She wanted to appreciate the full effect of her disguise. Her hands and feet did not seem much bigger. Her legs seemed more muscular and her knees bonier than they'd been before. But her shadow was no longer than before. She might be disguised as a man, but she was, after all, a Japanese man of average height.

She suppressed the incredulous grin that struggled to display itself, and frowned at Barnet instead.

"Well, what are you looking at?" she said. "I'm sure you've seen all this before."

She bent over Cameron, who was still groggy.

"What are you doing?" he said.

"I have to disguise you," she said. "Hold still—this might sting a bit."

She felt for his collarbone.

"Get off me!"

The next thing she knew, she was lying sprawled against the foundation stones, seeing stars. He had punched her in the face.

"What the devil was that for?" she cried, rubbing her jaw.

He stared at her wild-eyed, like a man gone mad.

"T-Taylor?" he stammered. "What the hell? Who the hell are you?"

She'd forgotten—already—that he wouldn't see her as she was.

"It's the dazzle buttons," she said. "The ones we took off the mantids in the boat. Noriyama's coming. We have to disguise ourselves."

"Over my dead body you're turning me into a Jap."

"She's right," Barnet said. "Do it, unless you want to be bug barbecue."

"Hold still and think of England," Jayne said meanly. She punched the button into his chest, and was gratified when he cried "Ow!" and tried to slap the device away.

She understood why Barnet had goggled at her like a beached fish.

Rawboned, sandy-haired Cameron, his skin pale under the collar and sunburned around the ears, had disappeared in an instant. Instead, she saw a man with thick black hair, dark eyes, and high, flat cheekbones. He was not bad-looking, she thought.

"You were better as a girl, Taylor," he said. "Definitely better."

Then his face twisted in a grimace of dismay.

"Oh, my God," he said. "A girl. I just hit a girl. I apologize. Oh, my God. I've never, ever—can you ever forgive me? I'm so sorry!"

She wanted to laugh, but his remorse was sincere, and they were in a hurry.

"Never mind," she said. "It wasn't your fault. You're not—er, not yourself. Now can we please get the hell out of here?"

They had to run crouching to the next turn in the street, as hot sparks flew overhead. The wind scorched their lungs.

And at the end of the alley, between them and cooler air, stood Noriyama's goons.

Barnet drew himself up to his full height, brushing an ember from his hair without flinching. The guards questioned him. Jayne could see he was answering them in the negative, waving them off toward some other destination. Then they gestured toward Jayne and Cameron. She maintained her slumped position, head down, doing her best to seem sullen and insignificant.

She heard Barnet say Lady Ko's name. Noriyama's men shrugged, finally, and jogged off smartly in the direction Barnet had indicated. She guessed that it didn't hurt that it was a direction away from the stifling smoke.

"I told him I thought you were some of the manservants attached to the convent," he said. "Let's hope they believe the foreigners have burned up."

Wearily, they emerged from the fire zone into clearer air. At the top of the cliff, on the road above the village, they found Lady Ko and another rescue party.

And then the rain began—water mixed with ash and mud, and dead cooked fish, falling from the sky.

By nightfall, the muddy rain had put the house fires out, but the beach was dotted with small cooking fires where people who were now without homes huddled for warmth. Jayne and Cameron built a small fire of their own, up on the headland, near the former site of the pavilions, far back under the shade of a grove of drippy trees. The pavilions themselves had been converted to emergency shelters.

Barnet joined them as the moon was rising. Clouds still built fantastic ziggurats in the skies. The explosion had created its own weather.

Barnet seated himself on a rock, insuring that he over-looked both of them. He brought cotton and oil. He gave some to Jayne so she could disassemble and dry her pre-cious, salt-stained Mauser, and he carefully cleaned and oiled his sword. Cameron could only watch enviously. His tommy gun had been confiscated, and he had no idea where it was.

Barnet finished the job and sheathed his sword.

"I've also come to give you instructions," he said, hitch-ing his salt-stained kimono into a more dignified drape.

"Really," Jayne said.

"Yes. I have to act against Noriyama tonight, or it will be too late. I don't know what the results will be. Cer-tainly, if he survives, and if he ever sees the two of you again, it will get ugly. They'll want to know exactly what happened on that boat, and believe me, they have a finely honed tradition of extracting information, even without help from the mantids.

"I want to make sure you're taken care of before I leave. Lady Ko will see that you're taken to a ship bound for the mainland, just as we planned originally. It will be a little more difficult now, because so many of the fishing boats have been wrecked. You'll have to travel to the other side of the island. Just follow her directions, and you'll be fine. I've given her a note for the American con-sul in Nagoya. It should explain your presence without reference to all this."

Jayne had assumed Barnet was a young man when they first met. He seemed to have aged a decade in the past week. Sharply shadowed in firelight, his face was lined and gaunt, more and more resembling the harsh mask of the *tengu*.

"Not so fast," Cameron said. "Maybe this morning, when we jumped out of the boat, I'd have taken you up on that. Not now. Not after what we've just seen. That was a bomb to crack open the earth. I'm not running home with my tail between my legs when something like that is on the loose."

"But don't you see," Barnet said between his teeth, "that's the very reason you *must* go. Noriyama was bragging over his dinner today, talking about his contacts in the Japanese military, and how they can use this weapon to advance their agenda. The next one could be smuggled onto our base in the Hawaiian Islands or even into San Francisco. To establish Japan as the preeminent power in the Pacific has long been a goal of certain factions here. They see your country as an obstacle. With this weapon, obstacles can be removed.

"Now *you* are an obstacle to my stopping them. I've made every effort to send you away safely. I don't think you understand the seriousness of my position. If you were to be captured, I would have to proceed without regard for your fate."

"I think I can handle my own fate," Cameron said. "You talk as if we're children to be sent home to nanny. I am an agent of the U.S. government, and I intend to act in the best interests of my country."

"And what does that mean to you, exactly?" Barnet said.

"If such weapons exist," Cameron said, "then it's in our best interests to obtain them. It's the only effective method of defense. So I'm not going home till I can bring one of these babies with me, or till I get a damn good look at the specs."

Barnet raised his hands as if calling on heaven for patience.

"And that is precisely the attitude that set all of Europe in flames," he said. "An eye for an eye! One side uses gas—the other must deploy a more frightful poison. One side commences a bombardment—the other must use bigger shells and throw them farther. Until all the world is a stinking no-man's-land."

"What are you—some kind of pacifist?" Cameron said. "All this peace talk is just a fleecy coat for the wolf. That's how it was last time around. What's your real angle? Whose interests are *you* working for?"

"I am working for the best interests of the whole human race," Barnet said carefully. Cameron, with a scornful noise, started to interrupt him, but Barnet held up a hand for silence. He did not speak again, but listened, and then his face relaxed a little. He rose to his feet.

Then Jayne, too, heard the light footsteps delicately picking their way through crackling undergrowth. Lady Ko bent to put aside a branch and stepped into the firelight.

"May I?" she said in French. She carried her cast-iron teakettle, and a basket with small porcelain cups.

"Pardon the interruption, Tengu-san, but if you must work through the night, please have some of my special tea first."

She crouched by the fire and placed stones to support the pot.

She looked up at Jayne and Cameron and blinked—the only sign of surprise she showed. Then she smiled behind her hand.

"I like you both very much as Japanese men," she said. "You are very handsome. Very nice! Perhaps you should stay this way.

"You know, down in the village they are telling stories about mysterious big-nosed *tengu* who came out of their mountain to help in time of need."

"I don't polly-voo," Cameron growled.

"Among the four of us, someone will have to use a translator," Barnet said. "Perhaps as a courtesy to the lady, you will consent to have Jayne translate for you, Mr. Cameron."

"With all due respect to the lady," Cameron said, "I'm not much interested in tea. I know it's kindly meant, but I have other things on my mind."

"Well, I'm not translating *that*," Jayne said. "I thought you believed in being polite to nuns."

She turned to Lady Ko.

"My partner says, in the frank and down-to-earth way peculiar to himself, that his concern about this thing that has happened is such that he worries he will not be able to properly appreciate your tea."

"Please tell him that I appreciate his concern," Lady Ko said. "I too am concerned, and this is why I've come."

"Good," Barnet said. "I was just telling them that you would be helping them get on a boat to leave the island—tomorrow."

Lady Ko smiled. "That reminds me of a saying. 'If you can empty your own boat, crossing the river of the world, no man will oppose you, no man will seek to harm you.'"

"What's that supposed to mean?" Cameron said, when Jayne had repeated it for him. Barnet looked almost equally disturbed.

"Today, Agent Cam Ron emptied his own boat!" Lady Ko said. "He met the obstacles without thought, without care, like the man of whom the Tao speaks. Therefore, I have been thinking that perhaps it is time for you, Tengu-san, to answer his questions."

"Well, all right then!" Cameron said. "I mean, thank you, ma'am. Sister."

"I've told him as much as he needs to know," Barnet said. "The boat can be emptied when they climb out of it—on the other shore."

"Pardon me, ma'am, but that's not true," Cameron said. "I need to know much more."

"Search into the origins of things, if you want to know the truth," Lady Ko said. The kettle boiled, and she poured carefully. A refreshing scent of herbs filled the air.

"You really think that I—" Barnet said.

"'If they will listen, sing them a song,'" Lady Ko said. "'If not, keep silent.'"

Barnet stared into the fire.

"I'll tell you this because Lady Ko advises it," he said. "But I'm not sure you can grasp the most important fact. The *kamakiri*—how shall I put this? They—"

"They're not from around here," Cameron said. "They come from somewhere else. Like eight-legged thoats from Barsoom."

"Why, Mr. Cameron!" Jayne said. "You *do* like to read!"

"Yeah, yeah," Cameron said. "We figured that out back in New Jersey."

Barnet's mouth opened and closed. It was the first time Jayne had seen him struck speechless.

Lady Ko smiled.

"Now that we've got that settled," Jayne said briskly, "what are they doing here? Do they want to conquer the Earth, like Mr. Wells's Martians?"

"There's the irony of our situation," Barnet said. "At first we assumed that. Now we think they came here by accident. Sometime during the war, their ship crashed to earth, somewhere in Eastern Europe. They passed unnoticed for a time, in the turmoil of conflict. All that they've done since is basically an attempt to leave."

"If they want to leave, why don't they just go?" Jayne said. "Why would they get involved with humans?"

"Their ship is damaged," Barnet said. "They need this Sun Substance for some reason. Perhaps to repair their ship, perhaps to power their engines. But humans have not yet discovered the substance, so it is unavailable in this world. They can't obtain it unless they put us to work for them."

Jayne tried to picture how the Sun Substance could power an engine, and failed.

"But they had that airplane," she said. "They had something that could lift it into the air without an engine. Why isn't that good enough?"

"We know they have some type of device that allows them to lift objects—but apparently it only works within a certain compass. It doesn't have the kind of power they need. Hot-air balloons took us a long way, too—but not to the moon."

"If they want to leave, why don't we help them along?" Cameron said. "Make a deal. Offer them American ingenuity and resources—a better deal than Noriyama could give them. They go wherever they want, we keep the engine."

"Now you're sounding like the German!" Jayne snapped. "That's exactly what he wanted, and you wouldn't even think about it when he offered it."

"I wouldn't take any deal from a crooked Boche and his bug buddies. A deal negotiated by properly constituted authorities is something else entirely."

"This is exactly why we cannot deal with the mantids," Barnet said. He clenched his fists in frustration. "Don't you see it? Greed for this power source is turning your head already. You aren't thinking straight. You've seen the mantids. They're monstrous. We have no reason to think that we could find any basis for negotiation with them. They would use us, and they would destroy us."

"Maybe I have more confidence in the human race than you do," Cameron said. "Maybe I think we can be trusted to look out for ourselves. It's the League of Nations all over again. We don't need an international nanny. All we need is a fair shot."

"How can you say that after what you saw today?" Barnet said. "No one can be trusted with that kind of power. It's like giving a loaded gun to a child. It is destructive in every way. It must be stopped before it goes any further."

"Why not say it's dangerous in some ways, and needs to be controlled by the right hands?" Cameron countered.

"You just can't see it, can you?" Barnet said. "The Sun Substance is a poison to humans. Mantid knowledge is like that. It can't be controlled. Whatever your original intentions, it will destroy you. Some knowledge is deadly."

"American knowledge, American know-how was the salvation of Europe in the last war!" Cameron said.

"American intervention prolonged the war and killed tens of thousands more!" Barnet said.

The two men glared at each other across the fire.

"Please," Lady Ko said. She handed each of them a cup, then offered one to Jayne.

"Tengu-san," she said, "whether or not our friends understand perfectly these secrets that you have learned, we must face the fact that you and I, alone, cannot overcome this great evil. We need help."

"I can't help you without knowing what I'm dealing with," Cameron said.

"And that is precisely what I cannot tell you," Barnet said. "The moment you understand what we're trying to protect you from, the damage would be done. As Miss Taylor said earlier, the knowledge that a thing can be done is the first step to knowing *how* it can be done. And once the method is known, someone will always find a motive for using it."

"But if we had just a sample of this stuff," Cameron said. "We could make sure our freedom would be defended against tyrants everywhere in the world, forever! We could make sure the last war really was the last one."

"I have to think of protecting the homeland of all mankind now," Barnet said. "That can only be done by destroying the *kamakiri* knowledge, not by seeking it out."

"'He lets the gold lie hidden in the mountain,'" Lady Ko said. "'He leaves the pearl lying in the deep. Had he all the world's power, he would not hold it as his own.' This is the true way, Cam Ron."

Cameron rolled his eyes.

"I remember this," he muttered. "The good sisters! They're all the same, shaved heads or veils. They quote you the Scriptures and say 'Now, boys, we trust you'll do the right thing.'"

"As I see it," Jayne said, "who the mantids are and what they want is really beside the point right now, isn't it? The point is, they're willing to give Noriyama whatever he wants if he'll help them run their operation. They seem quite willing to let him blow himself and all of us to kingdom come. And why not? What do they care what happens to us?

"The bottom line is simple—we can't let a man like Noriyama have and use that kind of power. And keep this in mind—once he starts using it, a smarter, more effective warlord will come and take it from him. It's like the speakeasy scene in Philadelphia. You start with local boys trying to make a few bucks, and end up with hardened thugs from New York muscling in. This has to be nipped in the bud."

Finally, Cameron laughed.

"I see your point, Taylor," he said. "All right, I'll go this far: We can work together to take this thing out of Noriyama's hands. After that—we may have to renegotiate."

Barnet hesitated for a split second. Then he reached across the circle and offered Cameron his hand. Jayne stuck her hand out, too, before he could return to his seat. But it seemed to her that he held her hand just a few seconds longer than he would have held the callused hand of a hardworking fisherman.

Of course, she thought. *It looks like a man's hand, but doesn't feel like one. He must have been struck by the incongruity.*

"It has to be done tonight," Barnet said. "This is our golden opportunity—while there's confusion on the island and many of the miners are working salvage operations. Noriyama is so enthusiastic about this that he'll redouble his efforts as soon as the emergency is over. We'd have great difficulty stopping him then."

"Whereas now it will be perfectly easy," Jayne said dryly.

Cameron laughed again. "All right, chief," he said, "how do we pull this off? Bear in mind the only thing I've seen on this island is the bottom of a birdcage."

"My original plan was to go down to the lower levels with a load of dynamite, and blow up their refining complex," Barnet said.

"That's a great idea, if you want to die," Cameron said. "I'm not that desperate. We have an old war ballad in America—'He who fights and runs, dear Mother, will live to fight another day!'"

"The plan has deficiencies quite apart from that," Barnet said. "The things I've done to keep you two alive have made the mantids suspicious enough of me that I doubt I could reach the secure levels with enough explosives to make a difference. Even if I were willing to sacrifice my life. Certainly you could not accompany me."

"We need a diversion," Jayne said.

Lady Ko refilled their cups. After sipping her tea, Jayne felt incredibly wide awake. Though it was dark, the world seemed to have a sparkle, a sharpness of detail, that she seldom felt even in the daytime.

As they discussed and discarded one plan after another, Lady Ko silently slipped squares of gossamer paper from her sleeve and began to fold them. Jayne tried to remember where she'd seen anything so delicate and precise, and then smiled as she recalled Maddie rolling out puff pastry.

The papers ended up as a squarish, double-sided shape with an opening in the bottom. Lady Ko lifted this to her lips and blew into it, and the flat shape unfolded into a ball, or a balloon.

She chose tiny, limber twigs and bound them together with silk thread, placing them across the opening so the balloon could not collapse. She wrapped a wad of oil-soaked cotton tightly to the twig crossbar, twisting up a thread to serve as a wick.

She picked up a stick with a live ember at the end of it, and just touched the fire to the cotton. The tiny wick lit, sputtered, and settled to a small but steady flame. Lady Ko held the paper balloon up between thumb and finger for a moment. The light of the flame glowed through the tissue paper, making it gleam like a precious stone.

Then she let go of it, and the gem flew away. The little lantern bumbled upward for a few minutes among the wet limbs of the overhanging trees, and then rose into the night sky like a tiny, wayward planet.

Cameron and Barnet were diverted from their argument long enough to watch it go.

"That's pretty," Cameron said. "But what is it for?"

"I was just thinking of what you said," Lady Ko said. "Of hot-air balloons, and sailing to the moon. I watched the little flame push the paper ball into the air. Perhaps the *kamakiri* would use Sun Substance to make a bigger flame—to push a ball into the air, past the air. Away from the earth."

Silence fell. They all stared upward, spellbound by the tiny flame, until it disappeared.

Cameron was the first to recover.

"You couldn't use a bomb like that for propellant," he said. "You'd blow yourself and your ship to smithereens. Wouldn't you?"

"The precursor substance, whatever that was, was enough to blow the wing off their airplane," Jayne said. "You took the lid off and provided a flame source. That was all it took. Remember?"

"Okay, okay, so I did a dumb thing. Is this all leading to something?"

"Yes. I don't want to go back into the mine."

"Does anyone?"

"No, but I mean it. I've been through the *tanuki* tunnels twice. Three times would be madness. Especially with dynamite strapped to my body. Isn't there some way to obtain explosives without going inside?"

She turned to Barnet.

"Where did they take what was left of the shipment we brought in with us?"

"It's still in storage in Aikawa," Barnet said. "They fished it out of the paddy with great caution. Something about having to dry it out before taking it inside the mine."

"So we could get those barrels from Aikawa. While no one is guarding the warehouse."

"Yes," Barnet said. "There's dynamite for mining stored there, too."

"I don't know much about explosives," Jayne said, "but wouldn't it make a bigger bomb if you could use the dynamite to ignite whatever was in those barrels? Maybe a big enough bomb to blow a hole in the lower tunnels—"

Barnet's eyes began to gleam with understanding and excitement.

"And flood them!" he said. "Yes! That would be a better way to stop the whole operation. Not just damaging the equipment, but making that level of the mine permanently unusable."

"I do know something about explosives," Cameron said. "Oil drums . . . I'm thinking . . . "

He and Barnet spoke at the same time.

"The Livens projector!"

Now it was Jayne's turn to be baffled.

"What?"

"Just another thing I picked up in France," Cameron said. "A captain in the Royal Engineers, named Livens, found a way to use old oil drums and spare parts for what he called a 'projector.' It took him a week to get his model up and running. By the end of the war, they were throwing gas canisters and grenades over twenty-five hundred yards into the German lines. We could build that."

Then his face fell.

"But what's the use? We have a delivery system—in theory—but no platform. How do we get it where we need to go? You couldn't take it through the tunnels—or into the elevator."

Jayne grinned, daring him.

"Why not fly their plane?"

The expression on his new face was hard to read. She knew the look on Barnet's face, though. Barnet was jealous.

"You said you could, before," she said.

"It's missing half a wing," he said.

"But if it's powered by some kind of lifting energy, maybe it doesn't need a wing. Maybe you could fly it, at least for a short way, with only half a wing," she said.

"Granting that, just for the sake of argument," he said, "that doesn't help us get inside the mine. You can't fly through the mountain."

"Maybe you can," Lady Ko said. "'How does the true man walk through walls without obstruction, walk through fire without being burnt?' It is possible."

"Oh, now it's you who are talking nonsense," Barnet said.

"I speak of the tunnel built by Kobo Daishi, the wandering monk," Lady Ko said. "Legend says it extends from one end of the island to the other. The opening to it is the cave where they are keeping the airplane, not far down the coast from Aikawa."

"Yes, but with all due respect, that's just another fairy story," Barnet said.

"No more than the *tanuki* paths, or the *tengu*," Lady Ko said. "There's a reality behind all of those stories, and there's a reality to the tunnel under Sado, too. Whether it was built by Kobo Daishi, I cannot say. But that the cave extends far under the mountain, I do know."

"You can't bet on that," Cameron said. "You can't fly blind into a mountain. That's just another way to die."

"We wouldn't be flying blind," Jayne said. "I've been there. The first time I went into the mines, when I was looking for you, I took the wrong turn. I ended up below the level of the mines, in a huge tunnel. Water was flowing there. It tasted salty. And now I know why the current was so strong. The water moves with the tide. It flows alongside the lower levels where the mantid machines are, and it goes all the way out to the sea. I'd stake my life on that."

They looked at her, then at each other, considering.

"My predecessors passed down accounts of the Kobo Daishi tunnel," Lady Ko said. "In all such accounts, I have found some truth."

"But is some truth going to be enough?" Barnet said.

"We have a long way to go before we even get to that point," Jayne said. "We could get started now and cross that bridge when we come to it."

"Cross that bridge or burn it," Cameron muttered.

"Cross that bridge and blow it up!" Jayne said.

"I thought I said goodbye to all that when the war ended," Cameron said.

"Who told you the war was over?" Barnet said.

CHAPTER THIRTEEN

THE WINGLESS BIRD FLIES THROUGH STONE

An hour later, Jayne, Cameron, and Lady Ko crouched on a rocky outcropping north of Aikawa, overlooking the road up to the mine entrance and, beyond the road, a group of warehouse buildings.

Jayne kept her eyes fixed anxiously on the road, believing that at any minute Barnet would cross it as he returned from his scouting foray. She could have sworn that she hadn't blinked, but Barnet appeared behind them without a sound.

"Is this what you wanted?" he whispered. He opened his fist to display a bag of firecrackers.

"Yes, good," Lady Ko said. She had occupied the time while they waited by folding a dozen more of the tiny fire balloons. Jayne joined her in blowing them up, tying on the delicate braces, and attaching the fuel source and the firecrackers. Barnet and Cameron fixed the length of the fuses.

They'd tested the wind with scraps of cotton fluff. When the balloons were ready, Barnet lit them and set them free. They drifted across the road and rose above the warehouse roof, still glowing gently. Jayne couldn't see them any more once they'd gone beyond the high roof peak. She waited, counting the seconds.

She jumped involuntarily, even though she'd been expecting it, when the firecrackers went off in a surprisingly loud fusillade. She heard agitated shouting on the far side of the warehouse, but only one voice. Barnet disappeared again.

"They left one old man with a rusty rifle up there," he said. "He said the others were watching over the gold shipments. He thought I was a bandit looking for gold."

"You didn't hurt him, did you?" Jayne said.

"I tied him up and gagged him—not very tightly," Barnet said. "I put him against a convenient post. He'll probably fall asleep waiting for rescue."

They dashed across the road and under the shadows of the eaves. Barnet had already scouted the location of the materials they needed. They piled empty oil drums into a handcart, padded them with sacking, and placed the smaller canisters inside, then the dynamite, wrapped in more sacking to keep it from rattling. Working quickly, Barnet and Cameron lashed a cover over the cart.

Barnet threw another coil of rope on top.

"Now comes the hardest part," he said. "Getting it down the road to the coast."

"Transportation is always the curse of the commando," Cameron said grimly. He sounded as if he spoke from personal experience.

"I developed a fondness for bicycles during the war," Barnet said. "They're better than horses because you don't have to feed them and they never make noises at an inopportune time. Oh, and they never, never step on your foot."

"Even a donkey would be nice right now," Jayne said.

The laden cart was extremely heavy, and soon it was a question not of pulling it but of keeping it from running away and careering disastrously downhill on its own. They tied ropes to it and walked behind, leaning their full weight against the cargo as the road became steeper.

They were headed not for Senkaku this time, but down the road to the port of Ogi, where the protective arms of Mano Bay had sheltered the coastal villages from destruction.

Barnet guided them to a path that cut away from the main road to narrow steps that descended to the beach in a secluded spot. By the time they'd lowered the cart successfully down the steps, their hands were scraped and bloody, and they all had bruises and cuts.

The wheels sank deep into the sand, refusing to turn. They had to drag the cart inch by inch to the water's edge.

"Now what?" Jayne said, rubbing her aching hands. "There's no way we can drag this all the way to the cave."

"There are still boats here with their hulls unbreached," Barnet said. They heard his feet splashing in the shallows, where moonlight gave the spray an eerie phosphorescence.

"Over here," his disembodied voice said, and they hauled the recalcitrant cart onto the wet, grainy sand until they reached him. He'd found a huddle of nets spread out to dry on poles, and next to them one of the round *taraibune* washtub boats, pulled up past the high-tide line.

Barnet untied his purse from his belt and hung it on the pole.

"The last of the *tanuki* money will pay for this," he said.

They unloaded their gear and shifted it into the boat. When all the containers were inside, it rode so low in the water that there was no room for passengers. Barnet knelt atop the heap of containers and explosives, and paddled the boat through shallow water. Jayne walked beside him, chest-deep, helping to guide the boat and keep it from tipping dangerously in the waves. Occasionally she stepped into a hollow and went in over her head.

Cameron and Lady Ko kept pace with them on shore until they saw the dark indentation in the cliff where the cave opened up. Then they all swam perilously out to sea, deeper into the cold, dark water, where the waves swelled over their heads. They came to the entrance from the sea, and swam in under the looming darkness of the mountainside, into the deeper darkness within.

Jayne panicked for a minute. She couldn't see anything, and inside the hollow space, the sound of the water boomed and rumbled. Then she saw a glimmer of light, and regained her orientation. Torches burned on the far wall, where the tide left a thin crescent of dry sand exposed. That was where the *kamakiri* airplane had been pulled in for repairs. The tail was anchored in the water, and a nose cable ran to a stake in the sand.

They pushed the *taraibune* up onto the narrow beach and splashed up out of the water, bedraggled and shivering. The cave seemed deserted. They saw no one.

The next problem was how to transfer the heavy canisters from the beach to the hold of the plane. They had to face the fact that even all four of them united didn't have the strength. They'd need a ramp, a winch, or some kind of mechanical assistance. Barnet stepped out from the plane's shadow to hunt for tools.

They heard a rasp of feet dragging on sand. It echoed loudly in the silent cave. Jayne flung herself flat to look out from under the belly of the plane.

She saw the German shuffling toward them, pale and sodden, like a zombie.

She reached for the Mauser tucked into her shirt like a talisman. But she knew it was soaked again and would never fire. The German had Cameron's tommy gun slung over one shoulder. He hugged something to his chest—an irregularly curved, vaguely trapezoidal plate of dull, bluish metal. It would effectively block any shot to the body—even if they had a gun.

Barnet moved in front of the German with a long, gliding stride. As he stepped forward, he unsheathed his sword. Somewhere in the tension of the moment, Jayne found time to be surprised. She knew he wore a sword, but she hadn't expected him to use it so effortlessly and with such assurance.

The sword flashed around his head and swept toward the German. It clanged against the metal plate and rebounded unhurt. Barnet slashed at the German's legs on the backswing—and the German soared up and over the sword like a high jumper.

He hung in the air at the top of his arc, and never descended. Barnet spun slowly, the tip of his sword tracking the German as he soared.

"That's why he went down with the bomb," Barnet shouted hoarsely, his voice echoing from the walls. "It wasn't suicide—he was going for the lifting plates! He knew that was the only way he'd get out of the destruction zone!"

Lifting plates, Jayne thought. So Barnet had known all along how that worked.

She tried to assimilate what Barnet was telling them. The German had survived—how? By detaching the devices from the bomb and using them to *fly* himself out of the explosion?

The German lunged at Barnet from the air. He had the gun, but he couldn't hold and aim it unless he let go of the lifting plate. He clawed at the sling with one hand as he passed over Barnet's head. He tilted in flight until he was facedown, the plate beneath him, and his legs kicking out awkwardly behind. He brought the gun around and trained the muzzle on Barnet.

Jayne needed a weapon. She ransacked her mind for one. She could not lie here on her belly while death danced overhead. She slid backward under the wing of the plane, disappearing from the German's view, to rummage among the odds and ends in the boat.

She briefly considered the oar, only to drop it in favor of the stout, well-worn rope. A swift double half-hitch created a sliding noose. The German's attention was all focused on Barnet as he took aim. Barnet retreated, dodging around the nose of the plane and bringing the German within arm's reach of Jayne.

She surged up off the ground, got a purchase with one foot on the side of the tub, and leapt into the air. She had no lifting plate to hold her at the height of her leap, but the arc of it carried her far enough to slip the noose over the German's feet before he knew what had captured him.

As she fell, the noose drew tight. She yanked on it hard and kept rolling. As she came faceup, she caught a glimpse of the German's look of shock and fear, as the plate flew on without him and he spun off into the air.

The gun flew wide. Barnet, too, made a mighty leap and severed the strap with one slash of the sword, and as he landed, Cameron launched himself into the air and intercepted the fall of the gun. He fell with feet planted wide to absorb the shock, and unleashed a deafening burst of fire as soon as his knees were braced on terra firma.

Jayne watched it as she would a ballet in slow motion. The German was the star of the show. He continued to spin, a spectacular barrel roll accentuated by the impact of the bullets. Dark fluid spurted out where the slugs punctured him. But it wasn't the color of blood. A line of holes stitched his arm, with a clangor as if the shots were being fired into a steel plate.

Jayne cringed in horror as the German's hand tore loose from his body and fell to the sand while his body plunged into the dark water. The reverberating echoes died, and silence fell.

Jayne jumped to her feet and ran to the place where the severed hand had fallen. She didn't want to see it, but she had to. Dark tendrils straggled out from the wrist. She had to swallow hard before she bent to touch them.

But they were not veins and ligaments. They felt flexible but firm, like woven cable, and the fluid drenching them was lubricant, not blood. Under the chill, dead-feeling skin, the hand was made of metal.

"It's a prosthetic," Cameron said. "That sure beats a wooden leg."

"I wonder," Jayne said. "I wonder if that was the only part of him that was artificial."

She glanced back at the dark water, but whatever he'd been made of, the German did not rise again.

The metal plate drifted to the ground like a snowflake, and rested there.

"It must have a fail-safe," Barnet said prosaically. "Fine—then we can use it to move our projectors onto the plane."

But Cameron was staring at the plane.

"We've got trouble," he said. "It's not just missing half a wing, it's missing both of 'em."

Now that she had time for a closer examination, Jayne could see it. The wings floated close to the body of the plane, but they were no longer attached. They were supported by a cradle of bamboo scaffolding where the restoration work was being done. The fuselage of the plane rested on the sand separately.

"It could still be all right," she said. "If it's lifted by the device, it might not need the wing surfaces to stay airborne."

"Yeah, but for control—" Cameron said.

"Look, we don't have much choice about this," Barnet said. "Get the bombs loaded. Then we'll make a test. If it doesn't work . . . well, we can try towing it!"

Barnet seemed to know more about the operation of the plane than he'd admitted, too. He used his jade claw to open the cargo door in the rear. Then he showed them the controls for the lifting plate. She wondered why he seemed so much less secretive suddenly. Maybe it was because he was showing them things they already knew about. Or maybe he didn't expect them to survive.

Cameron went to work on setting up the first projectors while the others were still loading the rest of the material.

"They have steel cable tiedowns for cargo here in the back," Barnet said. "They probably won't hold these barrels once you fire the projector—but we're only firing them once, so it doesn't matter as long as you get one good shot from each of them."

They'd had time and explosives enough for only four packets. The barrels were placed in pairs, set diagonally so they could fire through the open cargo door. They'd set off the starboard projectors first. The pilot would have to loop back to fire the barrels from the port side. It was the best they could do, since the fuselage held no gun emplacements and was airtight in flight.

When the cargo was loaded, Lady Ko cast off the nose cable for them, and took her leave.

"Will you be all right?" Barnet said.

"Yes, I've had much practice rowing these little boats," she said. "Maybe I'll catch a fish or two for breakfast on the way back."

She bowed to Barnet and Cameron, and smiled at Jayne.

"See you soon," she said.

The cargo door closed between them. The cabin lights came on, and Jayne felt her spirits rise. She knew she wasn't safe here, but she felt safe.

Barnet and Cameron bent over the controls. Cameron had pulled a splinter from the boat to use as a toggle, since Jayne had been out of hairpins for a long time. In tandem, they worked the switches. After a couple of shudders and jolts, they felt the fuselage lift from the ground. Barnet rolled the plane deliberately to port and starboard.

"We have control," he said. "Enough to get on with, anyway."

He lifted off into the tunnel, cautiously at first, the acceleration feather-light.

"Listen," he said, "we don't have safety belts. Or even seats. When the projectors go off, there will be a significant reaction. And when we come around for the second pass, I'll have to roll this thing. I'll try to do it in a controlled fashion, and I'll give you a warning, but that's the best I can do. Hit the deck and try to roll with it."

"Wait," Cameron said. "When *you* roll this thing? Since when are you flying?"

"Since you got your gun back," Barnet said. "You'll be needed in the rear. You have to protect Jayne and serve as backup gunner for the projectors. I can't match you as a marksman."

Jayne's heart beat faster as their speed increased. She had the job of firing off the blasting caps that would set off the dynamite and blast their projectiles into the rock wall. She checked the angle of the projectors again and again, trying to estimate when she should fire for maximum impact.

"We'll be under water in three . . . two . . . one!" Barnet announced calmly.

Jayne felt the ship shudder and rock as it struck the heavier medium of the water, but their flight leveled off and continued.

"We're going to horizontal direct visual now," Barnet said a few minutes later. "Jayne! Give me identifying marks."

"You're looking for a ladder," Jayne said. "Or remnants of one. It goes up a sheer rock wall. We should surface before we get there."

Barnet whistled.

"It's deep," he said. "I'm seeing a very deep shaft . . . still submerged . . . all right, there's air up above . . . surfacing . . . throttling back . . . when I see the ladder, I'm going to try to hover. I'll open the cargo door and give you a chance to aim. You call the shot. Then I'll close the door and roll, open it for the second shot. As soon as you give me the word, I'm going to button up and get out of here. Understood?"

"Yes, I get it," Jayne said. "Aye, sir" or something similar would have sounded better, she thought, but she'd never learned the vocabulary for this kind of thing.

Cameron came aft and braced himself on one knee next to her. She felt an unexpected glow of affection for him. He'd always been there to protect her, in his cranky way. They weren't a bad team.

"Jayne! I've got the ladder. Opening cargo door. . . ."

The plane bucked and wavered as Barnet tried to hold it stationary against currents of air and water.

The door slid open. Light spilled out, and Jayne saw fast-flowing black water just a couple of feet below her. Directly ahead of her was blackness. To her right she saw rough dark stone glistening with water. As the plane swayed in the air, horizontal marks on the wall became visible; from here they looked like ink slashed on with a wet brush, but she knew those were the same rusty rungs she had climbed.

Her fingers tightened on the plunger, but before she could press it, a shadow flashed between her and the wall. Blue lightning darted from it and sizzled over the skin of the fuselage. Jayne cried out.

"Jayne! Report!" Barnet shouted from the controls.

"We're being fired on," Cameron said. "But I can't see—aah!"

Another bolt of blue lightning crackled out of the dark, and cracked like a whip as it struck the deck inches from Cameron's foot.

"Close the door!" Jayne cried.

"No!" Cameron said. "We need to return fire. Can you see where they are?"

"I have visual on the attackers," Barnet said. "Two mantids . . . but they seem to be flying . . . it's not possible!"

"Yes it is," Jayne said. "*Move* us! We're a target!"

She braced herself against the rear bunk as Barnet rolled and swerved, barely missing the wall as he attempted to scrape the attackers off.

They swooped past again—two mantids, she now saw, riding plates like the one the German had been holding. But the mantids rode them standing up, balancing as the plates soared, controlling them with their taloned feet. In their hands, they held lightning rifles that spat out blue fire. Another bolt shot through the open door and left a charred mark on the interior wall.

"They're the ones who were in the boat with the German!" Jayne said.

Barnet rolled the plane again, and she slid across the floor. The steel cables still held the projectors in place, but she couldn't fire until she could see where she was aiming.

Cameron opened fire, but his target dropped out of sight—only to reappear from the other side of the plane and fire on them again.

"Dammit!" Cameron shouted. "Quit moving the plane! I can't see them!"

"Home me in," Barnet called back.

Cameron hooked his left arm over a cable and leaned farther out.

"Port!" he said. "Roll port . . . yaw port . . . more . . . more . . . no no, back starboard . . . hold it . . . hold it . . ."

He held the trigger down for a long burst.

"Roll port! Roll port!" he screamed. Leading the mantid who danced in his sights, he kept firing as the plane rolled and his feet left the floor. Sparks flew as his bullets struck the target. As the chatter of the gun fell silent, there was a splash. The lifting plate shot briefly upward, relieved of its burden, and then disappeared from sight.

"We got one, we got one!" Cameron shouted.

Barnet righted the plane.

"Jayne! Do you have a shot?"

The cabin rang with a direct hit from a lightning bolt at close range. Cameron screamed. His gun flew through the air as he dropped to the deck. Jayne dropped the plunger to seize the tommy gun as it flew past.

"Nose down!" she called frantically. "Cameron's down! He'll go overboard if you shake this thing."

She fired a burst into the darkness to discourage the mantid, though she couldn't see it. The recoil slammed her wrist back with a sharp pain. The gun fell from her hand and clattered away over the deck panels.

She stooped precariously to recover the plunger switch before it went out the door.

"Get me a shot," she said through gritted teeth.

The plane surged forward and tilted. Jayne saw the wall rise clear, angled for a penetrating shot. She grasped the switch. And waited, as the remaining mantid appeared in the corner of her eye and turned to cut in for another pass. She held her breath. Light gleamed along the silvery cylinder of his lightning gun.

She hit the switch.

She could have sworn she actually saw the lightning gathering along the barrel of the mantid's gun in the instant before the dynamite propellant went off and the projector fired. The explosion was louder than anything she'd ever heard—louder even than the mantid's bomb. It wasn't a sound at all—it was a force, and a pain, and a pressure that slammed her head to the deck like a fist.

She found herself sprawled flat, and didn't know if she'd jumped or been pushed. She'd thrown one arm across Cameron in automatic protection. They'd both escaped the boiling cloud of flame that had burst out of their explosive packet and was still eating its way through the roots of the mountain. Whatever had been in those barrels appeared to burn on its own once it was set free, and water didn't seem to discourage it much. Flame reflected luridly from the roiled water, and made it look as if they swam in a sea of fire. The heat scorched Jayne's bare head.

When she tried to report to Barnet, her voice didn't work.

She coughed convulsively and tried again.

"We have a hit!" she said. "Stand by for number two."

She searched the floor for the switch and found she'd fallen on top of it and was still clutching it. It took everything she had to push it again. This time she knew what was coming.

The roar was worse this time. Black spots danced before her eyes. The flames seemed to dance, too, and she realized it was because a growing cascade of rocks was falling from the breached wall to splash into the water.

"Number two hit!" she said. She wasn't sure Barnet could even hear her over the white-hot hissing rumble that echoed and re-echoed within the tunnel walls.

She heard Barnet say, "Coming about—secure the crew!"

Coming about? she thought. That couldn't be right. But she knew what he meant. She hugged Cameron close with one arm and clung to the base of an oil drum with the other, as the plane rolled completely over. She felt her head and feet swap stations, but when it was over, she was still in place and Cameron was still there, moaning. Which meant he was breathing, so that was a good thing.

Jayne crawled the few feet to the opposite side of the cabin and checked the line of sight of the second set of projectors. Her eyes blurred. She swiped at them and realized that sweat was pouring down her face. It was getting awfully hot in here.

"Port-side guns—firing!" she gasped. She shamelessly squeezed her eyes shut and buried her head in her arm as she hit the switch twice more in rapid succession. Pain and shock no longer had any meaning. She was barely conscious as Barnet closed the cargo door and gunned the plane out of the tunnel like a rocket from a bottle.

She came to slowly, called back by something cool, fresh, wonderful. . . . When she opened her eyes, she saw that the door was open again and they were loitering a few yards above a calm, mist-shrouded ocean that shone like mother-of-pearl in the predawn light. It was the moist, salt-scented, silent morning breeze that cooled her scorched skin. She gulped it like water.

She sat up and looked around. In spite of the beauty of the early morning, she was haunted by the feeling that she had been a part of something perfect and terrible. Something she was afraid she'd never be able to forget, and afraid she'd never be able to recapture.

Cameron, too, was trying to sit up. Jayne shook off the feeling and crawled toward him.

"How are you?" she said. "Where are you hurt?"

He stuck his foot out and examined it. Jayne could see a jagged burn mark running up his ankle. The skin was reddened, but not blistered.

"I guess I'm not," he said. "I got such a shock, it knocked the breath out of me. But I don't think it was a direct hit. It hit the deck right next to me, and I only got part of the charge. I'm never going out in a thunderstorm again, though. I can tell you that."

An odd, repetitive noise nagged at Jayne. She thought for a minute it was a ringing in her ears, and then realized it was something Barnet was doing at the controls. It sounded like Morse code.

"What are you doing?" she said.

"Just sending a distress call," he said. "There are a couple of castaways who are going to need a lift, and I spotted a freighter coming in this direction. They copy me and say they'll be here in a few minutes."

"Oh good," Jayne said vaguely. She wrinkled her lip. There was something stuck to her face.

"You need a good face wash," Cameron said. "It looks as if your nose has been bleeding. And—uh—there's one more thing."

"What?" She was poised for the worst—snot on her nose, a stain on her cheek.

"Would you mind losing the dazzle button?" he said. "I really liked you better as a girl."

"Thanks—I think," she said. Once more, she endured the pain of yanking the button free. She wondered for a minute if she should leave the translators in, but then she thought of the burns she had seen on the miners. She'd just have to let Barnet do the translating from now on. She popped them too.

"You're going to need stitches," Cameron said. She just shrugged. After all they'd been through, it couldn't hurt that much.

She felt around for something to wipe her nose on. In a heap of random objects stuffed into the starboard locker, she put her hand on something familiar—the leather bag. She seized it, and its heaviness gave her hope. She tugged it open to look inside. Yes! It was still full of gold.

She looked from the bag to Cameron, and back.

"I'm sorry," she said. "I'm sorry I thought it of you."

"What are you talking about now?" he said.

Jayne was afraid she might be blushing.

"I assumed you'd taken this. I apologize."

She clutched the bag to her chest. It was like a wonderful prize for all the trouble she'd been through. Something to look forward to when she got home. She missed Madeleine and the children more than ever. Her family! Now she'd be able to look after them.

"Well—how did we do?" she said to Barnet, with a pleasant feeling of anticipating praise for a job well done.

"You are a couple of heroes," he said warmly. That was even more than she'd expected.

"You probably saved thousands of lives last night," he continued. "In all honesty, I didn't think it was possible. My best working hypothesis was that we'd damage their operation, but not destroy it, and we'd probably lose our own lives in the process."

"You could have said something before," Jayne said indignantly.

"It doesn't matter now," he said. His voice was more resonant, more relaxed than she'd ever heard it. "We're alive. Noriyama will never get a chance to mine San Francisco Harbor. That's all that counts."

"Where are we?" Cameron said.

"About halfway across from Sado to Niigata," Barnet said.

"Can we make it to Honolulu?" Cameron said.

"I don't know that I'd want to take that chance," Barnet said. "I don't really know too much about the limits on the performance of this thing. I'd hate to find out halfway across the Pacific."

"You have a point," Cameron said grudgingly. "Okay, fine, land her in Tokyo. But I get to fly!"

"Whatever you say," Barnet said. "I owe you, and I know it. But could you do me a favor first?"

"Sure, what?"

"See that yellow package stowed in the aft baggage locker? Would you stand by to jettison that as soon as I open the cargo door? It's emergency supplies for those castaways I told you about."

"Standing by," Cameron said. "Stand back, Jayne—we don't want to have to fish you out of the drink."

The cargo door opened. Cameron shoved the heavy packet out.

Jayne watched idly as it hit the water. She judged that they weren't going very fast. There was really no danger of falling.

And then she was falling.

The plane tilted up, nose pointing to the sky, and she slid helplessly across the metal deck, grasped at a cable, but missed. She'd hit the water before she could fully realize that she was in the air.

The tremendous splash that drenched her again as she surfaced was Cameron—cursing incoherently as he tried in vain to hold his gun out of the water. Behind him the yellow packet inflated itself into an emergency raft, unfolding solemnly like some ponderous flower. The mournful horn of an approaching freighter sounded, indicating that they'd been seen and would soon be rescued.

"Castaways!" Jayne gasped. "Oh, my . . . sainted grandmother!"

Then she remembered.

"Hey! Come back here with my bag of gold!"

She shook her fist at the sky, where a slender silver shape bobbed briefly, as if bowing, and headed into the rising sun. When she'd blinked the dazzle away, it was gone.

Chapter Fourteen

BREAD AND ROSES

Jayne lounged on the porch steps, smelling the sweet-scented grass of a properly mowed front lawn and licking the last drops of strawberry jam off her fingers. She caught Madeleine's amused glance and smiled at her.

"That bread is so good, Maddie," she said. "Are you sure we still want to open a school? Maybe we should start a restaurant instead."

"You are joking, yes, Jayne?" Madeleine said. "You think it is 'ard to take care of the small children—you must run a kitchen sometime. Then you will know pain. My *tante* owned a small café. She told me many things."

They'd been having a picnic, in honor of many things. It was partly a welcome-home picnic—for though Jayne and Cameron had been home for several weeks, they'd been too busy picking up the threads of their lives to celebrate that fact.

The freighter had picked them up, and had dropped them off again in Niigata, where they'd spent a couple of wretched days without papers or money. Finally, on the road to Nagoya, they'd been met by a traveling monk who claimed, mysteriously, to know Lady Ko, and who spoke English as well. He'd escorted them as far as the American consul, and after that it had been merely a matter of much tedious explanation and waiting. Cables and diplomatic assurances had flown back and forth, and finally they'd been sent home on a respectable steamer, with letters of credit and Western clothing that hadn't quite fit.

After all the smoke and mirrors, Jayne was surprised to learn that Cameron was, in fact, a special agent. He'd done what he promised: he'd not only put Jayne up for a bonus, he'd talked to his boss about getting her a job. And since the Bureau was in the midst of a massive reorganization, and Cameron's boss was a wily man, Jayne was now safely tucked into the fold, under the designation of "J. Taylor." In possession of an office with a battered filing cabinet, a monthly check, and even a pension to look forward to, if she survived the next twenty years.

Also to her surprise, their tale of Germans smuggling contraband chemicals to the Japanese to build a super-bomb that, in the end, had blown up and destroyed the secret facility where it was built had been accepted by Cameron's Bureau chief as eminently credible. It sounded more believable, even to Jayne, than the truth.

She still thought wistfully about her vanished gold. She wished she could have brought home even a few pieces to show the children. It had been so pretty, and felt so good to hold. A government pension wasn't that pretty, she thought, but it was probably more useful. Just as well she hadn't kept the gold. It would only have created all kinds of trouble with various bureaucracies.

"Stop thinking so much, *chérie*," Madeleine said. "This is a party! You should be playing."

Madeleine finished brushing the crumbs off the white tablecloth that adorned the kitchen table she had moved out to the front porch. She was willing to find an American *déjeuner sur l'herbe* charming, but the idea of putting good food on the ground where ants could get into it still scandalized her. She'd insisted on a proper table for serving. There wasn't much left on the table now but the heel of a loaf of French country bread, a few strawberries, and the remnants of a *tarte aux pommes*.

She threw the crumbs to the white hen who was scratching under the azalea bushes, and came over to sit by Jayne. She gave a concerned look to the healing scar over Jayne's collarbone.

"How does it feel, *chérie*?" she said.

"Oh, it's fine, really. I never think of it anymore," Jayne said

Madeleine reached out and made a delicate adjustment to Kensie's lacy summer blouse, which she had insisted Jayne must wear.

"Then you must stop buttoning this top button," she said, too softly for anyone but Jayne to hear.

"Oh, stop it," Jayne said, her cheeks reddening. "Really, if it wasn't meant to be buttoned up, there wouldn't be a button, now would there."

"Just as you please—but if you do, the lace will not fall as it should," Madeleine said. "The look is important—especially today when we have guests."

Jayne glanced involuntarily over at the dogwood tree. Cameron lay on a plaid blanket in its shade, with a straw hat tipped forward over his eyes, sleeping off an afternoon spent teaching Jonny, Henri, and Hildy how to throw a baseball. Lucille had toddled around in the outfield picking clover.

Cameron didn't catch her looking, because his eyes were closed. But Kensie, who was gracefully seated on the corner of the blanket, smiled and raised her glass. It was a cool, dew-beaded glass of the finest lemonade, and out of respect for Jayne's new position, it was pure fruit juice and sugar, unenhanced by fermentation.

"Maddie, are you sure you've forgiven me for running off without a word of warning?" Jayne said.

"I 'ave said," Madeleine replied with patient dignity. "You had no choice. It was like in the war. And now, *voilà*. You have a job. A real job with no *pas-gentil* Boo Boo to make you trouble. You are happy, yes?"

She smiled, and Jayne was warmed to see that Maddie was happy too.

"*Et puis*, while you are gone I learn that now I have friends. I am not so alone here."

"Yes, Kensie is a brick," Jayne said.

Her first cable from Tokyo had been to Madeleine, care of Miss Millicent Kensington. When she'd come home, she'd found Kensie practically in residence, the guest bedroom nicely arranged for her convenience.

"I've decided to take my vacation at your summer home this year," Kensie had said, laughing. "You never told me you had such a charming country place. Much nicer than Bermuda."

"And Tante Clementina," Madeleine said. "She is a brick, too."

Clemmie and Salem sat together in the rocker swing— one of the few times Jayne had ever seen them doing nothing at all. In fact, even now they weren't doing strictly nothing. On her lap, Clemmie cradled Lucille, who had fallen asleep.

Madeleine strolled down to the garden fence, where the roses were blooming. She picked a Gloire de Dijon and tucked it into her curly hair, which had grown long enough in Jayne's absence to stray becomingly over her shoulders. The scent of the roses wafted up toward Jayne on the breeze, to mingle with cut grass and fresh-baked bread.

Apparently it was possible to have everything, Jayne thought—if only for a drowsy hour on a summer day. Dear friends, and a paying job, and the laughter of children, even though they weren't, technically, *her* children. Even a man lying around cluttering up the landscape— though he wasn't *her* man, technically nor by any stretch of the imagination. Bread and roses. And yet, it somehow wasn't quite enough. *Good grief*, she thought, *it can't be that I'm bored. That would be quite ridiculous.*

But she found herself thinking of the crumpled and stained postcard she kept upstairs in her jewelry box, along with Madame's latest letters. It had arrived a week after she'd come home, with a smudged postmark and a Chinese stamp.

Jayne Taylor: This is to apologize for parting without farewell, and in so discourteous a fashion. I meant all that I said. You are the comrade I would most wish to have at my side on any mission, if the choice were mine. But each of us has chosen another path. In spite of our differences, I wish you well and my hopes for a better future will be with you. Sincerely

—B.

She'd shown it to Cameron and to her boss, of course, and let them puzzle over the postmark and analyze the ink to their heart's content, but she'd refused to let them keep it for their files. This was America, after all. A person's private correspondence was her own.

She sometimes looked up at the sky and thought of him, wondered where he was and what mysterious mission he pursued. He obviously had known where to find her. If he ever needed to. . . .

Cameron had awakened from his nap, after Jonny rather too accidentally fell over his legs while trying to get his kite up into the air. Jayne saw Cameron's ruffled, sandy head bent conspiratorially toward Jonny's dark curls as they re-tied the tail of the kite.

Hildegarde had not yet given up on flying her kite all by herself. Starting at the very top of the backyard, she charged downhill, running with outstretched arms into the wind. She hurtled through the open gate, tossing the kite up with a final wild leap.

"I want to fly, I want to *fly*," she shouted as the kite wavered upward.

Jayne watched the kite catch the wind and soar, until it seemed to disappear into the sun dazzle.

You can take away the alien ships, she thought, *and drown their secrets under the mountain. Someday humans will trap the power of the sun, and seize those silver wings. Someday the secrets will be ours.*

"You'll fly," she said to herself. "Never fear—someday you will!"

ACKNOWLEDGMENTS

Among my research sources for this book, I'd like to give special acknowledgment to these:

The Making of the Atomic Bomb, by Richard Rhodes
Sado: Japan's Island in Exile, by Angus Waycott
The World Set Free, by H. G. Wells

They provided me with endless fascinating detail, inspiration, and food for thought. All errors, misinterpretations, and deliberate rearrangements of reality are, of course, my own responsibility.

Quotations on pp. 249, 253, and 258 are from *The Way of Chuang Tzu*, Thomas Merton, Shambala Pocket Classics.

ABOUT THE AUTHOR

Two-time Philip K. Dick Award nominee Ann Tonsor Zeddies spent her first three summers on a mountaintop in Idaho and wanted to be a cowboy until she realized that the frontier had moved off the planet. Her interest in biology began at an early age, when she collected a bucket of assorted amphibians and turned them loose in the tent where she was living with her parents and younger brother. Her brother became a professional biologist; Ann chose to deal with strange life-forms by writing science fiction.

While writing the water-based Typhon Universe novels *Typhon's Children* and *Riders of Leviathan* (written as Toni Anzetti), she swam in all of the Great Lakes and snorkeled in the Pacific between the Marianas Trench and the volcanic island of Pagan. She has camped in the Badlands and ridden horses in the Huron National

Forest and the vineyards of Quercy. Along with her husband and two of their four children, she earned a black belt in tae kwon do. After stays in Michigan, Kansas, and Texas, she now lives in Pennsylvania.

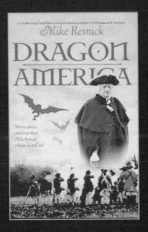

ALSO FROM PHOBOS BOOKS . . .

PHOBOS IMPACT . . . IMPACTING THE IMAGINATION

PHOBOS IMPACT
*An Imprint of Phobos Books LLC, 200 Park Ave South, New York, NY 10003
Voice: 347-683-8151 Fax: 718-228-3597
Distributed to the trade by National Book Network 1-800-462-6420*

PHOBOS IMPACT

An Imprint of Phobos Books LLC, 200 Park Ave South, New York, NY 10003
Voice: 347-683-8151 Fax: 718-228-3597
Distributed to the trade by National Book Network 1-800-462-6420

PHOBOS
IMPACT

Sandra Schulberg
Publisher

John J. Ordover
Editor-in-Chief

Kathleen David
Associate Editor

Matt Galemmo
Art Director

Terry McGarry
Production Editor

Julie Kirsch
Production Coordinator

Andy Heidel
Marketing Director

Keith Olexa
Webmaster

Chris Erkmann
Advertising Associate